LOOKING FOR LUCY JO

Praxos Academy

SG TURNER

Looking for Lucy Jo
A Praxos Academy novel
by SG Turner
Published by Chill Out Press
Copyright SG Turner 2014

For more information about the author
SG Turner and upcoming books, please visit:

www.chilloutpress.com/sgturner

PROLOGUE

She knew something was eating at him. It had consumed him day and night. Correctly, she'd assumed revenge was his greatest desire when she'd figured out he was trying to find a way to hurt them. Trying to come up with a plan to get his revenge on the Watchers. Ever since they'd thwarted his plot to acquire the Temporal Stone, he had become determined that they would pay.

From the darkness beyond the door, she stood listening to their conversation, careful to remain out of sight. Her fingers gently pressed against the wood, her ear straining to hear every last word when his other wife had spotted a photograph in his collection. A picture of a child.

'What a beautiful little girl,' she whispered into his ear. 'I do miss my children.'

Their husband laughed and hugged her to him.

'Perhaps it's time to have another, my love.'

Her small beady brown eyes lit up, 'Really, Sthen? We can have another?'

He picked up the photo and held it up to the light.

'How would you like this little one?'

'Really, Sthen? Really?'

She could just see Sthenelaus through the crack in the door, watching as he smiled wickedly before nodding. 'Yes, my dear. We will have a daughter this time. But shush... let's not tell Aria about this, not yet anyway.'

Gasping, she tiptoed away.

OoO

'STANLEY, WE HAVE TO DO THIS RIGHT,' HE BANGED HIS FISTS ON the desk. 'And that means everything, down to the tiniest detail,' he coughed.

The sounds of his coughing began to fill the room.

The younger man ran to his side, slapping his back. Sthenelaus pushed him away violently.

'Water,' he croaked.

Nodding, the man ran out of the room, returning seconds later with a large glass.

He snatched it, spilling almost half on the carpet before slugging it down. His coughing slowed, and he stood, trying to catch his breath.

'Dad?'

He held up his hand and shook his head angrily.

'Dad, you need to see a doctor.'

'You think I haven't seen every specialist in this damn country? Nobody knows what the problem is.'

'Then we must take you elsewhere. To America? There must be better doctors there? What about the witches?'

'What do you know about the medical profession? Not a damn thing. So keep your mouth shut. This has nothing to do with you, Stanley.'

The young man dropped his head and nodded. 'I'm sorry.'

'Now, back to business. I've already organised the helicopter to get you to the island. Are you listening, boy?'

Turning his attention back to his father, the young man nodded. He could have sworn he saw something move, out by the window, but he didn't dare go and look.

'Yes, Dad. I'm being flown out to Andilyse so I can snatch this child,' he said, pointing to the little girl in the picture. 'Before we fly out to the rig for a day and then, erm....'

'Then you fly to Portugal to meet the woman.'

'The woman?'

'Do you not listen to a damn thing I say?' he banged his fist on the desk again.

'I...I'm sorry. It's just a lot to take in. I've never kidnapped anyone before.'

Sthenelaus glared at his youngest son.

'Well, nobody that young before, anyway,' he said with his lip curled up slightly to one side.

'Your immature actions of the past couple of years mean nothing to me. From now on, you do what I say, do you hear?'

Immediately sitting up straight, Stanley nodded aggressively.

'That's better. Now, back to the plan. I've got everything in place, except for the memory clan but we're working on that.'

'The memory clan?'

'Yes, the memory clan. I told you about them earlier,' he said, shaking his head in disbelief. 'Do you not remember anything I tell you? Perhaps I should use the memory clan on you,' he laughed at his own joke. 'The Portuguese family that has the power to change people's memories.'

'But what's so impressive about that? There are loads of Skulls, witches—and even Watchers for that matter—who can do that.'

Suddenly he felt a sting on the back of his head where his father had slapped him so hard his eyes momentarily felt like they would pop out.

'Ow.'

'You think I don't know that? The memory clan are the only ones that can do it permanently.'

'But why do you want to do it in the first place?'

Sthenelaus rolled his eyes. 'Your mother wants that little girl. If she remembers her own life up until now, then she's not going to settle in very well, is she? I can't believe you're my son, have you no brain at all?'

'Why does Mother want another child? She's old enough to be a grandmother.'

This time, Sthenelaus held back his laughter at the sight of his oldest wife in the doorway, carrying a tray with a teapot and two cups.

'What did you just say?' she said, calmly placing it on the desk, before turning her attention to her son.

'Erm, nothing, Mum.'

Grabbing his ear, she pulled until he was forced to stand up. 'I might be old enough to be a grandma, but I can still whip your ass, young man.'

The boom of Sthenelaus' laugh made them both jump. 'A child, a little girl, will certainly change the dynamics in this house.'

'This house?' the woman asked, dropping her son's ear.

'Erm, well, no. The new house.'

Her grin made her features even scarier than usual. Madge had married into the Sophocles family when she was just sixteen years old. The union had been planned since her birth, and Sthenelaus had been powerless to stop it; both of their fathers (now deceased) were the most powerful Skulls in Greece at that time, and nobody said no to them, ever.

So he had simply taken a second wife, some twenty-five years later, when he'd found the perfect beauty to balance Madge's ugliness. Surprisingly, Madge had agreed to the marriage even though his younger bride initially had not.

'The new house?' asked their son.

'Yes, the Canadian house.'

'Oh, yes, right. I almost forgot about that.'

'How can you possibly forget about this?' Madge said, opening the large cupboard behind the desk and pulling out a thick magazine full of images of the most stunning log mansion. 'Our new home, our new life,' she said with a sigh, as she flicked through the pages.

'Not long now, my dear. We were just finalising the plans before you brought us tea. Where is Aria?

'She's out shopping. Don't worry, I haven't told her anything.'

'Good, she doesn't need to know about this. Not yet, anyway. Stanley, let's continue.'

'I shall leave you to it,' Madge whispered as she walked out of the room, closing the door behind her. Leaning back against it, she listened to the faint sounds of their voices, before curling her lips upwards and walking away.

❦ I ❦

Leaning against the lounge window with her legs tucked under her bottom, Emma Jane Morgan sighed at the most beautiful sight beyond. Snow fell hard and fast from the sky above, leaving a vast blanket of white completely covering the garden. Over a year ago, she wouldn't have even been able to look at it, let alone enjoy it.

Emma Jane had been terrified of storms – it didn't matter whether they were rainstorms or snowstorms, her irrational fear rendered her unable to do anything but hide indoors until the worst was over. That was until her sixteenth birthday when she discovered that she and her adopted sister, Lana Beth, were actually the daughters of an angel and a human male. Their entire lives changed in what seemed like an instant. Both girls grew strange tattoos that wound themselves around their bodies, finally settling at the base of their spines. The same stunning image of a winged eye, with different Latin words written beneath them, was just the start of a new life for them both. Lana had the words, Provehito in Altum written on her back, whereas Emma's tattoo said Lux In Tenebris Lucet.

Although Patrick and Audrey Morgan, their adoptive parents, were unaware of the truth, they had sent them to a unique academy in London where other young people in the same predicament were learning how to become Watchers. The girls were the happiest they'd ever been at the academy, even though their parents remained entirely in the dark, believing that their daughters had simply been invited to attend one of the finest A level colleges in the city.

'Come and give us a hand, Emma,' said Patrick.

Turning away from the white blanket and pushing her dark hair behind her ear, Emma smiled. Wrapped from head to foot in fairy lights, her sister, Lana, giggled as Patrick carefully unwound her, meticulously placing each light on the Christmas tree.

'How did you manage that?' Emma laughed, climbing up from the floor as Audrey appeared from the kitchen with a tray of mugs full of hot chocolate.

'Are those marshmallows?' shrieked Lucy Jo, her eyes wide in anticipation as she scrambled up, leaving the sketch she'd been poring over to fall off the coffee table, only to be trampled on by Fred, who barked at all the excitement.

'Shhhhh, Fred,' Lucy Jo scolded.

'Mmhm,' smiled Audrey.

'Yum.'

'Where's mine?' asked Greg, who suddenly appeared from behind the huge Christmas tree with countless baubles hanging from his clothes and ears.

Laughing, Audrey shook her head and handed him the marshmallow-topped hot chocolate with a grin. 'Maybe we should just forget the tree and stick you in the corner of the room instead. I think it's time you had a haircut,' she said, ruffling his slightly long hair.

'Nah, all the kids are wearing their hair like this these days, Mum. I'm thirteen now, not eight. It's cool.'

'What's wrong with being eight?' Lucy Jo pouted and placed her hand on her hip.

'Eight equals baby,' he taunted.

'Does not,' she yelled right back.

'Does too.'

'Does not!'

'Does too!'

'Alright, alright, that's enough. This is the time of year to be joyful, kids. Now, come and give me a hand, Greg. I'm ready for those baubles now.'

Finally free from the trail of fairy lights, Lana leaned her head on her mum's shoulder with a grin. 'Thanks for the yummy hot chocolate, Mum. You always spoil us, especially at Christmas.'

'Well, that's what Christmas is all about. I'm just glad you're still able to enjoy it. I dread to think about when you leave home for good.'

Emma put her arms around both her sister and her mum at the same time. 'You haven't got to worry about that for a while yet, Mum.'

'I suppose not,' she sighed as she peered outside for a moment, deep in thought.

'Even when they do leave us, I'm sure they'll be back for Christmas, love,' Patrick reassured her, as he stopped to take a long drink of his hot chocolate. Putting his mug down, everyone laughed at his huge melted marshmallow moustache.

'What? What? Have I got something on my face?'

'Dad, will you ever grow up?' laughed Lana.

Shaking his head, he licked off as much as he could before wiping his mouth with the back of his hand. 'I don't think we should ever grow up, not really. We should always keep some semblance of our youth, don't you agree, love?'

Audrey grinned and nodded as she leaned forward to peck him on the cheek. Fred seemed to agree, too, as he jumped up and began to lick Patrick's hand.

'I guess he likes marshmallows, Dad,' giggled Lucy Jo as she began to help her brother put baubles on the tree, resulting in yet another argument.

'Muuuuuum, tell him.'

'Greg, let your sister put some of them on the tree, sweetheart.'

'But she keeps putting them all on the bottom, and it looks stupid.'

A simple look from her made him back down. He looked to the floor and handed a few over to Lucy Jo. 'Here you go, Lucy,' he muttered.

Audrey and Patrick shared a smile, just as Fred started to bark again.

'I guess they've arrived.' Patrick grinned broadly.

'Who's here?' asked Lana and Emma at precisely the same time.

oOo

'SURPRISE!' DECLAN AND SALEENA YELLED. THEY CARRIED several large, perfectly wrapped gifts as Patrick led them into the living room.

'O-M-G!' shouted Lana.

'Declan, Saleena!' yelled Emma. 'What are you doing here?'

Hugging the girls, Declan grinned a cheeky, lop-sided smile, before shaking Greg's hand and picking up Lucy Jo, twirling her around. She giggled contagiously.

'Your parents invited us for Christmas,' Saleena gushed, as she hugged the girls.

'O-M-G,' repeated Lana. 'I can't believe it. And you didn't tell us?'

'We wanted it to be a surprise,' said Audrey. 'Oh, you're soaking wet. Come on, let me show you to your room so you can get out of those wet clothes.'

Patrick clapped Declan on the shoulder, grinning at the prospect of spending some quality time with his old pal and former work colleague. 'I'm so glad you're here, mate.'

Grinning, Declan nodded. 'We're gonna have a blast.'

Saleena rolled her eyes and laughed before she followed Audrey upstairs to the guest room. Declan followed right behind her, leaving the kids to happily finish off decorating the tree.

'That was sneaky,' Emma said as she plonked herself down onto the sofa next to Lana.

'I know, but way cool, though. I wonder how long they're staying?'

Emma shrugged. 'Hopefully, the whole school holidays.' She grinned. Pulling out her mobile phone from her jeans pocket, she started texting.

'Diarmuid?'

Without taking her eyes from her phone, Emma nodded. 'Course.'

Lana shook her head before letting it fall on to the back of the sofa, her dark curls flopping over her eyes. After a couple of minutes, she put her hand in her pocket and pulled out her own mobile and started texting.

'Barber?' asked Emma.

'Course,' Lana said seriously.

After a couple of seconds, both girls began to chuckle.

oOo

WEARING DARK, OVER-SIZED SUNGLASSES, LANA PULLED DOWN her stylish hat, so it covered her ears and shivered. Grinning, she watched as her oldest friend appeared from across the road. 'Scott, you're a bit early.'

He shrugged, careful not to skid on the icy street. 'Where's Emma?'

'She's just putting her boots on.'

'Oh right,' he rolled his eyes. 'The same old goth boots?'

Lana nodded with a grin. 'Way too many laces, takes forever.'

'Do you mind?' came a voice from the other side of the fence. The sound of crunching snow could be heard as Emma walked carefully over the thick white layer blanketing the ground. 'Stop criticising my choice of footwear.' She grinned the second she saw Scott.

'You'll never change, Ems,' he laughed, as they all stood facing one another in the bright sunlight. Scott and Emma both squinted, and Lana shook her head.

'You do know that sunglasses aren't only for summer, right?'

Emma rolled her eyes as they began walking away from the house.

'So, how's it going?' asked Scott.

'Great. How about you?' Lana linked arms with him.

'Pretty good.'

'How's work?'

'Not too bad. How's the academy?'

'Amazing,' grinned Emma, as she linked his other arm through hers.

'So, you ready to tell me what really goes on over there, then?' he said cheekily.

'Nope,' Lana said, looking off into the distance.

'What Lana means is that what really goes on there is a lot of studying, the occasional shopping trip into the city, hanging out with Barber and Diarmuid...'

'Oh, you're still together then?'

'Of course. Aren't you still with Lottie?' asked Emma.

Scott shook his head sadly.

'Oh, man, I'm so sorry. What happened?' Lana asked.

He shrugged, 'Just didn't work out. We're better as pals.'

Lana pouted. 'Really?'

He raised his eyebrows and nodded. 'Really. She's fun, but that was about it, really. You know what I mean?'

'I guess so,' Emma sighed. 'No-one else on the horizon?'

'Nah... can't be bothered with girls at the moment. Too much like trouble, if you ask me.'

'Hey!' Both girls unlinked arms with him and pushed him away; his feet skidded on the ice, and before they knew it, he was sitting on his backside.

Lana burst out laughing, while Emma's eyes nearly popped out of their sockets as she scrambled towards him, holding out her hand to help him up. 'I'm so sorry. Are you alright?'

Lana continued to laugh, tears falling down her cheeks.

'I can't believe you just did that,' Scott said, open-mouthed.

'I know, I'm sorry,' Emma breathed as she helped him to his feet.

'C'mon, let's just leave her,' Emma said, shaking her head as the two of them started to walk off, leaving Lana doubled over with laughter.

'Will she ever change?' Scott asked.

Emma shook her head. 'Nope. Never.'

As they started walking away from her, a huge black jeep skidded around the corner. The bright morning sun glared off the windscreen, and they couldn't see the driver as the vehicle seemed to hop along the treacherous ice.

Emma dropped Scott's arm and turned to look behind her, where Lana was still giggling with her hands on her hips, facing the opposite direction. She went running towards her sister, but her boots couldn't gain traction on the slippery surface, and she fell hard to the ground.

Scott watched in horror as the vehicle seemed to move in slow motion, getting closer and closer to Lana, who appeared to be oblivious to what was happening.

But, right at the last minute, she turned around, saw how close she was to being hit and ducked out of its way, throwing herself over a snow-covered hedge.

'Lana!' screeched Emma as she finally managed to stand up, her feet teetering. Scott grabbed her, and they both just about managed to run across the road as the jeep continued on its way.

'O-M-G!' squealed a voice from the garden.

'Are you okay?' Scott shouted as he ran to the nearby gate, Emma in tow.

'I...I think so,' she winced, rubbing her back. 'My bum and lower back took the brunt of the fall. I didn't land the way I usually do.'

'Huh?'

'Oh nothing,' she muttered as Emma pulled her to one side.

'Seriously, are you alright? Why didn't you land on your feet? You always land on your feet?'

'I think it's because it all happened so quickly. I didn't have time to even think. I'm okay, though. Honest.'

Emma hugged her.

'Was that a Hummer?' Scott asked, still watching as the giant black jeep sped off into the distance.

'I didn't get a chance to look at it, Scott. I was too busy running for my life,' Lana moaned.

'I think it might have been,' Emma replied. 'We don't get many of those on the island.'

'Many? I've never even seen one here before. It looked so cool.'

Both girls glared at him.

'Sorry. Point taken.'

OoO

'I CAN'T BELIEVE HE MADE YOU COME DOWN HERE,' STAN snarled at his more attractive brother, who was sat beside him.

'I'm just here to make sure you don't do anything stupid.'

'Oh, so now I'm stupid, huh? Doesn't he think I'm up to the job? All I have to do is snatch some snivelling little brat.'

'I guess he thinks this is more important than usual. He wants to be sure everything goes smoothly.'

'Smoothly? And he doesn't think I can do that? What does he think I am? I'm not a kid anymore.'

'Maybe he just wanted someone more mature to keep an eye on you, or something... Look out,' yelled the other man, pulling the steering wheel away from the girl in the road.

'What the hell?' shouted Stan. 'I did see her, you know?'

'You what? You almost killed her. Let's go back and make sure she's okay.'

'Hell no. We've got a job to do. We need to go and plan everything to the last detail. She's fine. She jumped over the hedge.'

Shaking his head, he closed his eyes for a second. 'Why does father want this little girl, anyway?'

Stan shrugged. 'Mum wants a daughter. Something like that, anyway.'

'So now we just take someone else's child? It's not right.'

'And you wanna tell him that?'

Archie stiffened.

'I didn't think so.'

'There must be more to it. If he could have any child he wanted, why this one? Why come all the way here? What's so special about her?' he said, glancing down at the photo of the cute girl holding hands with a slightly older boy as they walked along the beach. 'There must be another reason.'

Stan shrugged. 'Does it matter? Dad wants her, and we have to get her for him. If we don't...'

'He'll kill us. I know, Stan. I know.' Archie looked out of the window, off into the distance, wishing he'd been born into another family.

✾ 2 ✺

'Apparently, someone's bought old Josiah's house.' Patrick cradled a bottle of beer as he dunked a couple of Mexican chips into the chilli dip on the coffee table before popping them into his mouth.

'Oh, really?' Audrey replied.

Nodding, he turned to Declan, who was standing next to the Christmas tree admiring Lucy Jo's angel, perched on top. 'Josiah Grimshaw used to own the old farmhouse up on the hill on the other side of the island. He died earlier this year.'

'Yes, it was all very sad,' Audrey added.

Declan smiled sadly, glancing across at Lana and Emma knowingly. He knew all about Josiah, of course, because the man's ghost had travelled with the girls to London and had taken up residence at the academy for a short time before his mystery was solved.

'Who's the new owner, Dad?' asked Emma, in between texting her boyfriend.

'Nobody seems to know. It's a bit of a mystery,' he laughed.

Lana raised her eyebrows and elbowed her sister in the side; Emma promptly responded in the same way.

'What's for dinner, Mum? I'm starving,' Greg asked as he appeared in the doorway, rubbing his stomach.

'Lasagne. It'll be ready in ten minutes if you want to go and wash your hands? Go tell Lucy Jo to come downstairs, too.'

Turning, he almost ran straight into Saleena.

'Whoa, slow down there, kiddo.'

'Sorry,' he whispered, his cheeks turning a much darker shade of pink, before running up the stairs. The creaky stair squeaked loudly as he caught his foot on it.

'Lucy Jo was just showing me her Monster High dolls,' Saleena said, as she picked up her glass of white wine. 'They're really cool. I've never seen them before. Have you seen them, Dec?'

Shaking his head, his eyebrows knitted together. 'I'm more of an Action Man myself,' he chuckled, before placing his hand protectively on her lower back.

'They are really cool. If I weren't nearly seventeen, I'd have some myself,' Emma added.

'Well, perhaps you'll get one for Christmas,' Lana sniggered.

Emma rolled her eyes. 'So did you tell Mum and Dad about the idiot that nearly ran you over this morning?'

'What?' Patrick and Audrey both replied at the same time.

'What on Earth happened?' Patrick asked.

'It was nothing, Dad. Just an idiot in a jeep skidded on the ice, that's all.'

'Yeah, and nearly slammed into her. Luckily she just managed to jump over a garden hedge in time. It could have killed her. And it was driving way too fast, especially for those conditions.'

'Darling!' Audrey exclaimed. 'Were you hurt?'

'Just a sore back and bum, Mum. I'm okay.'

'Are you sure? Do you want me to have a look?'

Panic briefly filled Lana's eyes as she was quick to brush off the extent of her injuries. Since the tattoos had appeared, she and Emma had to be careful not to reveal them to their parents. So far, it had been easy.

'I still think I ought to have a look, darling. Just to be on the safe side.'

'No, Mum. I'm fine.'

'She really is, Mum. I saw earlier. There's just a little bruise starting to appear that's all.'

'Rub a little Arnica cream onto it, and you'll be right as rain,' Declan suggested. 'So, folks, what have you got planned for us next week?' he said, changing the subject.

Lana shot him a grateful glance before she and Emma stood up to go and set the table.

OoO

'WHO THE HELL ARE YOU?' STAN ASKED THE PRETTY YOUNG woman with short black hair as he carried a box of supplies into the farmhouse and found her sitting on the kitchen worktop, reading a newspaper.

'Kimberly. Hi, you must be Archie's brother,' she held out a hand.

He ignored it. 'He brought you here with him?'

'Yeah, I hope you don't mind.'

'Mind? You must be freakin' kidding me. Archie!' he yelled, opening the door into the living room.

'Erm, he's not here. He went for a walk around the farm.'

'I could kill him,' Stan muttered under his breath as he swung past her, back out into the cold.

'Charming,' Kim whispered, as she watched him stride down the garden, towards the old pigsty and out of sight.

'What the hell do you think you're doing?' Stan shouted the second he laid eyes on his brother.

'Hello to you too. What?' Archie replied.

'You brought a girl? A girl, Archie? What the hell? How are we gonna do this with a freakin' girl hanging around? Are you freakin' insane?' The vein in his temples pumped as he clenched and unclenched his fists.

'Stan, for God's sake, calm the hell down. It's just Kim. She's cool.'

'She's cool? Aw man, you've just signed your own death warrant.'

'Oh, don't be so melodramatic. Father knows she's here. In fact, it was his idea to have a woman come along to help look after the girl. Kim's my girlfriend, we've been together a couple of years. We can trust her, so leave her the hell alone. You hear me?'

It wasn't often that Archie lost his temper, but when he did,

Stan knew, from being his little brother for twenty years, to back down.

'Okay, okay.'

oOo

'Christmas day tomorrow,' squealed Lucy Jo as she ran down the stairs at speed, narrowly missing Fred who stood waiting, tail wagging, at the bottom. 'Hurry up, Greg!' she shouted as she quickly threw on her boots, warm coat, gloves and hat.

'We're ready, Dad,' she screeched, the moment she and her brother stood at the front door with Fred on his leash.

'Coming,' he shouted from the kitchen. Turning to his friend, he asked, 'Fancy joining us for a walk in the snow, Declan?'

Nodding, Declan gave Saleena a peck on the lips before he grabbed his own jacket and followed them out the door.

'Peace at last,' Emma sighed as she trampled down the stairs wearing her pyjamas and dressing gown.

'You don't mean that,' Audrey smiled from the kitchen. 'Tea?'

Emma nodded.

'Is Lana up yet?' her mum asked.

'Not really.'

'It's almost 10.30.' Audrey rolled her eyes.

'But it's also Christmas holidays.' Emma smiled.

'And we have guests.'

'Okay, I'll go and drag her out of bed, then.' Emma tightened her dressing gown around her and rushed up the stairs two at a time.

'Come on, sleepyhead. Mum said you've got to get up.'

'It's too early,' Lana muttered from beneath the duvet.

'Sis, it's almost half-past ten.'

'So?'

'So, we've got Declan and Saleena here.'

'They don't mind,' Lana groaned.

'That's not the point.'

'Urgh, just ten more minutes,' she muttered.

'If you stay in bed another ten minutes, Mum will probably set the kids on you – and the dog.' She grinned mischievously.

With that, Lana pulled back the duvet and poked her head out, squinting. 'It's so bright. What's going on?'

'It's called sunlight, now get up.'

'You're so bossy.'

'And you love me for it.' Emma promptly grabbed the end of the duvet and pulled it. Intending to merely remove it from the bed, she somehow managed to fling it across the other side of the bedroom, knocking the large lamp on the chest of drawers onto the floor with a crash.

'Oops,' she said.

'Girls? What's going on?' yelled their mother from downstairs.

'Now look what you've done,' Lana said as she jumped up. She put on her own dressing gown and walked out of the room, going downstairs and into the kitchen.

'It wasn't me,' she said as her mother handed her a cup of tea.

Audrey rolled her eyes, Saleena sniggered, and Emma appeared, looking guilty.

'What did you do?'

'I accidentally broke the lamp in our bedroom. Sorry, Mum.'

Shaking her head, Audrey passed her other daughter a cup of tea too.

'Morning, girls,' Saleena said brightly.

'Morning.' They grinned.

'So, you're still not morning people then?' she asked. 'Even after months at the academy? I figured you'd be raring to get up and go every day. There's so much to do,' she said with excitement.

'There is?' asked Lana, while Emma sat down with a smile.

'Of course. Everything that you've been learning can be put to good use - even here.'

'It can?'

'Sure it can,' she winked.

'Saleena's absolutely right, you two,' Audrey said as she washed the morning's breakfast dishes. 'You ought to be practising every-thing you've learned over in London.'

Lana gave Emma a sideways glance that wasn't lost on Saleena.

'You could go carol singing, for starters,' Audrey suggested. 'Put your music lessons to good use.'

'That's not a bad idea,' winked Saleena.

'Erm, I think we'll find something else to keep us occupied, won't we, sis?' Lana smirked, elbowing Emma in the side.

'Absolutely.' Emma nodded and rolled her eyes.

oOo

'Scott!' yelled Lana as she threw a little stone at his bedroom window.

'Why don't we just go and knock at the front door, like normal people?'

'Because we're not normal people, are we, Em?' Lana smirked as they waited for their best friend to appear.

After a couple of minutes, and a few more stones, the front door opened, and Scott's mother appeared with her hands on her hips and a cheeky grin on her face. 'He's gone for a ride, girls. Try his mobile,' she added, shaking her head before returning indoors and closing the door behind her.

'See, we should've just rung him in the first place.'

Lana dialled and let the phone ring, but there was no answer. 'He's not picking up.'

'Do you wanna just go for a ride and see if we can catch him up?'

'What, in the snow?'

'It's not that bad, there's only a bit of ice on the roads.'

Emma shrugged, and they hurried back home to pick up their bikes.

Shivering, they started cycling up the hill towards their favourite spot, the old castle ruins overlooking much of the island. As they approached, Lana grinned and sped up, seeing Scott's old bicycle leaning against the large broken stones at the entrance to the castle.

'He's very predictable,' laughed Emma as they hopped off, dropping their bikes by his and carefully walking through the snow.

'Scott!' yelled Lana. 'Where are you?'

'Over here,' came a voice from a little farther away.

They soon found Scott, sitting on a large flat rock. Grinning, he stood up and waved.

'Why didn't you call us? We'd have cycled up with you.'

He shrugged as the three of them sat down on the cold surface.

'You okay?' Emma asked.

He nodded, a little unconvincingly.

'C'mon, what aren't you telling us?' pressured Lana.

Again he shrugged, leaning his chin on his knees. 'It's nothing.'

'It's not nothing. What's on your mind?' Emma asked.

'I dunno, I guess I'm just a little...' he shrugged again, 'put out that you guys are having such great adventures in London without me and...'

'And what?' Lana whispered.

'And I feel like I'm in the dark with you two.'

'You're not in the dark, and we're not having that many adventures without you.'

He breathed out through his nose and shook his head. 'You're just not the same. It happened before you left Andilyse Island, and you won't come clean with me. I thought I could deal with it, but the truth is, I can't. And if you won't tell me the truth, then...' he glanced out across the island and shrugged yet again.

Lana glanced across at her sister. Both frowned before looking away.

'You're right, Scott. We do have a secret...' Lana said very quietly.

'But we can't tell you what it is,' Emma added.

'But why the hell not? We're supposed to be best friends. We've known each other since we were, like, babies.'

Emma sighed loudly. 'I know...'

'But if we told you... we'd have to kill you,' Lana said, more light-heartedly.

'Oh c'mon,' he said, leaning backwards. 'That's bull, and you know it.'

'Scott, if we could tell you the truth we would, you know we would. But it is practically life or death. Please just trust us, for now. Can we please just have a nice Christmas holiday with you? Please? Pretty please?' Lana fluttered her eyelashes at him and grinned, while Emma proceeded to tickle his side - it always worked.

'Okay, okay.' He gave in. 'But at some point or other, you are going to tell me what's going on.'

Emma looked across at her sister, and they said nothing. Instead, they both jumped on him and began to tickle him, making him laugh before he managed to get clear of them, falling onto the snow-covered grass below with a thump.

'Ow,' he groaned.

'Oh... are you okay?' Emma said, wide-eyed, as she peered over the rock only to find him not there.

'What the? Where did he go?'

A loud giggle could be heard from the other side of the rock where Scott was running back through the ruins towards their bikes.

'The last one's a wally!'

'Oh, we are so going to get you!' yelled Lana as they climbed down and ran after him.

⚜ 3 ⚜

T he fairy lights twinkled in the dark while Audrey, Patrick, Declan and Saleena silently placed a whole host of gifts under the tree and all over the sofa.

Just before they called it a night, Patrick drank the glass of sherry Lucy Jo had left for Father Christmas and handed the mince pie to Declan who took a bite, leaving a few crumbs on the plate. Rudolph's carrot was picked up by Audrey, who took a large bite before taking a large swig of the milk left for the reindeer.

Saleena watched from the doorway, smiling, touched by the annual tradition. When the room was set for the morning, all four grinned at each other, saying goodnight before they quietly went up to their rooms, careful to avoid the creaky step.

Declan and Saleena closed their door behind them, leaving the parents to peer into their children's bedrooms. Happy they were all sleeping peacefully, they went to bed for a good night's sleep before the chaos of Christmas morning.

oOo

EVER SINCE SHE COULD WALK AND UNDERSTAND THAT CHRISTMAS meant presents, Lucy Jo had always been the first to rush into her parents' bedroom and pounce on them on Christmas morning – usually not before six a.m., but no later than a quarter past.

At almost seven a.m., Audrey rolled over to look at the alarm clock on Patrick's side of the bed. Frowning, she rubbed her eyes and looked again. It was six fifty-seven.

Shaking her husband awake, he turned, opening his eyes with a grin. 'Is it time?' he whispered, like a small child.

She nodded and smiled. 'They've slept in today.'

Patrick glanced at the clock and frowned. 'That's not like her.'

Audrey sighed. 'It means we've got a few minutes to wake up properly this year.'

Grinning, he leaned over and pulled his wife close. 'Shall we go and pounce on them instead?'

She chuckled. 'At Christmas, you're such a child.'

'You love it, really.'

'I do,' she giggled. 'I love you.'

Giving her a long kiss, they both climbed out of bed and pulled on their dressing gowns and slippers. Before they opened the door, they glanced at each other childishly, then ran out, making lots of noise.

'Wakey, wakey! It's Christmas morning!'

Greg was first out onto the landing, followed by Emma, Lana, Declan and Saleena.

'Wow, it's freezing.' Lana shivered, pulling her dressing gown tightly around her. 'Does anyone else feel a draft?'

Seconds later, when they realised Lucy Jo still hadn't appeared, Audrey put her hand on her chest and looked across at her husband.

Rushing into the little girl's bedroom, Audrey screamed when she saw nothing but an empty bed... and an open window.

'Oh my god... my little girl! Lucy Jo!' she cried.

oOo

THE HOUSE WAS FULL OF PATRICK'S CO-WORKERS FROM THE police force, dusting for fingerprints, making notes and asking questions while a distraught Audrey, who wouldn't let Greg out of her sight, was being comforted by Saleena.

Patrick and Declan were combing the streets of Andilyse Island, hoping to find clues as to where the little girl was, or who had taken her. But they were getting nowhere.

Eventually, they trundled back home. Opening the front door, Audrey rushed to Patrick's side, looking for some trace of hope on his face. When she saw none, she burst into fresh tears and returned to the living room.

By this time, the forensics team and other police officers, except for one who stood by the main entrance, had left the house. It was eerily quiet.

Lana and Emma sat in the kitchen. They'd barely said a word all day.

'We've got to do something, Em,' Lana eventually whispered.

'I know.'

'We're Watchers, we can find her, I'm sure we can.'

'Yeah.'

'What about Eleanor? Maybe we should call her?' Lana suggested.

'Eleanor already knows,' said Declan, who was leaning against the kitchen doorframe.

'Oh. Is she sending help?' asked Lana.

Declan stepped forward and put his hands on both girl's shoulders. 'There's nothing she can do at the moment, not until the police uncover some more clues.'

'Huh, but why not?'

'Chances are Lucy Jo is still on the island. Eleanor is in London. It's up to the police to find her. We're going to help as much as we can, okay? We'll get her back.'

The girls looked distraught as he went back to the living room. Following him, they sat down beside Greg, whose eyes were red and puffy. Audrey tried to smile at them, but she just couldn't.

'I'll go make some tea,' Saleena said, standing up and walking out.

'Greg, can you go and give Saleena a hand in the kitchen, please?' Patrick asked his son, who nodded and followed her. And girls, why don't you go and make your mother some toast? I think she needs to eat something.'

'I'm not hungry.'

'You must eat, darling. You've not had anything all day.'

But she shook her head and looked out the window.

'Perhaps we ought to give your parents some time alone, girls?' suggested Declan.

Patrick looked up. 'Yes, thanks.'

Wandering slowly upstairs, Emma put her foot on the creaky step, making Lana jump.

'Why didn't we hear anything?' she said. 'We were right next door, we should have heard something.'

'I don't know, Lana. Nobody heard a thing.'

'But how? How can someone break in, take our sister, and not make a sound?'

Emma shook her head as they stood at the top of the stairs looking at Lucy Jo's bedroom door, with the little pink and silver sign on it that said 'Princess'.

Lana gingerly pushed the door open and stepped inside.

'I don't think we're supposed to go in, sis. It's a crime scene.'

'I don't care, this is our sist...'

Without finishing the sentence, Lana fell to the floor with a thud.

When she opened her eyes, it was dark. Letting them adjust to the lack of light, she looked around to see Lucy Jo, sleeping beneath her Disney Princess duvet, her gentle snores like heaven to her ears.

Standing up, Lana walked over and smiled. A sudden draft of air made her shiver, and she turned, startled at the sight of the bedroom window slowly opening.

Gasping, she ran over, trying to stop the kidnapper from entering, but it was no use. She wasn't really there; it was merely a vision, and her fingers went right through him.

Stepping backwards, she watched in horror as a person dressed entirely in black climbed in through the window. She tried to get a closer look, but she couldn't identify him. Yes, it was a man – but that was about all she could make out.

He carefully crept across the room and pulled back the duvet. Before picking little Lucy Jo up, he took something from his pocket and sprinkled it over her face. Then he put his hands underneath her and lifted her from the bed.

'Wake up, Lucy Jo, wake up!' Lana yelled as he crept back towards the window.

Seconds later, he and Lucy Jo were gone.

Lana started to sob loudly, tears rolling down her eyes as she felt the warmth of someone's arms wrap around and pull her into him. She stopped crying and breathed in the familiar scent of her father.

Opening her eyes, she looked up at his frowning face as he carried her into her own room. Declan and Emma stood behind them as he gently placed her on the bed.

'What happened?'

'I...I fell,' she said, rather unconvincingly.

Declan's eyes opened wide as he read her mind. 'Patrick, why don't you go back down to Audrey? I'll stay with the girls.'

Standing upright, Patrick turned to walk out of the room, but he stopped, turned back and asked. 'You just fell? Nothing else happened?'

'Erm...no, Dad.'

Frowning, he nodded and stepped out of the room, pulling the door closed behind him.

'What happened?' asked Emma again as she sat beside her.

'I saw him, Em. I saw the man who took Lucy Jo.'

'You did? Who? Who did this?' cried Emma before the door was suddenly flung open, and Patrick stood there, glaring at them all. 'You're going to tell me what's going on, and you're going to tell me right now,' he growled.

Emma grabbed Lana's hand as they both looked up at Declan.

'Patrick, I think you'd better sit down.'

'Declan, what the hell's going on?'

'Like I said, Patrick, sit.'

Doing as he was told, Patrick dropped down into the seat in the corner of the room.

'Girls, the truth was bound to get out at some point. And under the current circumstances, I feel it's only right that your parents should know.' Declan said sombrely.

'Know what?' Patrick said, barely opening his mouth.

'The truth about your girls.'

4

An hour later, Patrick remained in the same seat, totally dumb-founded. When Declan and the girls had finished telling him everything, he slowly stood up, rubbing his chin nervously.

Lana and Emma both looked pale. Both wanted so much for him to pull them into one of his bear hugs and tell them everything was going to be okay.

Instead, he opened the bedroom door and walked out without saying a word.

Emma couldn't hold it any longer, and she began to sob. Putting her arm around her, Lana leaned her head against her sister's shoulder and began to cry too.

Declan knelt down in front of them. 'Just give him a moment. He just needs to process it, that's all. Don't worry, please don't cry. He's still your dad, and he loves you so much more than you know. In fact, here he comes...' he stood up and stepped away from them as Patrick hurried back into the bedroom, crouched down and pulled his girls towards him.

'I always knew you were special,' he muttered beneath the tears. 'Your mother and I always used to say there was something about you, about both of you, that was different from other kids. But different in the best way possible. My daughters are angels, true angels.'

'Only half angels, Dad,' whispered Emma through her own tears.

Eventually, he let go and just looked at them.

'We need to find Lucy Jo, Dad,' Lana whispered.

He nodded and stood up, turning to Declan. Holding out his hand, Declan grinned and shook it before pulling him into a friendly hug. 'I'm sorry we had to keep the truth from you, mate.'

'It's alright. I understand now, I really do.'

'Right, Lana, you need to tell us everything about the vision.'

Lana looked up at her dad, who took a deep breath before nodding at her. 'Go on, love. Tell us everything.'

oOo

'So you think this person wasn't human?' Declan asked.

Patrick coughed nervously before she nodded. 'There was something about his eyes, something supernatural, Declan. I don't know how else to describe it. But he wasn't entirely human, I can tell you that much.'

'Perhaps that would explain the lack of footprints outside of Lucy Jo's window,' suggested Emma.

'We had some snowfall last night, which might have covered the tracks,' Patrick answered.

'But there is a possibility they didn't walk away from here, though,' Declan added.

Patrick shifted in his chair. 'If he didn't walk, then how?'

'He might have flown, Dad,' Emma said quietly.

'Flown? Jesus.'

The sound of the creaky step made Patrick jump up. The door opened, and Audrey appeared, looking pale and tired.

'Oh, love, perhaps you ought to get some sleep?'

'I can't eat, I can't sleep, I can't do anything until we've got our daughter back,' she snapped. 'Oh, I'm sorry, I just can't cope with this... I can't,' she cried into her husband's shoulder.

'I know, I know.'

'Right,' said Declan matter-of-factly. 'Audrey, I'm sending you to London with Saleena. No, I'm not taking no for an answer.

You're taking Greg with you, and you're going to stay with Eleanor. Patrick, you, me and the girls are going to get to the bottom of this. We're going to find Lucy Jo. Now that Lana has confirmed the presence of something supernatural, this is a case for the Watchers. You must trust us, okay?'

'Supernatural? Watchers? What are you talking about?' Audrey whispered.

'It's alright guys, I'll tell her,' Saleena said as she appeared in the doorway. 'Audrey, come and sit down in the lounge with me. Emma, would you and your sister mind going to make a very sweet cup of tea for your mum? She's going to need it. Patrick, perhaps a glass of brandy will be a good idea, as well. And, by the look on your face, you should join her.'

oOo

'I CAN'T BELIEVE THEY KNOW,' WHISPERED EMMA; THEY BOTH lay in the comfort of their beds, facing one another from across the room.

'I know it's kind of surreal, isn't it? Not having to hide anything from them ever again. It's cool.'

'They took it pretty well, didn't they?'

'If you mean drinking half a bottle of brandy, then I suppose so.'

'At least it helped her go to sleep for a while.'

'She'll be awake soon, though. The thought of Lucy Jo out there somewhere will stop her from sleeping for too long.'

'I know the feeling.'

'I can't believe they made us go to bed,' Lana tutted.

'Everyone needs sleep, sis.'

'I just can't help thinking about the kidnapper, you know? Those eyes. It's freaking me out. And why haven't we heard from him? Surely he's got demands? I mean, in the movies they always have demands.'

'Yeah, but this isn't a movie, Lana. This is real life.'

'Don't remind me.'

Both girls rolled over on to their backs, closed their eyes and sighed.

'Do you think she's okay?' Lana whispered.

'I hope so.'

'Why aren't we doing anything? We should be out there, scouring the island.'

'The police are doing that.'

'Yeah, and they won't let Dad join in. That sucks. He's the chief, he should be able to do what he wants.'

'He's too close, Lana. Too emotional. They need someone running the case that doesn't have such a strong connection to the victim.'

'You've been watching way too many episodes of CSI and Criminal Minds, you know, sis.' Lana smiled.

'But I'm right, though.'

'Yeah, I know.'

'Look, let's try and get some sleep and then, in the morning, we'll go hunting. Deal?'

'Deal. Night, sis.'

'Night.'

❄ 5 ❄

'Hi, Scott.' Lana sighed as she and Emma joined him on their bicycles a couple of days later.

'Hi. How are you coping?' he asked.

'Okay, I guess,' Emma sighed.

'Still no news?' Both of them shook their heads, and he frowned. 'You ready?"

They had planned to cycle over to the other side of the island, to see if they could spot anything suspicious. All three of them began cycling in the freezing cold air, determined to discover some kind of clue as to who took their little sister.

'Hey, there's that Hummer again,' yelled Scott, pointing further down the road as they watched it drive off into the distance for the second time in a week.

'That's a point, actually,' Lana said, 'That jeep only appeared on the scene a few days ago, just before Lucy Jo was taken.'

Speeding up, the three of them headed after it.

Eventually, out of breath and tired of pedalling, they arrived outside a traditional looking house just down the road from the Grimshaw farm.

The Hummer was parked in the driveway.

'Do you know who lives here?' asked Scott.

The girls shook their heads as they propped their bikes against the wall and crept around the back of the house, where a middle-aged woman was hanging out washing with two youngsters playing in the leftover snow just a few metres away.

'I recognise her,' whispered Lana. 'She works for Lady Denton. I think she's her cleaner.'

'Looks pretty normal to me,' Emma said quietly.

A bright-eyed young man appeared from within the house with a grin on his face.

'What you grinning at, son?' she asked in a high pitched squeaky voice, her face flushed from the cold breeze.

'I just bought a new car.' He grinned, almost jumping up and down with excitement.

'I didn't think there was anything wrong with the old one,' she said, pegging the last pair of oversized knickers to the line before turning to look at him.

'There wasn't, but I got an amazing deal on a Hummer,' he practically squealed.

Shaking her head, she picked up the basket and called to the kids to follow them back indoors.

'Do you fancy a ride in it, Mum? And how about you, kids? Want to come for a ride in Daddy's new jeep?'

'It's a jeep? What on Earth do you need a jeep for?' tutted his mum as they disappeared inside the house.

'So he just bought the jeep?' Scott said. 'So whoever owned it before nearly ran you over? We need to find out who owned it.'

'Why don't we just ask him?' asked Emma sensibly.

Lana shrugged as they walked back to the front of the house where the family was just climbing into the massive vehicle.

'Wow, what a car,' Scott said loudly.

'It is, isn't it?' said the young man.

'It's amazing. I've never seen one in the flesh before. Is it new?'

'Yup. Just bought it this morning.'

'Sweet,' Scott said. 'Can I come and check it out?' he asked as he stood at the front gate.

'Course, come and have a look,' the man said proudly.

The girls followed Scott as the middle-aged woman at the front door shook her head.

'Why on Earth would you spend all your hard-earned money on such a beast?'

'I think it's a boy thing,' Lana smiled.

'You're right there, love,' she said before nodding and going back inside, closing the door behind her.

'The guy I bought it off wanted to sell it quickly, so I got an outstanding deal.'

'Amazing. You'll be the envy of everyone on the island,' Scott said.

'Well, maybe all the men,' Emma smiled.

'So you just bought it this morning?' asked Lana.

He nodded.

'Who was the previous owner?'

'Nobody local.'

'What, just someone passing through?'

'I guess.'

'Do you know his name?'

The man knitted his eyebrows together, 'Yeah, it's right here. Let me have a look,' he climbed into the driver's seat and leaned forward, going through some papers in the front passenger seat. He didn't seem at all bothered about giving out the information.

'Stan something or other, I think. Yup. Stanley Sophokles.'

Lana's face dropped, and she turned to Emma. 'We've got to go now.'

'Huh?'

'We need to get home, like now, sis.'

Pulling her back towards their bikes, Scott had barely even noticed when he turned, and the girls were no longer there.

'Oh, wait up, I'm coming,' he yelled after them.

'Sorry,' he said to the new owner of the Hummer. 'Nice car.'

The man nodded his head before strapping his children into the vehicle.

'What's going on?' Emma asked as they cycled quicker than ever before, leaving Scott in their wake.

'Didn't you recognise the name?'

'No, I don't know anyone named Stan.'

'The surname, Emma, the surname.'

Emma looked puzzled as she puffed over the hill, letting herself freewheel for a few minutes to get her breath back.

'Sophokles? You really don't remember?'

Emma shook her head.

'That's Sthenelaus's surname.'

oOo

TELLING SCOTT THAT THEY WEREN'T FEELING VERY WELL AND needed to go and lie down, the sisters left him standing at the gate. He watched them disappear indoors, shrugged, and went home.

'Declan!' yelled Lana the second the door was closed. 'Declan!'

Both he and Patrick appeared from the kitchen, where they'd been poring over a map of the island. 'What is it?' he asked.

'We know who took Lucy Jo,' Emma gulped.

Lana glanced at her before blurting out, 'Sthenelaus.'

Declan's face dropped, and he sighed heavily.

'Who's Sthenelaus? Who is the man who has my daughter?'

'Sorry, mate, but you'd better sit down.'

Patrick shook his head. 'You're always telling me to sit down. I just want to know the truth.'

'And we're going to tell you. Please, have a seat, mate.'

Holding up his hands in surrender, Patrick walked back into the kitchen and sat down on a stool. 'Okay, I'm sitting down. Now, can you enlighten me?'

'Sthenelaus Sophokles is a very dangerous Skull.'

'What's a Skull?'

'They're like Watchers, but bad guys,' answered Lana.

'Yeah, they have a similar tattoo on their backs, but instead of a winged-eye, they have a skull with broken wings.'

'What do you mean by bad guys?'

'They fight for evil, not good.'

'But they have the same capabilities as the Watchers do?'

'Many of them have special abilities, yes,' Declan answered before continuing, 'and Sthenelaus is one of the worst. We recently came up against him in London, and it wasn't nice, mate.'

'We thought he'd killed Lana's boyfriend,' Emma whispered.

'But Barber managed to escape, and we think Sthenelaus might have been injured in the process.'

'So you think he's taken Lucy Jo to get back at Barber?' Patrick said, confused.

'Something like that,' Declan replied. 'But we can't be sure.'

'How bad is he?' Patrick whispered.

'Honestly?' Declan asked, and Patrick nodded. 'We're not really sure about the extent of his powers because he always uses other Skulls to do his dirty work, but he must be pretty evil for them all to look up to him. Girls, why do you think it's him?'

Lana explained how they'd come to the conclusion, and Declan nodded, rubbing his forehead.

'But it wasn't Sthenelaus that broke into the house,' Lana suddenly whispered. 'I would have known if it was him. I'd have recognised him for sure.'

'So maybe this Stan is a relative?'

'I reckon that's quite likely,' Declan said as he pulled out his mobile phone and dialled Praxos.

'Hey, Wilbur, Dec here. Can I have a quick word with Ellie? Thanks.' He waited a few moments before continuing. 'Hey, Ellie. Everything okay over there? Great. No, but we think we're on to something. Can you do some digging on a Stan Sophokles? Uh, huh, yeah. We think so too. Okay, I'll wait to hear from you. Thanks. Yeah, they're fine. Sure, hang on a sec,' he said, handing the phone to Patrick. 'Audrey wants a word.'

The girls and Declan left Patrick alone in the kitchen to speak to his wife.

'Eleanor is going to see what she can find out, but in the meantime, we need to find out where on the island this guy has been staying.'

'Oh, I just thought of something,' Emma said. 'Remember Mum told us someone had bought the old Grimshaw farm? She said that it was a mystery who'd bought it. What's the bet it's the same guy who sold the Hummer?'

'Where's the farm?' Declan asked.

'I'll drive,' Patrick said, sneaking up behind them. 'Come on.'

oOo

WITH LITTLE TRAFFIC ON THE ROAD, THEY ARRIVED IN NO TIME at all.

Climbing out of the car, Lana and Declan raced round to the farmhouse's back door, and Emma and Patrick ran towards the front. With his hand on the knob, Patrick twisted it. The door opened easily.

'Unlocked,' he whispered, pushing her behind him as they tiptoed in.

The house was completely devoid of all contents.

'I don't think there's anyone here, nor has there been for a while.'

'Then why was the door unlocked?' Emma whispered.

'Downstairs is empty,' Declan said as they all met up in the kitchen.

A thud from above silenced them.

Declan took the lead, with Patrick closely behind. 'Girls, wait down here,' their father said protectively.

'Dad, you forget what we are,' Lana tutted.

'You're still my girls, and I want to keep you out of danger, okay? Got that?'

Emma nodded, pulling Lana by the hand so that they stood leaning against the worktop.

Nodding, Patrick disappeared upstairs.

'It's weird, isn't it?' Emma whispered.

'What?'

'The house being all empty, this guy Stan and the Hummer, Dad knowing the truth about us... shall I go on?'

'Yeah, I know what you mean. I think we should go upstairs. You coming?'

Emma rolled her eyes but followed as they gingerly crept up the stairs, two at a time. Peering around the first door, they found nothing but an empty room. The second door was the same, the third just the bathroom and then, there behind the fifth door was Declan, standing beside Patrick, who was sobbing.

'What?' Lana asked as she pushed open the door.

'What is it, Dad?' Emma cried. She hated seeing him cry.

In his hands was Lucy Jo's favourite Monster High doll, and on the floor was a large dead blackbird.

$$\text{❦} \quad 6 \quad \text{❦}$$

Stan Sophokles was a twenty-year-old punk with an attitude. He was also the son of Sthenelaus Sophokles.

Eleanor had managed to find out all there was to know about him. What she couldn't find out, though, was his current whereabouts.

'I'm sorry, Declan, but that's all we know. We're still searching. I'll let you know the moment we have more details. What I can tell you is that nobody resembling Stan or Sthenelaus has arrived back on the mainland since Lucy Jo went missing. What have you discovered?'

'Very little, I'm afraid. Only that the old Grimshaw farm was purchased by Stan some time ago. It looks like he'd been hiding out there for the past two months. We're heading back up there shortly. Lana's hoping she'll have a vision. Keep your fingers crossed it'll work.'

After finishing his conversation with Eleanor, Declan turned to face the others.

'Eleanor's going to email all the details to us. We can study it tonight. I think you guys ought to have something to eat before we go anywhere, though. Audrey will do her nut if she finds out you're not looking after yourselves.'

Patrick nodded. He was tired, too, but he didn't care; sleep was the last thing on his mind.

oOo

THEY'D BEEN WALKING AROUND THE FARM FOR WHAT SEEMED like hours, but Lana had yet to experience one of her visions.

'I don't understand. Usually, they happen quicker than this.' She sighed as she plonked herself down on the floor of the room where they'd found Lucy Jo's doll. Emma sat down carefully beside her.

'Don't worry, sis. It'll happen, I'm sure it will.'

When the door flew open, Emma gasped in fright.

'Sorry,' Declan said. 'The front door's open and it's a bit windy out there. Anything?'

Lana shook her head.

'Don't worry, we're going to find her.'

'Dec?' shouted Patrick, who had been scouring the farmland for clues, and now stood at the bottom of the stairs.

The three of them walked to the top, peering down at him.

'I think I've found something,' he said quietly.

Rushing down as quickly as they could, they followed him back outdoors. Lana and Emma wrapped their scarves around their necks and put their gloves back on. The wind was biting cold.

'Down here, I think it's where old Mr Grimshaw used to keep his pigs,' he said, almost sliding down a slippery bank of ice and mud.

As they approached the old stone shelter, Lana looked across at her sister and physically heaved at the horrendous stench.

'What is that?'

Patrick shook his head. 'What?'

'That smell?'

'I don't smell anything,' Declan answered, looking at her with a weird expression.

'You don't?'

Patrick, Declan and Emma all shook their heads.

'That's weird,' she said, almost choking, 'It's disgusting,' she said, and began coughing, leaning forward with her hands on her knees.

'Are you alright, sis?'

'I... I think so.'

Two seconds later, Lana collapsed on the dirt.

Rushing to her side, both men carefully lifted her off the ground and were about to carry her back towards the house when Emma spoke.

'No, I think she's having a vision, Dad. She should stay here until it's over.'

Nodding, they looked around, before Declan's eyes settled on the little stone building.

As if reading Declan's mind for a change, Patrick nodded, and they carried her inside. Emma followed, her eyes adjusting to the dark.

'There – put her down there,' she suggested, pointing to a bed of fresh hay.

'That's odd,' Patrick whispered.

'What?' Emma asked as she sat on the hay beside her sister, holding her hand.

'The hay,' Declan answered. 'This place should be empty. It hasn't been used for a long time.'

'I think that's where you're wrong,' Emma whispered. 'I have a feeling this might have been where they kept Lucy Jo.'

Patrick clenched his fists and let out an angry sigh.

oOo

THE SMELL WAS NAUSEATING. LANA COULD BARELY BREATHE. Looking around, she shrieked. She was surrounded by pigs.

'O-M-G, I've died and gone to hell,' she muttered. 'This isn't the vision I wanted.'

Climbing up from the floor, Lana ran outside into the fresh air. Breathing deeply, the warmth of the sun enveloped her freezing cold body, and she sighed. Thousands of beautiful yellow butter-cups covered the fields surrounding her. Mr Grimshaw's farm stood proudly at the top of the hill, just a few hundred metres away.

Squinting, she shielded her eyes with her hand and watched as a young man walked towards her. He was dressed a little strangely, but Lana did nothing as he walked right past her and into the pigpen, where he fed and watered them, before returning back up the hill.

'What's going on?' She whispered under her breath as the sound of something unfamiliar filled her ears. Hooves?

Following him, she noticed a couple of horses in the field and then, just beyond the house, a horse and cart driven by a pretty red-haired woman covered in freckles appeared. The man grinned and hurried forward, helping her down.

They then walked back into the house.

Lana sighed. 'I need to get back to our time.'

Suddenly, another more familiar sound filled the air, and she looked towards the sky. It sounded like a propeller, a helicopter.

'But they didn't exist in this time,' she whispered to herself as she came over all dizzy, stumbling back onto the wall behind her where she fell.

'Lana, Lana?'

'Just give her a minute, Dad. She'll be okay.'

'What is that?' Lana whispered. 'It sounds like a chopper,' she said as she came out of the vision, opening her eyes to see three sets of worried eyes looking at her.

'A what?' Patrick asked.

'A helicopter. She thinks she can hear a helicopter,' Declan added.

The others quietened down, all listening in the distance.

Emma shook her head, 'No, there's nothing. It must've been in your vision.'

Lana shook her head as she lifted herself up off the floor, with the help of the others, 'No, it can't have been, because I wasn't in the right vision. I went back in time to... I dunno, maybe a couple of hundred years ago.'

'What did you see?' asked her sister.

'Nothing, really. Just one of the old owners of the farm, some pigs, a horse and cart and a pretty redhead. That was about it.'

'But the helicopter?' asked her dad.

Shrugging, Lana brushed the back of her coat, 'I definitely heard it.'

'Perhaps you were about to go into another vision?' Emma suggested.

'Maybe, but then why didn't I?'

Declan rubbed his chin, 'It doesn't matter. You might have given us the info we needed anyway. If you heard a helicopter, perhaps that's how Stan took Lucy Jo away.'

'Good point,' Patrick said as he took his mobile phone out of his pocket. 'I'll see if there have been any registered helicopter flights around the island over the past few days.'

Shivering as they exited the pigsty, Emma linked arms with Lana and smiled. 'You did good.'

'You think? But it was useless.'

Emma shook her head. 'Not quite. If he was using a helicopter, then that's a huge clue. We wouldn't have thought about it without you.'

'Thanks, sis, you always seem to make me feel better.'

Emma squeezed her arm, and they walked back towards the car and waited for Patrick to finish on the phone.

'There's been no registered activity, but a couple of locals did report a lot of noise on the night of the 25th, around here. One of them said it sounded like a helicopter.'

'So she was taken off the island by helicopter?' Emma whispered, tears falling down her cheeks.

'It certainly seems that way,' Declan answered, as Patrick pulled his girls towards him and hugged them tightly.

'Where would he have taken her, Dad? And why? Why did he take Lucy Jo and not me?' sobbed Lana.

'I don't know, sweetheart, I don't know.'

'It's all my fault,' she cried.

'No, Lana,' he whispered. 'It's not your fault, not at all. Don't think that, sweetheart. We'll get him, we'll get him for this.'

7

That night, wind blasted against the walls of the property and howled through the rest of the house, even though all the windows were closed. It was a haunting sound that made Lana shiver as she and Emma sat in front of the fire, drinking hot chocolate to warm themselves.

Nobody said a word, wrapped up in their own dark thoughts.

'It's like being on a ship,' she muttered.

'Huh?' said Emma.

'It makes me think of those storm movies, you know like The Perfect Storm or something. It's kind of creepy.'

'What?' Declan said from across the room, where he and Patrick were poring over a map of the British Isles.

'The noise of the wind, it reminds me of being on a big ship, you know, the ones you see in the movies.'

'Lana, you're a genius,' he answered as Patrick looked up at him in confusion.

'I bet he's taken them to a ship.'

'You think so?'

'It's a definite possibility.'

'But where?'

'That's the million-dollar question.'

'There must be something we can do,' Lana said as she stood up and walked over to look at the map. 'She could be anywhere in the world by now. Why would he keep her in Britain if he has a helicopter and a ship?'

'Because he's goading us. I doubt he'd take her too far away because he wants us to follow him. Lucy Jo is merely a pawn in his little game.'

'So you reckon they're on a boat somewhere? Not too far away?'

Declan nodded. 'That's my theory.'

'So where would he go?' Emma interrupted as she walked towards them and looked over her dad's shoulder.

'Where would you be on a ship in this weather, that's not too far away, and that's accessible by helicopter?'

All four of them looked down at the map.

'They've got to be in the North Sea somewhere,' Declan answered.

'Good God, I hope not. Lucy Jo will be absolutely terrified in this weather,' Patrick whispered, rubbing his eyes.

Placing her hands on his shoulders, Lana leaned forward and squeezed. 'Don't worry, Dad. We'll find her.'

Immediately picking up his phone, Declan dialled Praxos and explained his theory to Eleanor, who promised to get right on to it.

'Right, come on, girls, you need to get some sleep,' their father insisted.

'Only if you do, Dad,' Emma said.

'I will, I promise. Now go to bed.'

oOo

ALTHOUGH THE WIND HAD CALMED DOWN SINCE THE PREVIOUS night, the sea remained angry and rough. Striding towards it, Emma took a deep breath and looked out as far as she could see.

'Where are you, Lucy Jo?' she whispered, before shouting, 'Lucy Jo, we're going to find you!'

Without giving it a single thought, she took off her shoes and walked forward, wincing at the sudden plummet in temperature. Soon though, her gift kicked in, and her feet warmed up to match the rest of her body. Temporarily walking back out of the water, she thought nothing of removing the rest of her clothes, except for her black underwear, before running and diving into the sea.

Breathless just for a second, she trod water, waiting for her temperature to adjust to normal. When she felt comfortable, she ducked beneath the waves, opening her eyes as she swam farther and farther out, thinking of nothing but her little sister, out there somewhere, frightened and alone.

The thoughts made her swim faster and faster, until she swam upwards, breaking the surface like a dolphin gracefully jumping out of the water.

Looking around, Emma could see nothing but water, but she didn't care. With her newfound love of the sea and deep, inexplicable understanding of it, she knew she could always find her way home. But that was far from her mind. She was thinking solely of Lucy Jo and the evil that had taken her.

'Where are you?' she shouted.

In the distance, she could see fishing trawlers busy at work but dismissed them as being too small for a helicopter to land on.

Swimming farther and farther into the deep, she watched as huge tankers slowly made their way across the water and wondered if Lucy Jo could be hidden deep within their bowels. But she shook her head; even if she was, she could do nothing. Yes, she could haul herself from the water onto the ship, but then what? She was alone, she had no backup. And even if she did find her little sister, how would she return her safely to Andilyse Island? Lucy Jo would undoubtedly die of hypothermia.

Tears as salty as the water she drifted in rolled down her cheeks, and Emma realised had no choice but to go home. Floating on her back for a few moments, she let the water take her. Closing her eyes, she listened to the sounds surrounding her. Focussing hard, she could hear the tankers gliding through the water, the wind rushing across the surface and... what was that? Straining, she listened to what sounded like metal hitting metal, something far away, echoing through the water. Opening her eyes, she gazed up, watching as a plane flew across the sky, miles and miles above her.

Sighing, she was about to start swimming back home, but a different sound could be heard in the distance. It was familiar, a soft whirring getting closer and closer. As she recognised it, she stopped still, looking to catch sight of it. After another minute, she spotted it flying towards her. Eyes wide, Emma swallowed hard and watched the spinning propellers as the helicopter passed by at high-speed overhead.

Immediately following, she swam and swam until she spotted its destination: an oil rig.

Eventually stopping in the water, she watched as the helicopter deftly slowed, before landing on the specially designed helipad.

Without even giving it a thought, Emma swam as close to the rig as possible, sizing it up before deciding to climb up. It wasn't easy, but eventually, she managed to climb all the way to the top and peered over. She watched as several oil rig workers busied themselves, some joking as they walked past the helicopter, which had now come to a standstill, the sound of its engine no longer echoing through the air.

Emma knew instinctively that Lucy Jo wouldn't be found on the rig, but it had sparked an idea in her mind. She remembered reading something about some defunct oil rigs in the North Sea, and wouldn't one of them make a perfect hiding place for an evil gang and his captive?

Careful not to be seen, Emma turned and dived back into the cold water below, heading back to Andilyse Island as quickly as she possibly could.

oOo

Walking along the beach, whistling, Scott squinted at the sight of what appeared to be a pile of clothes in the distance. Removing his hands from his pockets, he ran forward, picked up the purple coat, and gasped. He recognised it at once. It belonged to Emma.

Picking up the rest of the items, he shook his head in shock.

'No, Emma,' he shouted, instantly thinking the worst. Looking around, he scoured the beach for signs of her body. 'No!' he wailed. Why would she do it? Surely she didn't blame herself for Lucy Jo's kidnapping?

Falling to the sand, he buried his face in her coat, crying loudly, sniffing and roughly wiping the tears from his face.

'Oh, Emma, no.'

'Scott?' said a voice behind him. 'Scott, what's going on?'

'Lana, I found Emma's clothes. She must've... she must've...' he gazed out at the freezing cold water of the North Sea and let out an involuntary sob.

Rushing forward, Lana realised she had to tell him. She couldn't let him think Emma was dead. It was time he knew the truth.

Taking the clothes from him, she dropped them onto the sand, took his gloved hands in hers and looked into his eyes. 'Scott, Emma isn't dead. Far from it.'

'What?' he muttered, barely able to focus on her because of his salty tears.

'She's not dead, Scott. She's swimming.'

'Exactly. No-one could survive that. It's... it's the middle of winter. She'll have gotten hypothermia, she'll have drowned.'

'Scott, look at me,' she demanded.

Immediately, he pulled one hand from hers and rubbed his eyes clear. When he'd finished, she took his hand back in hers and made him look at her.

'Emma is special, Scott. She can swim like a fish, a dolphin. The water temperature isn't a problem for her. She could stay out there for ages, maybe even days, and she wouldn't be hurt. I promise you, she's very much alive.'

'Wh...what?' he said suddenly climbing to his feet, looking at her disgust. 'Is this some kind of sick joke?'

'No, Scott. I promise you it isn't.'

'Well, it isn't funny. You can come out now, Emma. Joke's over,' he spat.

'Scott Spencer, stop right there and listen to me,' Lana shouted at his back. 'You've wanted to know the truth for some time now, and I'm trying to tell you what's going on, but if you're going to carry on being a stupid, pig-headed idiot, then that's up to you.' Lana stood up and turned with her head high. She stormed away from him. 'Boys,' she muttered exasperatedly.

'W—wait,' he semi-shouted.

Stopping abruptly, she turned to face him, angry tears stinging her eyes. 'What?'

'You're... you're really telling me the truth?'

'No, I'm just making up some pathetic lies to make you feel better. What do you think?'

'I...I... erm, Emma's okay, then?'

Crossing her arms, Lana nodded.

'She's out there?' He pointed towards the freezing sea.

'Yes,' Lana sighed as she walked back towards him.

'She has special... powers?' he whispered.

'Yes.'

'And you do, too?'

She nodded.

'So that time when you threw yourself off the cliff...?'

'Yes.'

'Jesus.'

Scott sat down on the sand with a thud. Lana joined him, placing Emma's clothes in between them.

'Why?'

Lana shrugged. 'It's in our genes.'

Scott coughed, half laughing. 'What exactly does that mean?'

'Emma and I are what are called Watchers. We're descended from angels.'

'Huh? Angels? For real? Come on, now you're really having me on.'

Lana shook her head. 'Nope. I'm telling you the truth. We actually found out that we have the same mother, who was an angel, but different fathers - obviously,' she added with a smile. 'We are kind of twins. Our mother carried us together, but had us on different days.'

'Huh? How is that possible?'

'She was an angel, Scott. Anything is possible for angels.'

'But I don't get it. Why you? Why are you here? Do your parents know? That Declan guy, he's one of you too, isn't he? And that place in London? It's connected, isn't it?'

'Whoa, slow down, slow down. For a start, I don't know why us. And we're here because our real mother decided Patrick and Audrey Morgan were the right parents for us. Yes, Declan is a

Watcher. Well, he's a Mentor, but still a Watcher. Oh and that place in London? Yes, it's an academy for others just like us.'

Scott's white face was motionless.

'Scott, say something, do something,' she said, pushing him hard on the shoulder.

'I...I... I don't know what to say,' he whispered.

'You must keep this a secret, Scott. You must do. We can't have the general population knowing the truth about us and all the other supernaturals out there - it could cause outrage, and God knows what.'

'Did you say other supernaturals?'

Laughing, Lana leaned forward. 'All those things you assume are just in fairy tales?'

He nodded.

'They're real.'

'No way.'

'Yes, way. So, you swear on your life that you won't tell a soul about us?'

'I swear on my life,' he whispered. 'Your secret is safe with me, Lana. I promise. You can trust me.'

'I always knew that, but Emma is going to go ape when she finds out I told you.'

'Emma is what?' said a voice approaching them.

'Emma!' Scott exclaimed, grabbing her clothes and handing them to her.

'What's going on?' she asked, as she quickly got dressed.

Scott looked away nervously.

'I told him, sis.'

'You told him what?'

'The truth.'

Emma looked up, her long-sleeved T-shirt halfway over her head.

'I had to. I found him here on the beach, crying his eyes out. He thought you were dead.'

'Oh.'

'You should never leave your clothes in plain sight like this. Jeeze, Em. What were you thinking?'

'Oh, I erm... sorry.'

Once she was fully clothed, she turned to look at Scott, who had turned his back towards her while she got dressed. 'I'm dressed now.'

Slowly he turned to face her.

'You thought I was dead?' she whispered.

Nodding, he plunged his hands into his pockets.

'Sorry.'

'Now, do you get why I had to tell him?'

Emma nodded and shivered. She would never understand why she could swim in freezing temperatures, but the moment she stepped out of the water, she couldn't stop shivering.

'Come on, let's head back and get you into some warm clothes.'

They turned to walk up the beach. After a couple of seconds, Emma turned to find Scott still stuck in the same spot.

'Coming?'

'You want me to come with you?'

Emma smiled. 'You know who we really are. You may as well come back to the house and help us find our sister.'

He looked down and kicked a pebble towards the sea.

'Plus, you're our best friend, Scott. I'm sorry we had to leave you out before. We won't keep the truth from you again.'

His face lit up, and he walked forward, linking his arms with theirs.

'You okay?' Lana asked.

'Yeah, I think I'll be fine once this has all sunk in.'

Emma chuckled. 'You think?'

$$\approx \quad 8 \quad \approx$$

'Emma, you were absolutely right,' grinned Declan. 'About two months ago, a former oil rig owned by Peliogas Ltd. was about to be decommissioned. However, in a last-ditch attempt to sell it off, they found a buyer called...'

'Let me guess, Sthenelaus Sophokles,' Emma answered.

'Close.' He smiled. 'Sophokles Inc.'

Lana and Emma jumped up and down while Patrick smiled at their reaction.

Scott sat nervously in the corner of the living room, holding onto a now very cold cup of tea.

'We're going to get her back, Dad,' Lana said once they'd calmed down.

'It's not going to be easy, though,' Patrick replied. 'How are we going to get there?'

Declan smiled. 'Patrick, you clearly don't know very much about Praxos. 'Raising his eyebrows, Patrick turned to look at Declan, who winked. 'We have our resources.'

'So what are we waiting for?'

'Slow down, mate,' Declan said. 'We can't just fly in, all guns blazing. They'll have eyes everywhere. We need to keep Lucy Jo's safety at the front of our minds, and for that, we need to be sneaky. We're going to need Emma to swim... again.'

Emma grinned. 'Finally, I can do something to help,' she sighed.

'Erm, can I do anything?' whispered Scott.

Turning to look at him, Declan stood up, making Scott jump and move back in the sofa. 'We might be able to use you,' he said thoughtfully. 'There's a possibility we might need some bait.'

Scott swallowed loudly, and Declan's face creased up.

'Oh man, you should have seen your face.'

Scott laughed nervously.

'Declan!' scolded Lana.

'Seriously, though, we could use an extra pair of hands, couldn't we?' asked Emma.

'Perhaps, but I'm not putting young Scott in any danger if we don't have to,' Patrick added.

'But you'll take me with you, won't you?' Scott asked, standing up and putting the cold cup on the coffee table. 'I really want to help. Your daughters are my best friends, sir. I want to do everything possible to get Lucy Jo back safe and sound.'

'And I appreciate it, Scott. Thank you.'

Declan patted him on the back. 'I don't want you getting in the way or putting any of us in danger. You're not as strong as Lana and Emma, Scott. You're not a Watcher. So you can't come with us. I'm sorry, mate, but it's just too dangerous.'

'B—but...'

'No buts, mate.' Declan shook his head.

'Sorry, Scott,' Lana said sadly.

oOo

Piling everything they were going to need into the large boat, the group climbed aboard, leaving Scott standing on the dockside alone.

'Please let me come with you,' he pleaded, wringing his hands in front of him. 'I must be able to do something. Don't leave me behind... again.'

Lana and Emma looked at each other and then back at Declan, who had disappeared with their father below deck.

Hurrying, they leaned forward and grabbed him, pulling him onto the boat.

Grinning, Scott quietly hid away in a corner until they were well out at sea.

After about an hour, Declan stepped out on the deck and looked for the girls, who were sitting quietly chatting.

'Do you think I'm stupid or something?' he asked.

'Huh?'

Pointing to his own head, he shook it. 'Are you forgetting I can read minds? Get out here, Scotty boy.'

Emma winced, and Lana actually smacked herself on the forehead. 'I forgot about that.'

Scott nervously appeared, shivering and frowning with his head hanging low.

'What am I supposed to tell your mother?' said Patrick, peering out from where he'd been chatting to the captain.

'I'm sorry, sir,' Scott muttered.

Patrick shook his head before looking at his daughters. 'You should know better than to put your friend in danger.'

'Sorry, Dad, but he really wants to help. We couldn't just leave him there,' Emma said.

'Yes, actually, you could,' Declan scolded. 'But he's here now. Unless we throw him overboard, there's not much we can do.'

Scott took a step backwards and gulped.

'You must be freezing. Get out of the cold, and go and get warmed up. In fact, why don't you make yourself useful and go make us all a cup of tea.'

Relieved at not being thrown into the freezing cold North Sea, Scott attempted a weak smile before disappearing below deck.

'I'll call his mother. I'm sure I can reassure her he'll be fine with the girls.'

'What will you tell her, Dad?' asked Lana.

'Not much I can tell her, really, except for the fact he's going to be spending a few days away with us.'

'It'll be alright, mate,' Declan interrupted. 'You're the Chief of Police. That boy could move in permanently with you, and she'd be okay with it.'

Patrick smiled and went inside to make the call.

'That was a stupid thing you've just done, you two. Now we've got another person to worry about.'

Both girls hung their heads down. They were unused to being told off by Declan. Usually, he was the cool guy.

But his mood didn't last. When Scott re-appeared, trying hard not to spill the tea he was carrying in both hands, Declan shook his head with a cheeky grin as he took the first cup.

Taking a sip, he nodded appreciatively. 'Well, at the least we've got ourselves a decent tea boy.'

oOo

IT SEEMED LIKE THEY'D BEEN TRAVELLING FOR AGES WHEN THE captain began to slow the vessel down.

'There.' He pointed far off into the distance. 'That's the rig you're looking for.'

'I guess it's over to me, then,' grinned Emma as she hurried inside to put on the wetsuit Patrick insisted she wear.

'Whoa, not so fast, Em,' Declan said as they followed her indoors. 'We need to talk about—'

'No, we don't. Just let me go and find out where he's hiding her and then—'

'No,' Patrick and Declan said at the same time.

'You're not going in there until we've discussed how we're going to handle this. It could be a trap. We don't want him taking you hostage too.' Patrick's brow furrowed.

Sighing, Emma plonked herself down on the uncomfortable sofa and waited as the two men discussed the best way to handle the situation.

Both Lana and Scott said nothing.

Nobody noticed, after twenty minutes of discussion, that Emma was no longer sitting in the room with them.

oOo

FINALLY, SHE THOUGHT, AS SHE SWAM THROUGH THE WATER, feeling a little guilty at just disappearing like that. But she couldn't wait any longer. Lucy Jo was so close. She couldn't just sit and wait for them to finish talking. She had to do something.

Sooner or later she'd be swimming anyway; it may as well be sooner.

As she approached the now-defunct oil rig, Emma was careful to remain below the waterline. For all she knew, this Stan character could be waiting for her. Did they know about her power? She had no idea. But at this point, she didn't care. All she cared about was little Lucy Jo.

Slowly surfacing for air almost directly beneath the rig, she was careful to keep herself hidden beneath the structure. Scouring above her, she waited patiently, listening, straining her ears for any sound other than the soft swishing of the sea.

But there was little more than the faint clanging of steel above. Slowly emerging from the cold water, Emma stretched, reaching for a low hanging pipe which she grabbed and used to pull herself upwards. Climbing, she didn't stop until she was safely standing beside the only door in sight. Shivering, she looked around. Not a sound and no sign of anyone, so she slowly concentrated on her inner warmth, allowing her light to emanate upwards from her core, the heat beginning to dry her. When she'd stopped shivering, she opened the door and walked through, careful not to make a sound. But she couldn't shake the bad feeling creeping into her mind. The thought that she wasn't going to find her little sister. The notion that this was just some crazy ruse by a mad man, trying to drive the Watchers insane. It was working, just a bit.

Unable to shake the sensation, Emma began running down the corridor, pushing open every door. But behind each one was nothing. No sign of her sister, no sign of any kind of life. What was going on? They were so sure this was where she would be. The rig belonged to the Sophokles clan, didn't it?

Moving faster than she ever thought possible, Emma soon found herself in front of the last door. Taking a deep breath, she slowly pushed it open. But before she could see anything, she knew. She knew Lucy Jo wouldn't be there.

❊ 9 ❊

'I can't believe you did that,' Lana shrieked, as Emma climbed back on board the fishing boat, rushing towards her with a towel. Emma took it gratefully.

'What the hell do you think you're doing? You could have been killed,' yelled her father as he climbed the steps from the lower deck.

'I...I'm sorry, Dad, but I couldn't just sit here and do nothing.'

Roughly towel drying her hair, she looked guilty as he continued to berate her.

'Yes, you could. We're handling this. Me and Declan. Don't ever pull a stunt like that again, do you hear me?'

'But Dad,' she almost wailed.

'No,' he interrupted. 'I've already lost one daughter, I'm not losing another.'

'Patrick, come on. I think that's enough. As much as you don't want to hear it, you have to rely on the Watchers sometimes. Emma, what happened?'

She shook her head.

'Nothing at all?'

Standing looking down, she slowly lifted her arm. Everyone looked down as she opened the palm of her hand.

'That's, ...that's Lucy's bracelet,' cried Lana, falling into her dad's arms and sobbing.

'So we were right. They did bring her here.'

Nodding, Emma looked towards Declan. 'There was nothing else there. Just this, on a chair in the middle of the last room I looked in.'

'But when did they get away?' Lana whispered. Scott gently placed his hand on her shoulder as her father walked away from them and stood silently looking towards the rig.

'It's all been a ruse. This whole thing. Nothing but a ruse to bring us here. But why?' he asked, turning around to face them all. 'What does he want with us?'

Declan shook his head. 'Some kind of revenge, maybe. Or he just wants to play.'

'Play? This is a game to him?' Anger clouded Patrick's face.

Declan nodded. 'I think so, mate. I'm sorry we haven't found her, but we will. We're going to get Lucy Jo back.'

oOo

EMERGING FROM THE TINY CABIN WEARING DRY CLOTHES, EMMA caught her breath when Lana appeared out of nowhere and headed towards her.

'I still can't believe you did that. It's so unlike you,' she smiled.
'What?'

'Disregarding what Dad said and diving into the water to try and rescue Lucy Jo all on your own. It's more like something I would do.'

'If only you could swim like me,' Emma joked as she took her sister's hand and they walked back up to where the rest of the gang were.

Declan was on the phone as the boat trawled through the water at its fastest speed – which really wasn't very fast at all.

'...yep, nothing. Huh? Where? Are you sure about that? We're on our way.'

He turned to the others who stood eagerly awaiting news.
'Well?' asked Patrick.
'There's been a sighting.'
Lana's eyes opened wide. 'Of Lucy Jo? Where?'

'Of Stan... in Portugal.'

'Portugal? What the heck is he doing in Portugal? And does he have my daughter?' Patrick asked.

'The reports suggest he might be holding someone captive there,' Declan added. 'But we don't know for sure that it is Lucy Jo.'

'But it's our best shot. We must go.'

'I agree, and so does Eleanor. She's organised a small plane to take us there from the mainland.'

Patrick nodded and looked at his other daughters and Scott. 'It's going to be a long night. Why don't you go and try and get some sleep? We'll wake you when we arrive.'

Lana and Emma both scurried into his arms and gave him a long hug.

'We'll find her, Dad. Don't worry,' Emma assured him.

Patrick, careful to not let them see the tears collecting in his eyes, merely nodded and pushed them in the direction of the door. 'Go and sleep. You too, Scott.'

'Yes, sir,' Scott replied as he led the girls out to the bunk beds.

'So what really happened over there?' asked Scott when they were all lying in their berths and trying, but failing, to get some shuteye.

'Nothing,' murmured Emma.

'Didn't you see anything?'

'Nope.'

'There must have been something.'

'Scott, listen to what she's saying. She said nothing else happened. Now stop asking stupid questions.'

'Sorry,' he mumbled, turning on his side to face the wall. 'It's just that, well, you know. I'm not a Watcher, so I don't really understand anything, and I'd like to know details to try and get my head around all this stuff.'

Emma turned around and held her hand into the middle of the room, tapping him gently on his shoulder. When he turned back over to face her, she smiled. 'Honestly, there really isn't much to tell. I dived into the water and swam to the rig, where I climbed up and scoured the area until I found Lucy's bracelet on that chair. I had another good look around to see if I'd missed anything, but there was nothing there at all. It was almost like it was staged for us.'

'I think that's exactly what it was,' Lana whispered. 'They wanted to get us away from the island so they could disappear without being seen.'

'And go to Portugal,' Scott said.

'Do you really think that's where they've taken her?' asked Lana.

Emma nodded. 'Far away from London, far away from Andilyse Island. Yep, sounds about right.'

'But why Portugal? Of all places, why there?'

Emma shrugged. 'That's something we're just going to have to figure out, isn't it?' she said, as she leaned forward and looked at her sister who was lying face upwards on the bottom bunk.

'Absolutely.' Lana grinned.

'Do you think your dad's going to let me go with you?' whispered Scott, after a few minutes of silence.

'Honestly?' Emma said, and he nodded. 'No way.'

Sighing heavily, Scott turned onto his stomach and closed his eyes. 'That sucks.'

oOo

'PLEASE, MR MORGAN, SIR. I WANT TO DO EVERYTHING I CAN TO help you find Lucy Jo. Please let me come with you. I won't get in your way. I'll do everything you tell me to. Just please, please let me come with you.'

Patrick shook his head and placed both of his hands on Scott's shoulders as he looked down into the teenager's eyes. 'Scott, son, you know I can't do that. I can't let you come and put yourself in danger. I'm sorry, but no. This time, you have to stay here.'

Scott cursed silently under his breath and turned away.

'And there's no creeping onto the plane, this time, either.' Declan smiled. 'Trust me, mate. You're much better off staying here. If anything happened to you, the girls would be heartbroken. Stay and wait for us to come back with little Lucy Jo. Just support them, Scott. That's all we can ask you to do. And most importantly, don't tell a soul about what you know. Okay?'

Scott nodded silently as both Lana and Emma approached him, each taking one of his hands in theirs and pulling him across the tarmac to the little cafe beside the runway.

Emma let go as she went and ordered herself a cup of green tea, a coffee for Lana and a hot chocolate for Scott.

Returning with the drinks, she carefully placed the tray on the table and sat down. Nobody said a word as they sipped quietly.

After ten minutes, Lana sighed loudly.

'I know,' Emma agreed.

'It just sucks,' Scott said, slamming his drink down so hard that some of the dark liquid sloshed out of the top and dripped down the side, leaving a ring on the table.

'But it's probably for the best,' sighed Emma as she wiped it with a paper napkin.

'You can't possibly mean that.'

'I do, Scott. We don't know what's out there. You can't...' she sighed and looked around before continuing, 'fight like we can. You don't have our... skills.'

'She's right, you know,' Lana agreed.

Scott looked forlorn.

'But that doesn't mean we don't want you to come. Of course we do. It's just that, well, you can't, and there's nothing we can do about it. I'm sorry, Scott. I really am.'

'I know,' he sighed, looking across the runway at Patrick and Declan. The soft sound of an aircraft in the distance made him look away. 'That must be your plane.'

Looking up, the girls nodded, watching as it made its way towards them, slowly descending out of the sky. Soon, it was approaching the runway, and within a few more minutes had touched down. Turning, it eventually came to a halt just a few hundred metres away.

'Have you got everything ready, girls?' Declan asked.

They nodded, standing.

Reaching for Scott's hand, Declan smiled. 'We'll see you soon, mate. Take care of yourself.'

Shaking his hand, Scott attempted to smile as Patrick put his hand on his shoulder. 'We'll keep you updated about what's going on. Hopefully, we'll be back in no time at all. Girls, you've got a couple of minutes,' he said as he picked up their heavier bags and headed towards the plane.

'So,' Scott said as he kicked the tarmac with the front of his shoe.

'So,' Emma smiled. 'I guess we'll see you soon?'

'Guess so.'

'Oh, come here,' Lana said as she pulled him towards her into a big hug.

'Lana!' yelled a voice from the plane as the door opened.

Letting Scott go, Lana looked up in surprise. Her gaze followed the sounds, and a grin appeared on her face. 'Barber?' she shouted. 'Barber!' she squealed as she ran towards him, and he ran down the steps of the private plane.

Before she reached him, though, she stopped and turned back to look at Scott. 'I'll call you, Scott!' she waved before rushing into her boyfriend's arms and climbing the steps, disappearing inside.

'Well, I didn't expect that,' Scott mumbled.

'Yeah, me neither. Sorry.'

'For what?'

'You know.'

'Huh?'

Emma smiled and said nothing.

'What?' he asked again.

'Never mind.'

'I guess you should go too.'

'Yeah, we have to go find my sister. I'm sorry you can't come, Scott. I really am. But we'll call you all the time to let you know what's going on.'

'Yeah, I know. It's cool,' he said unconvincingly.

Pulling him into a hug, Emma sighed when Patrick called out her name. 'I guess it's time.'

'Be careful, Emma.'

'I will, I promise. Speak soon, Scott.'

He smiled and pushed her gently away. Walking backwards, she grinned at him before turning and running towards the plane.

oOo

'HE'S A WHAT?' YELLED PATRICK AS HE STOOD UP AND TURNED to glare at his daughter and the incredibly handsome young man sitting beside her.

'Calm down, mate,' Declan said, trying to pull his friend back down but he was having none of it as he stormed over to Lana who was looking increasingly worried.

'Take your hands off my daughter.'

Barber immediately removed his hand from Lana's and looked over at Declan, who was trying to calm the situation down before it got out of hand.

'Dad?' Lana whispered.

'You're dating a...a... a vampire?'

Lana shook her head before slowly turning the movement into a nod.

'I don't believe this,' he said through gritted teeth. 'Declan, how could you let this happen? This is preposterous.'

'Mate, look, you're blowing things way out of proportion, here.'

'You just told me he's a vampire,' Patrick said, pointing a finger at Barber, who was still sitting calmly, yet looking a little concerned.

'Dad, he's not like your everyday vampire. You've got nothing to worry about,' Lana tried to reassure him.

'Stand up,' Patrick said.

Turning to look at Lana, who let out a deep sigh, Barber stood.

'Get away from my daughter, you beast.'

Barber looked down and shook his head. 'Sir, you've got this all wrong.'

'So you're telling me you're not a vampire?'

'Erm, well no. I am.'

'Then get the hell away from my little girl.'

'That's enough, Dad. And I'm not a little girl. Not anymore. I'm a Watcher, I'm supernatural, just like Barber is. There's no difference between us,' she cried.

'Really, you should know better than this, Lana Beth. I said, step away from my daughter.'

Barber stepped away from his girlfriend and just stood, looking at Declan as he approached.

'Patrick,' Declan placed a hand on his friend's shoulder. 'Lana is safer with Barber than any other young lad. He may be a vampire, but he's one of us,' he said, putting his hand on his heart. 'He would never do anything to harm your girl. In fact, he would die for her. I know that for a fact.'

Barber nodded as Lana stood up and grabbed his hand.

'It's true, sir. She means the world to me. I'm sorry that I'm not an ordinary boy. I wish I were, but I'm not, and there's nothing I can do to change that. But Lana means more to me than anyone ever has. Please, I know it's hard to accept, but we want to be together. '

With his nostrils flaring, Patrick looked away for a minute before returning is gaze to the two of them. 'So you're not going to drink her blood and try to turn her into one of...you?'

Barber shook his head. 'She is totally safe with me.'

'It's true, Dad. Barber's not like the vampires you see on TV. He's a really good guy, and we all trust him implicitly,' Emma said from her seat.

'Dad, chill out,' Lana said with a sad smile. 'We've got much more important things to worry about, and Barber's here to help us with that. Trust him, Dad. He's a good guy.' She stepped forward. 'I know you're upset, but please stop. You don't need to worry about me.'

'I will always worry about you and Emma. You mean the world to me.'

'I know, Dad,' she said as she hugged him tightly.

As she pulled away, he looked at her and then at Barber before he nodded. 'Alright, but if you ever do anything to hurt my daughter, I will hunt you down. You understand?'

Barber tried to hide his smile. 'Yes, sir, absolutely.'

🙞 10 🙜

'J eeze, I thought it was gonna be warm,' Lana said with chattering teeth as Barber laughed, pulling her into him and rubbing her bare shoulders. She grinned, looking up into his dark eyes. 'I'm so glad you were able to come.'

'I will always come when you need me,' he replied as she continued to shiver.

'Lana, it's nearly January. Please tell me you brought some winter clothes with you?' Emma tutted.

'Yeah, I did. Kind of,' she sniffed. 'I thought it would be warmer. I mean, look at this incredible blue sky. It should be hot, not f-f-freezing cold.'

'For goodness' sake, Lana, what is with you? This is Portugal, not the Caribbean. You'll have to borrow some of mine.' Emma walked towards her suitcase and rifled about in it for a couple of seconds before pulling out a thick, warm black hoodie and a pair of purple jeans. She handed them to her sister.

'You've got to be joking. I can't wear that.'

'What's wrong with it?' asked Emma as she looked down at her clothes.

'It's just so not me, Em,' Lana said in disgust.

'Well, in that case, you can just stay freezing cold then, can't you?'

'Maybe I could go shopping?'

Emma's nostrils flared as she tried to stay calm.

'What?'

'Lana Beth Morgan, we're here to rescue our little sister, not go to a freaking fashion show. Now put the damn clothes on and stop being so ridiculous.'

'She does have a point, hon.' Barber half laughed where he sat on the kerb.

'Oh God, you're so right, Em. I'm sorry.' Lana took the clothes from Emma and smiled. 'Thanks. Where can I change?'

'I think the toilets are through there,' Emma pointed.

'I'll come with you,' Barber smiled.

Patrick raised his eyebrows at them before Barber added, 'I'll wait outside.'

They were standing outside Faro Airport, waiting for their pick-up, and although the sun shone down from a glorious blue sky, it was still pretty cold. Emma was glad she'd dressed sensibly, unlike her sister who had been wearing thin leggings with what looked like a summer dress over the top.

'Here she is,' Declan announced as a large black van drove down the road towards them and stopped just a few metres away.

When the driver's door opened, a beautiful woman in her late twenties with long dark hair hopped out. With a huge grin, she removed her sunglasses and walked towards them. 'Declan!' she yelled. 'It's so good to see you!'

'Bella, mate. Long-time no see. How you doing?'

'Awesome, Declan. I'm awesome,' she winked as she turned to look at the others. When her face stopped on Patrick's, her expression changed immediately, and she took his hand. 'You must be Patrick Morgan. I'm so sorry about Lucy Jo. But don't worry, we're going to find her. Know that, okay?'

Patrick nodded and smiled. 'Thank you. That means a lot.'

'I'm Arabella, by the way. Please call me Bella. It's a pleasure to meet you.'

'It's good to meet you too, Ara...bella.'

'And this is Emma Jane, Patrick's daughter.'

Emma smiled as Arabella leaned forward and kissed her on both cheeks.

'I've heard a lot about you, Emma Jane. It's lovely to finally meet you.'

'You have?'

Arabella nodded. 'Eleanor talks about you and Lana Beth quite a lot, actually. Where is Lana Beth?' she asked, looking around.

'Erm, she had to go and change. Lana usually likes to make a bit of a fashion statement, but she kind of got it wrong today.'

'Let me guess. She wore summer clothes, right?'

Chuckling, Emma nodded. 'She has to borrow some of my clothes, and she's not too happy about it.'

Arabella looked Emma up and down and laughed. 'I take it she's not much of a goth?'

'No way.' Emma smiled as Lana and Barber finally appeared from the airport.

'There she is.' Emma pointed to her sister, who was looking pretty disgusted at her outfit. Barber was holding her hand, reassuring her that she looked fine.

'Hey,' Lana smiled.

'Hi, Lana, I'm Arabella. It's great to meet you.'

After introducing Barber, and all the pleasantries were out of the way, the group climbed into the black van. Declan whistled as he settled in. 'Nice wheels, Bella.'

'I know, right? It's new. We just bought it a couple of months ago. It's got all the mod cons you could ask for – plus a few special extras.' She grinned as they pulled away from the airport and headed out into the sparse traffic on the main road.

Lana let out a shriek the moment they did so, causing Arabella to quickly pull over and lean backwards. 'What? What's happened?'

'You're... you're...?'

'What's wrong, Lana? asked Patrick.

Declan sniggered from the front passenger seat and shook his head as he read her mind.

'Don't worry about her, Bella. She's just never been abroad before. She didn't realise you drive on the other side of the road.'

Everyone shook their heads in disbelief as Arabella giggled and slowly pulled back out into the traffic. 'Don't worry, Lana. I'll be careful.' She winked, looking at her via the rearview mirror.

Lana looked embarrassed as she shrank down into her seat and covered her face with her hand, leaning her head on Barber's shoulder. He gently patted her knee and squeezed her hand.

'So, Barber. You're a vampire, right?' asked Arabella.

Barber nodded. 'That's right.'

'That must be weird for you, Patrick.'

'Weird? That's one word for it,' Patrick replied, looking away from them both.

'We've actually got a few vamps living with us in Monchique. It'll be nice for you guys to meet.'

'Monchique?' asked Emma.

Arabella nodded as she focussed on the road. 'That's where we live. Well, where our Praxos HQ is located. It's in the mountains.'

'Cool. Is that where we're headed now?'

Arabella nodded. 'I think we should get settled in and then start work immediately.'

'Absolutely,' Declan agreed.

'The sooner we do that, the sooner we get my little girl back.' Patrick smiled grimly and fixed his gaze out of the window as they hurried towards their destination.

oOo

The journey from the airport to Monchique was a quiet one. There was very little traffic on the roads, and everyone was so curious about their surroundings that they'd mostly just looked out the window silently. When they eventually turned off the motorway, the group had sat up and taken more notice of the winding roads and the pretty old houses dotted on either side of the hills.

'There are a few entrances to HQ, but the main one—the one we like to use the most—is just off Monchique town itself. Plus, it's well camouflaged. To the general public, they think it's merely an attractive villa in the hills.' Arabella grinned. 'Monchique town is just up there,' she pointed as they turned right off the roundabout and then right again behind an old building where several old men were sitting chatting away.

'It's a pretty awesome view up here,' she said as they followed a winding road around a few bends before they found themselves looking down on the whole of the Algarve beyond.

'Wow,' said Lana. 'It's breathtaking.'

'It is, isn't it? The villa is just around the corner,' she said as they turned left down a country lane. At the end was a large gate. Opening her window, Arabella inputted a code on a keypad and sat back while she waited for it to open.

As it did, it revealed the most stunning contemporary property the girls had ever seen.

'Whoa... are we actually staying here?' Lana shrieked.

'As a matter of speaking, yes,' Arabella smiled. 'When you're not needed downstairs, you can hang out here, of course.'

'Downstairs?' asked Patrick.

'It's just our term for HQ – because it's located deep within the mountain. Access is by elevator or stairs inside the villa. And, of course, as I mentioned before, several other points throughout Monchique.'

'You mean there are other villas like this one?'

'Yes, but some are old buildings too.'

'Is HQ a number of tunnels, like in London?' asked Barber.

Arabella nodded. 'It's a similar design.'

'Nice,' he replied.

As they parked close to the main entrance, Emma and Lana hopped out and ran around the front to check out the view.

'O-M-G there's an infinity pool!' squealed Lana. 'And look at that view. It's like being on a plane. It's just... amazing,' she sighed.

'Just remember why we're here, sis,' Emma whispered.

'Yeah, I know. I can't forget Lucy Jo. But maybe, when we've got her back, we can spend some time here? Maybe fly Mum and Greg over for a holiday?'

Emma smiled as Patrick walked up behind them. 'It's a nice thought, Lana, but let's not get ahead of ourselves. Let's just concentrate on getting her back. Lucy Jo is all that matters now.'

❧ 11 ❧

Arabella stood in front of a large map of Portugal, poring over it with Declan, Barber and Patrick, as well as a few other Portuguese Watchers.

Lana and Emma sat quietly, waiting for the time when they could actually do something.

A massive wooden door, with the Praxos Eye carved into it, was pushed open silently and a little teenage girl appeared. When she spotted the sisters, she smiled and walked over.

'Ola.'

'Hi.' Emma grinned. Lana just smiled.

'Are you Emma and Lana?'

The girls nodded.

'I heard about you from Arabella. She asked me to come and take you for a walk, for fresh air.' She pointed upwards.

'That would be great, thanks,' Emma replied as she pulled Lana up off the sofa.

'I'm Sonia. Follow me, please.'

Arabella looked up and nodded to the girls with a smile before returning her attention to a tall, dark man who Lana assumed was one of the vampires she'd mentioned earlier. They hadn't had time to meet them because Patrick had been keen to get straight down to business.

Taking a different route back to the main villa, the girls walked behind Sonia, noting her long dark hair, fashioned into two plaits that reached just below her bottom. They continued walking until they came out into a room with a large indoor swimming pool and jacuzzi.

'Wow, this place is amazing,' said Lana.

'Yes, it is like a playground, no?' Sonia smiled.

'Do you live here?'

'No, not really. My main house is towards the bottom of the mountain, but I am allowed to come here when I want – along with the other Watchers. We use the pool sometimes.' She grinned. 'It's heated,' she added.

'Cool.'

'Maybe I can show you around my house sometime?'

'That would be nice,' Emma smiled as they walked up some more stairs that led into a large open plan kitchen, dining room and living room, with walls of thick glass that looked out onto that stunning view they'd seen earlier, with the outdoor pool just steps away.

'I could get used to this,' sighed Lana.

'Yes, it is very nice,' Sonia smiled. 'Come, let's walk.'

Following the girl, the sisters were forced to stop when she suddenly disappeared right in front of them.

'Erm, Sonia?' Lana whispered.

'Oops, sorry. It sometimes happens without me realising,' said a voice from thin air before she materialised again.

'Now that is one cool power,' whistled Lana.

'Yes but I am still trying to control it. I am not allowed to go anywhere alone until I have control. Anywhere out of Praxos, that is.'

'That's a bummer,' Lana said as they continued walking through the immaculate gardens in front of the house.

'Yes, a bummer,' Sonia said.

Emma laughed at her accent, making Sonia smile.

'I am told you two are sisters? You don't look like sisters.'

'Yes, we get that a lot, but we are. We have the same mother – an angel – and different fathers. But, we are actually twins. One of the wonders of having an angel mother, I suppose.'

'Yes, I have heard lots of interesting stories about Watchers. Yours is most intriguing, though. Do you know your real parents?'

Both the girls shook their heads sadly.

'Our real fathers died, and our mother had to return up there, apparently. You know the drill?' said Lana.

Sonia looked confused. 'The drill?'

'Oh, that's just a funny phrase. You know the truth about the angels?'

'Oh, yes, of course. My mother also had to return. But my father is still here, and he is a Watcher too. He lives in the house down the mountain.'

'Oh right, that's cool.'

Sonia nodded. 'He is a very good man. He looks after my sister and me very well.'

'Your sister?'

'A young sister. She is only three. She is not a full Watcher, though. She has a different mother.'

'So your father remarried?'

'My step-mother is a little... strange,' she said, with a weird expression on her face.

'Strange?'

Sonia shrugged and sped up a little.

Emma shook her head. 'I don't think she wants to talk about her,' she whispered, just as Lana was about to ask.

'I think you're right. Maybe she'll elaborate when she's a bit more comfortable with us,' Lana whispered back.

Suddenly, Sonia disappeared right in front of their eyes again, and Emma found herself bumping into something solid.

'Ooh,' Sonia said before they heard the sounds of something falling.

'Huh? What's going on?' Lana said from behind her sister.

'Erm, I don't know. Sonia disappeared, and then, erm, I really don't know.

'Sonia?' they both asked together.

Suddenly she re-appeared further down the steep garden, curled up on the ground, holding her leg. Her face was drained of colour.

'What happened? Are you alright?' Emma asked as she leaned forward to help the girl up. 'You disappeared.'

'I stumbled and fell down through the bushes, my leg... it hurts,' she said, rubbing her ankle.

'Ewww, Sonia I think you've broken it,' Lana said, pulling a face at the oddly-positioned leg. 'I'll go and get help.'

Sonia nodded, and a couple of heavy tears slowly fell from the corners of her eyes as she tried to stand up.

'No, Sonia,' Emma almost yelled at the poor girl. 'Don't stand up. You'll make it worse. Just stay sitting down until the others get here to help. Don't worry, you'll be fine. I'll stay with you.'

'I...I've never broken a bone before,' Sonia cried.

'Me neither. It looks pretty bad, though.'

'It hurts so much, the pain is... is... getting... worse...'

And with that, Sonia slumped sideways, passing out amongst the sticky bushes behind her.

'Oh, shoot,' Emma muttered under her breath as she carefully tried to hold onto the other girl. She had absolutely no idea what to do. It was only then that she realised in all the classes they took at Praxos, first aid hadn't been amongst them.

Eleanor... I think we need to add a new class, she thought to herself.

'Exactly what I was just thinking,' said a voice behind her.

Startled, Emma breathed a sigh of relief at the sight of Declan, followed by a few others close behind him.

'She passed out. I didn't know what to do.'

'It's okay, we've got her. She'll be fine,' he said as he very gently hoisted her up into his arms. He winced when she saw the state of her ankle.

'It's definitely broken,' Arabella said as she carefully held the injured leg up.

'Oh God, I think I might throw up,' Lana said as they approached her by the pool.

Suddenly, Sonia began to groan, and slowly her body began to disappear.

'Oh!'

'It's okay, Declan. She has the power of invisibility, as I'm sure you were already aware. The problem is she's only just discovered it, and she can't control it,' Arabella said as they both kept a firm hold of the invisible girl.

'Oh God, this must be my fault. She disappeared, and I bumped into something. It must have been her,' Emma cried.

'No, it's not your fault at all. Don't blame yourself,' Arabella whispered.

'Don't worry, my love', you're going be just fine,' Declan reassured Sonia.

'Se doi... Doi tanto. Sinto-me tonta Arabella.'

'Não te preocupes minha linda. Tu vais sobreviver.' Arabella smiled as she led them indoors. Sonia reappeared again as they laid her down on the large leather sofa in the living room.

Arabella immediately pulled out a mobile phone and seconds later, began speaking incredibly fast in a language the girls didn't understand.

'She can't be taken to a hospital,' Declan told them.

'Why?' Lana asked as Barber appeared from downstairs.

'Is she okay?' he asked.

'I think she'll be alright in time. She's broken her ankle – I think in two places,' Declan answered before turning to look at Lana with raised eyebrows.

'Oh, yeah, her invisibility thing.'

Ignoring everyone else, Emma had gone into the kitchen and put the kettle on, returning a few minutes later to hand a cup of sweet tea to Sonia.

'Sonia,' she whispered, pushing the girl's damp fringe from her eyes. 'Here, drink this. I've heard that sweet tea is good for shock. I'm so sorry for bumping into you.'

Arabella and Declan shared a smile as Sonia carefully took a few sips before handing it back and collapsing on the sofa.

'Can't we do anything?' Emma asked.

'Don't worry,' Arabella said, 'the Praxos doctor is on his way, and in the meantime, one of the Mentors is coming to help with the pain relief. She'll be fine. The sweet tea was an excellent idea. You're a natural carer, Emma Jane. Did you realise that?'

'Always been the same,' said Patrick as he pushed open the door from downstairs and walked in, looking exhausted. 'She's always tried to look after us all, even when she was a little girl.' He smiled.

'Any news?' asked Declan.

'I've just spoken to Eleanor. She's got a group together, and they're coming over as soon as possible. Apparently, there's been some unusual erm... paranormal activity, along the coast. She's waiting to speak to you, Arabella.'

'I'll call her immediately, thank you. When Theodore arrives, please show him to Sonia. He'll know what to do before the doctor gets here.'

Declan nodded as Patrick and Arabella returned downstairs.

oOo

THEODORE WASN'T WHAT EMMA JANE WAS EXPECTING AT ALL. IN fact, she wasn't quite sure what she'd been expecting, but it certainly wasn't him.

About six foot six, Theodore was nothing less than a hulk. His massive bulk of muscles were covered from head to toe in tattoos... well, not his head. From neck to toe. If they'd seen him from behind, they'd probably have run a mile, but the moment Emma and Lana looked at his face, they knew instantly that he was nothing but a gentle giant.

His eyes were so warm and friendly; it was easy to imagine that they twinkled a little bit too. He had long dark hair, which he wore loose as he arrived, but before he approached Sonia, he twisted it up into a kind of masculine chignon – if a chignon could ever be masculine. But with Theodore, it just worked. He had a long droopy moustache, which Lana thought looked a lot like the ones sported by those heavy-looking bikers that drive Harleys in America. He nodded to everyone but didn't say a word; his only concern was Sonia. And for that reason, Emma Jane smiled.

Approaching the young girl, Theodore bent his knees so that he was on a level with her and he took both her hands in his large ones. She opened her eyes to see who it was, and at first, she visibly shook with fright, but it lasted mere seconds. As her eyes sought out his, the girls watched as she relaxed, a faint smile forming on her pale lips.

'Don't worry lassie, yer gonna be fine,' said Theodore in an unexpectedly gentle voice.

'Scottish?' Lana almost shrieked before her eyes opened wide and she covered her mouth with her hands, embarrassed at her gut reaction.

'Aye,' he replied with a wink before returning his attention to his patient.

'Sorry,' she whispered, shrugging as Emma and Barber tried not to laugh.

Theodore smirked before he released Sonia's hands and proceeded to hover them above the broken bones.

Emma was intrigued as she watched a faint glow appear from beneath his fingers and wind itself around the leg.

Sonia opened her eyes again and gasped. 'The pain, it's gone.'

Theodore smiled and continued to control the glow for a few more minutes before leaning forward and whispering something into Sonia's ear. She smiled and closed her eyes before relaxing further into the soft leather. Seconds later, the sound of her gentle breathing in sleep was all that could be heard.

'Wow,' Emma said. 'That's fantastic. I wish I could do that. My boyfriend has a similar skill.'

Standing to his full height, Theodore grinned. 'Am guessin your boyfriend's Diarmuid, then?'

'How did you know?'

'I have me ways, lassie.'

Looking confused, Emma wished she could interrogate him, but the door from downstairs burst open and Patrick appeared looking like he'd seen a ghost.

'Dad?' Lana gulped. 'What is it? What's happened.'

'They've... they've found a...a....bo—' Unable to say anything further, Patrick stumbled, choking on his tears.

Theodore rushed forward and helped him to the nearest chair.

Arabella appeared looking a little pale.

'Arabella, Dad... what's going on?' Emma asked.

'We've received news that the body of a child has been found.'

'No, it's not her, it's not. I know it's not Lucy Jo,' Lana said as she tried to get everyone's attention.

'What do you mean?' asked Barber.

'I don't know what it is, but I can feel something, and I just know that it's not her. Dad, Declan, Arabella you've got to believe me. Lucy Jo is alive. I just know it.'

'Then who is the little lassie?' asked Theodore.

Arabella and Declan looked at each other sadly.

'I wish we knew.' replied Arabella.

'Let's go and find out. Maybe there's something we can do. Maybe we can help her?' said Emma.

Arabella shook her head. 'I'm afraid that's impossible, Emma. She's dead. We can't bring her back to life. That's just... impossible.'

'But... But...'

'There are no buts, I'm afraid,' said Declan. 'I wish there were. If only I could somehow pass on my ability to arise from the dead, but I can't. I'm sorry.'

'Are we... are we... absolutely certain that the little girl isn't my Lu...Lu...Lucy Jo?' Patrick could barely utter the words.

'If Lana has a feeling, then I trust her one hundred per cent. And you should, too,' replied Declan.

'But... perhaps we should go to the...' Emma swallowed loudly. 'The morgue. So Dad can see for himself?'

'No need, we have someone working there who will send us a picture as soon as the body arrives. Let's just sit tight and wait,' Arabella said quietly, looking at her watch. 'The doctor should be here shortly. Theo, could you please carry Sonia through into one of the bedrooms?'

Nodding, he bent down and picked her up as if she weighed nothing at all, before walking down a bright corridor adjacent to the kitchen.

Patrick didn't say a word, he just sat with his face in his hands. It broke Emma's heart looking at him. Standing, she approached him and put her arms around his shoulders.

'Don't worry, Dad. Lucy Jo is going to be fine. We're going to find her.'

He nodded sadly and hugged her back before Lana walked over and hugged them too.

oOo

THE LITTLE GIRL WHO HAD DIED WAS A SEVEN-YEAR-OLD Bulgarian child who had wandered off from her parents in a nearby town and walked down to the beach. Her parents were beside themselves with worry until the scream of a passer-by had alerted them to her lifeless body, floating on the water's edge. All life had disappeared from her previously bright blue eyes, and her scraggly blonde hair had wrapped itself around her neck. Her sobbing father and wailing mother had carried her away from the waves and laid her carefully on the sand, hoping against hope that she wasn't dead, just unconscious. Sadly that simply wasn't the case. The little girl had drowned. It had only taken a matter of minutes.

❧ 12 ❧

It had taken him a few days to convince her, but eventually, Eleanor had given in and allowed Diarmuid and his classmates to board the plane with her and the other supernaturals. Destination: Algarve.

Diarmuid was determined to be there for his girl, Emma Jane, and to help in the search for her kidnapped little sister.

Although the mood was rather sombre during the flight, the group had tried to cheer themselves up, playing tricks on each other, taking advantage of being surrounded solely by other supernaturals and using their powers for fun.

Eleanor had turned a blind eye, instead concentrating on the large file she had created over the past few days. In it were details of every unusual occurrence that had happened in the Algarve region and beyond since Lucy Jo's disappearance. She had fought the likes of Sthenelaus for hundreds of years, but never before had anyone made such a personal attack on her students or their families. Anger grew in the pit of her stomach, and she felt the stress rise until she wanted to scream.

Are you alright, Eleanor?

The voice hadn't spoken aloud, the words merely popping into her head. Turning, Eleanor watched Ava, who stood and left the others. Walking towards her Guardian, Ava practised her power.

You look troubled.

Eleanor smiled and nodded sadly. 'You're quite right, my dear.'

'Anything I can do to help?' Ava asked, aloud this time.

'You're already doing it, by being here. I had wanted to avoid bringing any of my students towards any sign of danger, but I think in this case, it was probably a good idea. That poor little girl,' she said, looking out of the window.

Ava placed her hand momentarily on Eleanor's before she turned away, going back to her seat.

'These students are pretty special,' Beau Madigan said from the seat opposite Eleanor.

'Your daughter among them,' she smiled back as they both looked over at the fifteen-year-old with a mass of red curls at the other end of the plane. She was sitting next to Cassie, who also had a mass of curls, but hers were blonde. She was tall and strong, quite different from Daisy's more petite frame. Even though there was a year between them, the two had bonded over their ability to move exceedingly quickly. Eleanor and Beau watched as they murmured, looking very serious.

'Yes,' Beau muttered. 'She has grown into a remarkable young woman.'

He fidgeted slightly with his fingers and sighed.

'Beau,' said Eleanor, 'don't blame yourself for what happened. It is done now, and you are back together, where you belong. It was a tough year for both of you. Don't forget that. We all deal with grief in different ways. Besides, that year alone,' she said, nodding her head towards the back of the plane, 'has made her a much stronger Watcher. She's special, Daisy is. But I think you knew that already.'

Beau's smile belied the pain he still felt at the loss of his wife, Esther, but smile he did. He was determined to give his only daughter a better life, and that began with Praxos.

'Thank you, Eleanor. For everything.'

'You know you really must stop thanking me,' she laughed. 'You do it almost every day.'

Beau's smile reached his eyes this time. 'I don't think I'll ever stop.'

Undoing her seatbelt, Eleanor stood and patted him on the shoulder before turning her attention to the group of supernaturals she'd gathered together to help in the hunt for Lucy Jo. They were silently sitting at the other end of the plane, a couple of them clearly uncomfortable in the air.

Eleanor approached and took a seat next to a handsome man with chiselled features. He smiled warmly at her.

'Glad you came?' she asked.

'I'm glad you asked me to come,' he replied cheekily.

'I knew a man of your skills would come in very handy.'

'Is that the only reason you invited me along?'

Eleanor blushed slightly. 'You already know the answer to that question, Giovanni.'

'I'm sorry I can only stay for a couple of days, but I will do everything I can to help.'

'I know, and for that, I am exceedingly grateful.'

She and the leader of the London Werewolves had become close since his assistance with finding the Temporal Stone, several months earlier, much to the amusement of her students, who often made silly quips about her being a dog lover. But Eleanor took it all in her stride. She knew everyone was delighted with the pairing, especially her.

Giovanni wasn't a shy man, and he took her hand in his and smiled, before closing his eyes. 'Why don't you try and get some shuteye before we land?' he whispered.

She thought for a second and then followed suit.

oOo

'DIARMUID!' SCREECHED EMMA JANE AS SHE RAN DOWN THE steps by the pool and straight into his open arms. They ignored the other teenagers' stupid comments and kissed each other, laughing. 'I didn't know you were coming. I didn't know you were all coming,' she said as Lana joined them, hugging each and every one of them—except for Liam, of course. That would be too weird after they'd broken up before the summer. Plus, she didn't think Ava would appreciate it. Maybe Barber wouldn't, either.

Liam whistled appreciatively as they all followed them up the steps and out onto the terrace where they stood for a moment eyeing the view.

'It's quite special, isn't it?' asked Emma.

'You can say that again, Em,' Imran laughed as Nisha grabbed his hand.

'Hey... you two finally got together huh?' Lana laughed, pointing, making them both blush.

'Yeah,' Nisha said quietly. 'A few weeks ago.'

'Perfect couple,' Emma added before they all followed her indoors, where Arabella, Eleanor, Declan, Beau, Patrick and all the other supernaturals were filling each other in. Even Theodore had stuck around to lend a hand, much to Eleanor's delight.

'Theo, it's been so long,' she said as they hugged. 'I'd forgotten you'd moved to Portugal after Inverness.'

'I needed some sun, lassie,' he chuckled before they all headed downstairs to what had become the hub for the search for Lucy Jo.

'You kids hang out for a while. Help yourselves to anything in the kitchen,' Arabella said.

'Except the beer,' Declan added, looking specifically at Liam and Rupert, who put his hand to his forehead in a salute.

'Shouldn't we come and give you a hand?' asked Emma, who was practically glued to Diarmuid's side.

'No need, not just yet, Emma,' Eleanor replied. 'Let us get settled. Don't worry, we'll call you when we need you. If you go out, please stay close.'

The teenagers all nodded as the adults left them to it.

'This is wicked,' Rupert said, falling onto the large sofa.

Emma gave him a dirty look.

'Oh, man, Emma. I'm sorry,' he muttered, sitting upright. 'For a second there, I forgot why we're here. Sorry, girls.'

'That's okay, Rupert,' Lana replied.

'What news has there been so far?' asked Elliot, who had stayed pretty quiet throughout the whole journey.

'We had an awful scare this morning. A little girl turned up dead. But it wasn't Lucy Jo, thank God. I mean, it's so sad for her and her family... erm, y...you know what I mean,' Emma stuttered.

'It's okay, sis. We know.'

'That's it? Nothing else?' asked Rupert.

Both girls shook their heads.

'No visions, nothing?' asked Cassie.

'Nothing,' Emma sighed.

'Oh man,' Rupert mumbled.

'I know, right? I feel so helpless. I wish there were something we could do to find her,' Lana said quietly.

'Have you started an actual search... you know, like a door to door?' Daisy suggested.

'It's not as easy as that, unfortunately. The Algarve's a big place when you look at it like that. We need a starting point,' Lana replied.

'So what are they doing downstairs?'

'Trying to find that starting point, I guess.' Emma said, as she and Diarmuid sat down at the dining table.

'Why don't I put the kettle on while we have a brainstorm of our own?' asked Moira, who yawned and stretched like a cat before she took off her glasses, gave them a quick wipe and went into the kitchen.

'Sounds like a plan to me. Thanks, Moira,' Emma smiled.

'My pleasure, honey. Now, who wants what?'

oOo

'...THE MAIN ISSUE HERE IS THAT SINCE WE PUT OUT A PRAXOS alert, we've been absolutely inundated with possible sightings covering the length and breadth of the Algarve and beyond. So, unless we bring in more Watchers from around Europe, we'll never be able to look into every single sighting.' Eleanor sighed as she placed the last of the red dots on to the map. A map that looked like a giant red dot, considering how many were actually placed on it.

Patrick nodded, as did the others. 'But you guys are superhuman, right?' he asked gingerly. 'There must be something you can do with your powers to narrow down the search area? '

Eleanor smiled warmly as Barber opened the door and tiptoed in before she looked at the rest of the group. 'We've already used some of our abilities, but it hasn't helped enormously, I'm afraid. Giovanni sent word to the local wolves, who are still out there now. We gave them one of Lucy Jo's teddy bears, so they have a good scent to follow, but as yet, nothing.'

'What if this guy has already taken her out of the country?' Patrick asked.

'We don't think that's the case. We are being led to believe that he is toying with us. He's playing a game of cat and mouse. And he's unlikely to remove the one thing we want from him,' Declan added.

Patrick let out a deep sigh. 'And the general search?'

'So far it has brought us nothing,' Arabella answered as she sat down on the armchair.

'This guy must want something from you?' Patrick asked.

'So far, we're unsure about that,' Eleanor replied.

'Didn't you say something about a stone? The... Temporal Stone, or something? You mentioned he tried to steal it from you? Maybe that's what he's after?' said Patrick

'It's a possibility, but an unlikely one. I fear he wants people, not objects.'

'People?'

'Maybe Barber, maybe Lana Beth, maybe even me. Who knows?' she replied.

'Can we send him a message?' Barber asked.

'Probably. What are you thinking?' she replied.

'We make a trade. Me for the little girl?' Barber offered.

'Barber, no. He'll kill you this time.'

'I'm prepared for that.'

Patrick put his hand on his daughter's boyfriend's shoulder and shook his head. 'Thank you, Barber, but nobody dies. Not on my watch. Not even a vampire.'

'Spoken like a true copper,' said Declan, from the corner of the room, 'but Barber has a point. We could send out the message that we're prepared to negotiate. It doesn't mean we give him what he wants. We just let him think that.'

Everyone nodded.

'Okay then, let's do it. Start spreading the word. Prepared to negotiate. Got that?' Eleanor asked as people started making phone calls to their contacts on the street.

'Now what?' asked Arabella.

'Now we wait.' said Eleanor.

OoO

'I DON'T LIKE THIS, I CAN'T UNDERSTAND A WORD THEY'RE saying,' grumbled the little girl as she crossed her arms and pouted.

Kimberly chuckled and stood up from the dining table where she'd been reading the newspaper. Grabbing the remote control, she flicked through the channels until she found some English cartoons playing on the screen. 'How's that? Better?'

The girl's eyes grew round, and a broad grin appeared on her face. 'Monster High!' she squealed. 'That's my favourite!'

Kimberly smiled and sat down beside her. After a couple of minutes, she was laughing with the child. 'You're right. This is really cool.'

'Told you.'

Archie stood watching from the doorway when Stan suddenly appeared. 'Why isn't she pining for home? She's not mentioned her mum or dad since we left the rig.'

Stanley shrugged with a smirk.

Turning to face him, Archie's face became darker. 'What did you do?'

'Nothing, nothing.'

'Stanley,' Archie growled.

'Nothing to hurt her, Jeeze, Archie. I just did what Dad told me to do. It's just a temporary spell until he finds the memory clan, that's all.'

'A spell? There's a witch here?'

'Not now. She came, she did the spell, and she left.'

'And she did nothing to hurt her?' Archie asked, glancing at the little girl giggling in front of the TV.

'Nothing, I swear.'

13

Lana Beth had kept Lucy Jo's Monster High doll with her ever since they'd discovered it lying there on its own at the old farmhouse on Andilyse Island. She was hoping it would help her to have another vision, but so far there'd been nothing. Not a single stir.

Feeling helpless, she went to open the door to go downstairs when she bumped into Barber, who was on his way up.

'Oops, sorry, babe,' he said, taking her hand and pulling her away from the doorway.

'What's going on?' she asked.

The other teenagers looked over, waiting to hear the latest news.

Barber filled them in. 'Now we're just waiting.'

Lana sighed. 'Just waiting? That's all you've all come up with? It's crazy.'

Barber squeezed her hand. 'Be patient,' he whispered. 'You look exhausted. Why don't you try and take a nap?'

Lana shook her head. 'Impossible.' But as she sat down next to him, she found her eyes closing involuntarily, and soon she was breathing heavily, fast asleep.

'I think I'm going to swim,' Emma said quietly, as she stood up. 'I think better when I'm under the water.'

Diarmuid stood up too. 'Want some company?'

'Honestly? I'd like to swim alone. Plus, it's probably a bit cold for you. You don't mind, do you?'

'Of course not,' he replied, kissing her forehead, thankful that she hadn't wanted him to go into the freezing cold pool. She hadn't shown him the heated one yet.

As she went to change, he went back to sit with the other Watchers, who were still trying to think of ways to find her sister.

Although she'd have preferred to swim in the ocean, the outdoor pool enticed her, pulling at something deep inside her. She dived in, settling at the bottom of the deep end, where she managed to sit cross-legged beneath the water.

With her eyes closed, Emma focussed her entire being on Lucy Jo. She thought back to the day her parents had brought her back from the hospital, a couple of days after she was born. She and Lana had been ecstatic at having a little sister, and they'd spent hours just looking at her, until she started crying, and then they'd left their mum alone. Emma smiled at the memory. About how delighted she'd been when they'd brought Fred home from old Josiah's house. She thought about the days before Christmas, the fun they'd had decorating the tree, Declan and Saleena's arrival, messing about with Scott and then she thought about Christmas Eve, when Audrey and Patrick had put Lucy Jo and Greg to bed at the same time; it had been the only night they hadn't complained about going to bed before everyone else. So excited about the next day, they were eager to sleep in readiness for all the fun and presents of Christmas day. But that wasn't meant to be, was it? Because she had been taken in the middle of the night.

Emma's brow furrowed at the thought, but she stayed still and focussed on the bedroom, the sounds of the night, and she remembered Lana's vision as if it was her own. Someone climbing in through the bedroom window and tiptoeing across the little room, picking up Lucy Jo's favourite rabbit slippers and Princess dressing gown, waking the little girl who didn't appear frightened in a strange woozy state, as if she'd been drugged. He then tenderly put on the slippers and nightgown and carried her out of the window.

Suddenly, Emma's eyes flew open, and she propelled herself off the tiles until she stood beside the pool, dripping water everywhere. She didn't even bother with the towel, she just ran into the house. The others watched in confusion, seeing the look on her face. The look of wonder that she'd just had a vision of her own.

Breathless, she ran down the stairs until she reached Eleanor, leaving a trail of glistening water in her wake.

'Emma? Emma? What is it?' shouted Lana, who ran closely behind, careful not to slip on the wet tiles.

The other teens followed until everybody was standing around Emma as she briefly caught her breath.

'What is it, Emma?' Patrick asked as he stood before her and held her arms.

'I had a... I had a...'

'A what? Slow down,' Eleanor said. 'Take a deep breath.'

Breathing in through her nose, Emma closed her eyes and let the breath out slowly before she spoke. 'I had a vision.'

Lana gasped and put her hand on her sister's arm. 'A vision?' she said, looking delighted.

'I saw him come to Lucy Jo's bedroom. He drugged her somehow, with something he blew into her face. But the thing is, the weird thing....'

'What, Emma, what?' Patrick said, shaking her arms slightly. 'Please tell me what happened.'

'He was so gentle with her. He cared, Dad. He didn't want to hurt her. Plus, something we didn't even notice before. He dressed her in her favourite slippers and dressing gown. He didn't want her to be cold or uncomfortable. He cared, Dad. He was gentle. Why?' Emma sat down, not bothered that she was still soaking wet.

'That's very interesting, Emma. Thank you...' Eleanor smiled.

'But what does it mean?' Lana asked. 'I don't get it?'

'It means that he won't hurt her. He might be an evil son of a b...erm, sorry,' Patrick muttered, letting his daughter go. 'But he doesn't intend to harm her. Which can mean only one thing.'

'What, Dad?'

Patrick's expression was grim. 'That he means to keep her as his own.'

Lana and Emma gasped at the same time.

'So it was never a game?' Arabella whispered.

'He thinks she's a Watcher too,' Eleanor suddenly said. 'That's why. He found out that Emma Jane and Lana Beth Morgan have the potential to be two of our strongest Watchers, and he wanted that for himself. So he took their sibling. Their youngest. The one he can make forget,' she continued, talking to herself.

'Forget? Forget what?' asked Patrick.

'Everything.'

$\maltese$ I4 $\maltese$

'**B**ut why would he bring her to Portugal? And why wouldn't he leave?' Diarmuid asked the other teens later that day.

They all shook their heads in dismay.

'What if...' Elliott suggested, 'there's someone in Portugal, or in the Algarve, that possesses the power to make people forget and can give them new memories. If that person exists, then that is what Sthenelaus will want. He'll want to make Lucy Jo think that he is her father.'

'Absolutely,' said Arabella. 'After talking this through with everyone downstairs, that's exactly what we think he will do. It is believed that there are four people here in the Algarve that can do exactly that. Apparently, they all belong to the same family, but there was a feud many hundreds of years ago, and each went their separate ways. The trouble is, we don't know where they went. And I doubt that Sthenelaus knows, either. All we know is that they are Portuguese, and they were born and raised in the Algarve. Specifically, in the city of Silves. They may have left, they may not. Unfortunately, they have always been a very secretive family, and so we know very little about them. But we will find them. Before he does. We will.'

Everybody was given an hour to prepare for their first day out in the Algarve. They were on the hunt for four people, and as yet, nobody knew what they looked like. Eleanor was busy trying to find a clue—something, anything—that would help track them down first.

'Are they good, these people? Are they on our side?' asked Daisy as she searched her father's face.

'Hopefully, Eleanor will be able to tell us, sweetheart. Let's just wait and see.'

Daisy nodded and went outside to sit with Sammy, who was leaning against a large oak tree with a smile on her face. 'What are you smiling at?'

'This tree. It's a happy tree,' Sammy said simply.

'O...kay,' Daisy muttered.

'Yeah, it's been here for a hundred years, it loves the sun here. It says it's not too hot.'

'Right...'

'She can talk to animals as well as plants, you know,' said a voice behind them.

Turning, Daisy smiled at the sight of Emma Jane. 'Hey.'

'Hey, you. How are you doing? I haven't had much of a chance to speak to you in a while.'

'I'm good... I'm happier now. Thanks to you.'

Emma just smiled and looked at the water over in the pool.

'That was pretty cool what you did earlier, you know?'

'What? Having a vision in the water?'

Daisy nodded. 'It's clear that you have an affinity with the water like Sammy has an affinity with trees, I guess,' she laughed.

'Yeah, maybe you're right.'

'No maybe about it. I am right. I usually am,' Daisy grinned.

'Hey, guys!' Lana shouted from indoors. 'We think we have something.'

Eleanor was handing out sheets of A4 paper to all the different groups. On each layer was the same pencil-drawn image of what looked like an old hag. Lana thought she looked like something out of Hansel and Gretel.

'Are they witches?' she asked as everybody stood quietly looking at the picture.

'No, although you might think they resemble something out of a fairy tale book.' Eleanor smiled. 'But they're not witches. It is said that they have the power to change memories permanently –

we're not sure how, yet, but we're trying to track down some people that might be able to enlighten us.'

'So what do we do when we find them? What if they try and change our memories?' asked one of the other kids.

'We believe that they are good people who won't use their power unless they are in danger—or are forced to, of course. Our main problem is tracking them down. We believe there are four in existence here in Portugal, the only ones in Europe. We must find them before he does.'

'But how are we going to do that? We know virtually nothing about them,' moaned Imran.

'Our colleagues are working on that. They've given us some coordinates in several different towns along the Algarve. We're going to split up into groups and head off and investigate. We'll keep doing that until we find something—anything—that might help us.'

Patrick nodded. 'What are we waiting for? Let's move.'

The Morgan sisters were teamed with Barber, Diarmuid (much to their delight), Declan and Arabella, while the other groups all hopped into their designated vehicles, which had been delivered that morning. They drove through the gate and started heading back down the mountain. Nobody said a word until they approached a beautiful, large old building on the left. Outside stood a familiar smiling face, leaning on a pair of crutches.

'Sonia!' yelled Emma as they pulled over for a moment.

Arabella hopped out, saying, 'I'll be right back.'

Winding down the window, Emma leaned sideways with a grin. 'How are you? How's your leg? I'm so sorry about your fall, I feel responsible.'

'I'm okay, I think, and please don't think that. It's my fault. I should have told you about my... erm, invisibility problem. Don't worry, I'll be okay. Thank you for helping me before.'

'It's our pleasure, lovely,' Declan said from the front passenger seat. 'Are you feeling better?'

Sonia nodded shyly. 'Whatever Theodore did, it helped... a lot.'

'I'm glad,' replied Emma.

'We need to sign your cast,' Lana added, leaning forward.

'Sign it?'

'Yes, it makes having a broken leg a little bit better... if everyone signs it or draws funny pictures.'

'Oh, okay. Maybe later.' Sonia grinned.

'You ought to be lying down,' Declan added.

'Yes, I know. I've been horizontal since yesterday. I just wanted to come out and wave to you as you went by. I did not know Arabella was going to stop. I should go indoors. Good luck today— I believe my father is joining you.'

'That's great,' Emma said. 'Hopefully we'll see you later.'

Sonia nodded and turned, struggling to walk on her crutches. As she approached the front door, it opened, and Arabella appeared with a man in his forties by her side. He wasn't the most attractive of men, but his face exuded friendliness. Lana thought he looked like fun. They watched as he carefully kissed Sonia on the forehead, helping her through the door before closing it behind him and heading towards the blue van they were in today.

'Hello! I am Luis. It is an honour to meet you all. I have heard much about you. I am just sorry it is under such horrible circumstances,' he said as he climbed in and shut the door behind him.

'Luis, this is Declan, Barber, Diarmuid and these two young ladies are Emma Jane and Lana Beth.'

After the greetings, Arabella slowly drove back onto the main road, and they continued their journey towards Silves. Occasionally, Arabella or Luis would comment on something outside, pointing out places that were well known in the region.

'Wow, are they storks?' Lana pointed as they drove past a number of high nests, each containing two or three huge white birds with long necks.

'Yes. Beautiful, aren't they?'

'I've never seen so many at once.'

'You'll notice them all over the Algarve,' Luis said. 'Sometimes I think they're a bit creepy.'

Declan laughed.

'How can they possibly be creepy?' asked Emma.

Luis shrugged. 'I guess I have quite the imagination. I sometimes think they're going to take over the world.'

The group cracked up as his voice changed to that of an evil cartoon character. It was then that everyone realised that Luis was good fun, as well as super friendly.

After another ten minutes of winding roads full of potholes, the group finally arrived in Silves, where Arabella found a parking spot and they climbed out, stretching their arms and legs.

As they walked through the narrow streets towards the castle, Emma was a little disappointed when they headed off in a different direction.

'I thought we were going to the castle?'

'No, we know that no supernaturals live in there. The coordinates we have are for over here,' Arabella pointed to a square not far from the entrance, where there was a cafe and restaurant.

'Oh,' Emma said.

'Why don't you guys start from the other end of the road?' Arabella suggested to Luis, who nodded, taking Barber and Declan with him.

The others waited outside while Arabella went into the cafe with the picture. There were hardly any people around, just a couple of old men sitting a few metres away, enjoying the warmth of the sun on their faces.

'How are you feeling?' Lana asked her sister, who shrugged in response.

'Okay, I guess. What about you?'

Lana shrugged too and waited a moment before replying, 'I guess I'm still in shock that your visions are more accurate than mine.'

'Huh?'

Lana nodded, 'They are. You were able to see way more than I could. I guess I'm a bit bummed, but it's okay. I'll get over it,' she smiled.

Emma put her arm around her shoulders and squeezed. 'I never expected to be able to have any visions at all. Maybe your powers will start to increase soon as well.'

'I hope so,' Lana whispered before Arabella came out of the cafe shaking her head. Then they moved on to the next building, asking people, showing the picture to them. But nobody knew the old woman.

'What about up there?' pointed Lana Beth.

'That's the Camara Municipal,' Arabella replied. 'The local council?'

'You mean the Town Council?'

'Exactly. We don't need to go in there. We have a few contacts there. I emailed them this morning. They're looking into it.'

As they moved on to a house across the road, an ancient lady opened the door. She didn't have any teeth.

Arabella spoke in Portuguese with her for a few moments and showed her the picture. The old lady beckoned them inside.

'She needs her glasses,' Arabella whispered, 'and she doesn't like too much sun. She's invited us in.'

As they stepped over the threshold, the overwhelming odour of mothballs filled their nostrils, making Lana almost gag. She stepped backwards and tripped on something on the floor. Her hand flew out to steady herself, landing on the door handle.

Suddenly, she found herself alone in the same room. The smell of mothballs had disappeared entirely.

'What the? Hello?' she whispered as she stepped forward.

She heard the sounds of someone moving in another room and the scent of cooking started to fill the air. Tiptoeing through the little house, Lana soon found herself face to face with a pretty red-haired young woman, wearing a scarf on her head and an apron over her simple blouse and skirt. She was humming softly as she cooked what looked like vegetable soup.

Lana hovered in the corner of the room, knowing that there must be something useful about the vision, otherwise, why would she have it? She waited, watching as the woman cooked. Soon, a knock on the door made her remove the scarf from her head and the apron from around her torso. Lana followed her out into the hall where she checked her face in the little mirror before opening the front door.

Standing there with a broad grin was the woman from the picture. She looked almost the same, except for the fact that her nose was even longer in real life, and her hair much thicker and darker.

The old lady and the young one chatted in Portuguese for a couple of moments before they walked through to the kitchen and sat down for lunch together.

Lana tried to force herself to snap out of the vision. She'd got what she needed. She now knew that the old woman they were looking for had been here before. But who was the young woman? Could she possibly be the toothless woman?

Suddenly, her sight blurred slightly, and the feeling of wooziness overcame her.

'Lana... Lana, are you alright?' said a familiar voice.

As she opened her eyes, the smell of mothballs almost made her choke again.

'Wh...what happened?'

'I think you must have had a vision. Tell us,' said Emma as she helped her sister up from the old lady's ancient, uncomfortable sofa.

'Yeah, yes, I did. The old woman we're looking for was here before. But it seemed a long time ago, I dunno, maybe seventy years or so? She was with a red-haired woman who lived here.'

As she stood up, her eye was caught by a faded picture on the mantelpiece.

'That's her, there,' she pointed, rushing over to get a better look.

The toothless woman grinned and pointed to herself, before muttering something to Arabella.

'She says that's her when she was a young woman.'

'Then she knew the woman we're looking for.'

Arabella showed her the picture again, and she put her glasses back on, but she shook her head.

Lana nodded, and the woman shook her head. But Lana insisted, nodding enthusiastically. The old lady began to get a little annoyed, muttering something or other in the strange language.

'She says she's ninety-eight years old, her memory isn't what it used to be.'

Lana sighed. Emma put her hand on her sister's arm to calm her down.

'What can we do? Hypnotise her?' Lana joked. 'She knew that woman. I saw them together.'

'I understand,' Arabella answered. 'But there's little we can do at the moment.'

'Wait, what about Penny?' Emma suddenly interjected.

Lana sighed and nodded, 'Of course.'

'What can Penny do?' asked Arabella.

'She can make people speak the truth. Opera et Veritate – that's her tattoo,' Emma squealed.

The old lady looked tired all of a sudden and went to sit down.

Arabella moved to her side and said a few words. The lady nodded.

'You call Eleanor immediately and get her to send Penny from wherever she went this morning. I'm going to make Maria Augusta a cup of tea.'

oOo

IT ONLY TOOK HALF AN HOUR FOR PENNY TO RETURN FROM Alcantarilha, a small town south-east of Silves. The moment she walked through the door and put her hands on Maria Augusta's shoulders, the old lady started talking about her younger years when her neighbour, Almerinda, had taken her under her wing. They had become firm friends, and she was devastated when she had to leave.

'Why did she have to leave?' asked Penny.

After the translations, they discovered the old lady had moved in with her even more elderly sister to look after her.

'Where was that?'

'Lagos.'

'Can you be more specific?'

The old lady shrugged.

'She never saw her again. She has no idea where in Lagos she moved to. But, she did say that Almerinda attended church every Sunday.'

'Well, at least we've found out where she went. It looks like we're heading to Lagos, people,' Arabella said, as she thanked the old lady for all her help. The poor woman was exhausted, but she smiled and walked them to the door, politely asking them to return again, but secretly hoping they wouldn't.

❦ 15 ❦

Lagos was a very different place to Silves, with its large marina and people buzzing around, even though it was the middle of winter. Christmas decorations lined the avenue and hippies walked along the street, mingling with surf dudes and very arty looking characters alike. Emma Jane liked the feel of it.

They parked in an underground car park and, when they appeared back above ground, they headed towards a small church nearby.

'Do you know where we're going?' asked Lana.

'We figured we'd ask the local vicar about this Almerinda character,' Declan smiled.

'We'll wait outside, then?' Emma replied.

'No, I think you should come in. You never know when your visions might happen again.'

The girls nodded, both holding their boyfriends' hands as they walked through the door and into the freezing cold of the church.

'O-M-G, it's so... so... ornate,' exclaimed Lana, not knowing how else to describe it.

'It certainly is,' Arabella whispered before finding the man she was looking for.

The girls hovered in the background as she did the talking before they noticed Barber looking a little lost.

'Babe? You okay?' asked Lana.

He nodded.

'No, you don't look okay.'

Declan appeared and quietly led him back outdoors. The girls followed.

'What is it? What's wrong?' Lana almost cried.

'It's nothing to worry about,' Declan said. 'It's just that some vampires can't cope well with churches. I'd completely forgotten. You alright, mate?'

Barber nodded, taking a deep breath before forcing a smile for the girls. 'I'll be fine. Just give me a moment.'

Lana didn't leave his side for a second, rubbing his arms and hands until he looked better.

'That's so weird,' Diarmuid said. 'Why did that happen?'

Declan shrugged. 'It's a bit of a mystery. Most of the really old vampires are fine with it, but some of the younger ones seem to... react strangely. They can't breathe and feel like they're going to pass out. I completely forgot that Barber is a vamp.' He shook his head. 'Sorry, mate.'

'It's fine,' Barber said. 'I'm alright, I feel better. You don't have to fuss,' he smiled at Lana who breathed a sigh of relief as Arabella approached them.

'Everything okay?' she asked.

Everyone nodded.

'Any news?' asked Declan.

She smiled. 'Two elderly sisters, Almerinda and Selma, lived in a house not far from here, up until about five years ago. Selma passed away, and Almerinda left soon afterwards. He's not sure, but he thinks she went to live in Portimão, to be near her other sister.'

'But I thought there'd been some big family feud?' asked Emma.

Arabella shrugged. 'I don't know about that, but I guess our next stop is Portimão.'

Lana's stomach rumbled noisily.

'After lunch, then, perhaps?' Arabella suggested.

'No, I'm fine. We need to continue.'

'Okay, let's grab something to eat in the car then,' Declan suggested. 'I'm starving myself.'

After checking in with Eleanor and the others, the group drove to Portimão, starting with the church in the centre of town. Unfortunately, the local vicar had no recollection of ever seeing Almerinda during any of his regular services.

'So we've drawn a blank?' Diarmuid said as they stood outside the pretty little church.

'Not necessarily,' said Lana.

'What do you mean?' he asked.

'I don't know about you, but I got a strange feeling about that priest—vicar, whatever you call him.'

'Did you?' Arabella asked. 'That's strange because I was kind of feeling the same thing.'

Suddenly, Declan ran back inside the church, searching high and low for the man they'd spoken to. But all he found was the man's clerical shirt crumpled on the floor behind the altar.

Cursing under his breath, he picked it up. 'We've been duped. I'm guessing that was one of the Skulls.'

'Which means they're ahead of us,' said Arabella.

'Where's the real vicar?' asked Emma.

'If only we knew,' Declan answered.

'I hope they haven't hurt him,' whispered Emma.

'This is the Skulls we're dealing with, Emma. I'm afraid that is a possibility.'

'I'll call Eleanor at once.' Arabella dialled her mobile immediately and walked away to talk. The others followed her out of the church.

'We need to speak to some other regular church-goers here. Girls, go and ask some of the local shopkeepers if they know of Almerinda.'

Lana and Emma disappeared, carrying the rough drawing of the old lady, while Declan stood alongside Arabella with his arms crossed, deep in thought.

'Go with them, guys. There might be more Skulls around here,' he said to Diarmuid and Barber, who nodded and followed the girls.

'I keep thinking about Lucy Jo,' Emma whispered as they walked out of their third shop with nothing, the boys hovering behind.

'Me too. Do you think she's okay?'

'I just hope he's keeping her safe and warm and fed. Oh, Lana.' Emma suddenly burst into tears.

'Oh, hon, I'm sure she's okay. Remember your vision? You said whoever took her was really gentle with her. He made sure she had her favourite slippers and nightgown. He was so careful with her. That's what you said, wasn't it?'

Emma nodded, wiping her eyes. Diarmuid wanted to go to her, but Lana shook her head behind her sister's back, mouthing, 'wait'.

'But she'll be terrified, won't she?'

'You forget what a strong little girl Lucy Jo really is. She's special, really special. I know she's not a Watcher, but she's still a Morgan. She'll be fighting back, I'm sure she is. Remember how feisty she is?'

Emma Jane smiled and nodded.

'Also, remember, in your vision, somehow he kept her in a gentle woozy state? Maybe she's still the same? In which case, she might not realise what's really going on. But there's one thing she will know, and that's that we're looking for her. She knows we'll never stop looking.'

Emma Jane smiled again. 'You're right.'

Lana hugged her and then nodded to Diarmuid, who came forward and put his arms around Emma.

'Is she alright?' Barber whispered to Lana.

'She's just anxious about Lucy Jo. We all are. We've got to find her, Barber. We've got to find her soon.'

Barber squeezed her hand before letting go. The girls walked into the next shop, a really old fashioned haberdashery full of buttons, wool, fabrics and everything you could possibly think of when it came to making clothes. Two women behind the counter looked at them quizzically.

'Posso ajudar?' said the first lady, a woman in her late sixties with immaculately coiffured hair, sprayed to within an inch of its life.

'Erm, sorry, do you speak English?' asked Lana self-consciously.'

The other woman (who looked decidedly more friendly) nodded. 'A little,' she said with a smile as she held up her thumb and forefinger, indicating only a small amount.

'We're wondering if you know this lady?' Lana said, handing the paper to the shopkeeper.

'Almerinda?' the woman replied.

'Yes,' squealed Emma. 'Do you know where she lives?'

'Of course! She live above,' she said, pointing upwards. 'But she not home now.'

'No?' asked Lana.

Both ladies shook their heads.

'Where will we find her?' asked Lana.

'Almerinda is in Lisbon. Two days.'

'When does she come back?'

'Tomorrow,' the kind lady said.

The shoulders of both girls slumped forward.

'You need speak with her?'

'Desperately,' Emma pleaded.

The lady took a piece of paper from the counter and a pen from beneath it and then scribbled something down.

'Here.'

Lana took the paper. It was a phone number.

'Almerinda's.' She pointed. 'You call her.'

'Thank you so very much,' Emma said before they walked out of the shop and bumped into Declan, who had been talking to the boys.

Lana immediately handed Declan the piece of paper, explaining what had happened.

'I'll call her,' Arabella said. 'I must warn her not to return yet. Hopefully, she'll tell me where her other family members are.'

'Good job, girls,' Declan said, giving them both a gentle slap on the back.

❄ 16 ❄

pparently, Almerinda was horrified when she heard about the kidnap of a little girl and had given them all the information they needed. The only problem was that there was some truth about what they'd been told regarding a family feud; Almerinda's youngest sister had turned her back on them some fifty years ago, and she had no idea where she was. Willing to do everything possible to help track her down, Almerinda had promised to leave Lisbon immediately and head straight to Praxos HQ, where Lana—and possibly even Emma—could try to have a vision. She assured them she'd be there in a matter of hours.

Almerinda looked almost identical to the woman Lana had seen in her vision – she hadn't aged one bit—and she was just as friendly and jolly now as she had been then. Getting in her car in the centre of Lisbon, she'd sped through the city and down the motorway, not stopping until she reached the villa in Monchique, where she'd enthusiastically offered to help in any way possible.

She hadn't been the slightest bit surprised at meeting all the 'gifted' people, as she described them in a perfect English accent.

'Aren't you Portuguese?' asked Lana, as the old lady gulped back a large glass of water, before putting it down on the table and nodding.

'But you sound English?'

Almerinda smiled. 'Yes, I also have a special ability with

languages and accents. I can speak all the languages of the world and sound like I am from every single country.' She grinned.

'Wow, that's totally cool.'

'I agree.' She laughed, before returning her attention back to Eleanor, who had reappeared from downstairs, carrying all her notes from the past few days.

'We'll give you half an hour to read through everything. Maybe something will catch your eye and give us a clue about where your sister might be.'

The old lady nodded. 'Let's just hope we can find her before that evil man does,' she said, before putting on a pair of glasses and glancing down.

'Come, everyone, let's leave Almerinda alone for a bit,' Eleanor said, shooing the teenagers out of the room and out onto the terrace, where Patrick and Declan sat with Arabella drinking coffee. Deep dark circles ringed Patrick's eyes, but he attempted to smile at his two older daughters.

Noticing, Lana pulled Emma away from the rest of the gang. They walked towards the pool, where they sat down. Emma took off her shoes and socks and let her feet dangle over the edge. 'Isn't that too cold?' Lana asked, without thinking. 'Look, have you seen the state of Dad?'

Emma just raised her eyebrows, and they both turned to look at him. 'I know. It's a lot for him to take in. It's not just Lucy Jo's kidnap, but it's us too.' Emma shook her head.

'What do you mean?' Lana asked.

'He hasn't really had the time to take in the truth about us. I mean, we're half angels, and you're dating a vampire.'

'Yeah, I see your point. But we can't worry about that, right now. We've got to do something, sis. We've got to do something about Lucy Jo.'

'Like what?'

'I've been thinking, since you had your vision – which was totally cool by the way – we haven't had much chance to talk about it yet, but...'

Emma smiled, 'I didn't think I would get them as well. It was pretty scary, though.'

'You'll get used to them.'

'I hope so.'

'So what have you been thinking about?'

Lana dropped her head slightly to the side and looked up towards the sky. 'I was thinking that maybe two visions are better than one.'

'Yeah? What exactly do you mean?'

'Well, I was wondering if there is any way we could try and have a vision together.'

'You mean like both of us there at the same time?'

Lana nodded.

'The only problem with that is I think my visions might be prompted by the water. Like, literally being in the water.'

'Oh, really?'

'It's the only time I've ever had one, and it was while I was at the bottom of the pool.'

'Oh,' Lana looked a little downtrodden.

'But we could still try it?'

Lana raised her eyebrows before looking down into the deep end. 'I'd have to go in there, wouldn't I?'

Nodding, Emma held her sister's hand. 'But we'd do anything for Lucy Jo, right?'

Lana grinned and nodded and, before she could even think about it, Emma had slid into the cold water, pulling her sister down with her.

They barely even heard their father yell their names.

'What are they doing?' he shouted from the side of the pool. 'It's freezing in there! I know that Emma can withstand the cold and the water, but Lana can't, can she?'

'Just watch, mate,' Declan said, putting his hand on his shoulder.

The men stood there, surrounded by the rest of the girls' classmates and watched as a glow appeared from the deep end. If they looked closely, they could tell that the glow was coming from Emma, who had her arms wrapped tightly around her sister.

'What are they doing?' asked Arabella.

Grinning, Declan said, 'They're trying to combine visions. Smart.'

'But Lana can't breathe down there,' their father muttered.

'With Emma's help she can, I'm sure. Don't worry, they're absolutely fine. But if it works, they'll be knackered when they come up, so can someone go and get some towels and hot drinks ready? Thanks, Cassie.'

oOo

THE ONLY OTHER TIME THAT LANA HAD BEEN UNDERWATER LIKE this was when the two of them were in the Thames, in London, but then they'd come up for air at regular intervals. Now, though, Emma seemed to have been able to create a little air pocket for Lana to breathe in. It felt peculiar, but she was okay; she felt safe and, thanks to the heat glow Emma was emitting, she felt relatively warm too.

After about a minute, Emma loosened her grip around Lana and they took each other's hands instead. They both opened their eyes for a second and nodded to each other, before closing them again and focussing all their energy on one thing: Lucy Jo.

Both girls felt it at the same time, strange dizziness that rose from their stomachs to their heads and back again, causing a slightly nauseous sensation in both of them, but they didn't let go. Instead, they focussed harder.

Lana opened her eyes first. 'Sis? Are you coming?' she asked as she tried to take in her surroundings, but it was so dark she couldn't see a thing.

'Emma, I need you. I can't see.'

'Erm... I'm here,' Emma whispered in the blackness that encased them. 'Just a sec.'

Soon, her body began to emit a light that shone from within, slowly brightening until they could see all around them.

'We did it,' Lana squealed. 'I knew we could.'

Emma smiled. 'It was a great idea. The problem is, how do we know this is related to Lucy Jo? We could be anywhere.'

'Were you focussing all your energy on finding our little sister?'

Emma nodded. 'Absolutely.'

'Then believe me, this place, wherever it is, has definitely got something to do with her.'

'Wait, I recognise this and that smell, that's the North Sea, Lana. We're on the oil rig.'

Lana sighed. 'But they left the oil rig ages ago and if they were... did you hear that?'

'What?'

'Voices.'

Straining to listen, both girls held their breaths and waited.

'Lucy Jo!' they said at precisely the same time before running towards the sound of a little girl sobbing. Leaving the darkness behind, they soon found themselves in an illuminated corridor, with doors along each side.

They listened, trying to follow the sounds of the sobbing, walking as quickly as they could.

But she wasn't sobbing, she was singing.

They found her in a kitchen of sorts, sitting at a table with a large slice of cake and a glass of milk in front of her. She was singing one of her favourite songs, and she was smiling. She looked quite happy, actually.

'Lucy Jo,' Emma cried as she hurried to her side and tried to hug her. 'Oh, I wish I could hold her right now. Why can't I hold her, sis, why can't I?' she wailed.

Lana stood beside her. 'It's just a vision, hon, nothing more. We can't touch her. She doesn't know we're here. We just have to find out as much as we can before the vision fades, okay?'

Emma slowly stood, nodding, tears collecting in the corners of her eyes.

Both looking around, they noticed a woman standing at the other side of the kitchen, making herself a cup of tea. They watched as she finished stirring in two teaspoons of sugar before turning back towards the little girl.

'Are you enjoying the cake, little one?' she asked. 'I made it especially for you, you know?'

Lucy Jo nodded. 'It's yummy.'

'I can make you another one tomorrow if you like? What's your favourite kind?'

'Chocolate and vanilla, with lots of chocolate sprinkles,' the little girl shouted across the room. 'Can I help? I help mummy bake cakes all the time. I love baking. Mummy says I'm a natural.'

The woman pushed a hand through her short black hair and nodded. 'Of course you can. In fact, I'd like that very much. Don't forget to drink your milk, too. I'll be right back,' she said, before walking out the room, leaving Lucy Jo to finish off her cake in silence.

'Let's follow her,' Lana suggested. 'Come on, Em. We can't just stay here staring at her. I know it's so good to see her, but we can't help by watching her. Let's go.'

Tearing herself away, Emma brushed the tears from her cheeks and followed her sister out of the room.

Ahead, the woman sauntered down the passageway until she reached a door at the end of the corridor. Pushing it open, she smiled at the sight of a man standing with a mobile phone to his ear.

'Yes, Father, she's fine. What now? Erm, she's...' He turned to the woman and asked, 'What's she doing now?'

'Eating cake, drinking milk, singing her favourite songs. She's fine.'

'Did you hear that Father?... okay ... but why there? When? We'll be ready. Don't worry, we'll take good care of her.'

Putting the phone down, the young man turned to face the woman and held out his hand to her. 'Thank you for doing this. I would never have heard the end of it if we couldn't pull this off.'

'I know. You just want to make him happy. It's what we all want for our parents. Well, sometimes, anyway,' she smiled as he pulled her forward and kissed her.

'Your parents were happy with you before they died, weren't they?'

'I don't know. I guess so. Probably. I think they were just glad I wasn't anything like my brother. Drake is such a badass.'

'You can be a badass too,' the man joked.

'Yeah, maybe, but Drake? He's totally nuts. Having said that, here we are on an oil rig in the middle of the sea with a child who doesn't belong to us. The things we do for your dad, right?'

He nodded.

'I'm glad your dad asked us to do this, and not your stupid little brother. Stan is so messed up, I think he might have hurt her.'

'At least we know Dad's not gonna hurt her. She's sweet. I kinda like her. Maybe we'll have one of our own, one day?'

'Really? You want me to have your babies?'

The guy smiled. 'Come on, let's go make sure she's okay. Did you put something in her milk to help her sleep?'

'A little bit.'

'Then she'll be fast asleep for the journey to Portugal.'

'I've never been to Portugal before. Where exactly are we going?'

'That's a secret.' He grinned, tapping her nose.

'Awww, c'mon, give us a clue.'

He stopped halfway down the middle of the corridor and turned to her. 'You'll see little but ocean for miles around, and the cliffs are like nothing you've seen before, babe. It's spectacular.'

'But what's it called, where we're going?'

'I said it's a secret. That would be telling.'

'Aww, babe, I want to know,' she said, pulling his arms and stopping him from going any farther.

He chuckled and took her in his arms again. 'We're going to the most south-westerly point, okay? Does that satisfy your inquisitiveness? Or should I say nosiness?'

He leaned forward and rubbed his nose against hers before Lana suddenly started coughing and spluttering.

'Jeeze, Em, I can't breathe. Oh God... the water, Emma, the water.'

And then everything went black.

❦ 17 ❦

'**G**et them out, get them out now! There's something wrong, look...' Eleanor yelled from the side of the pool.

Both Declan and Patrick dived in, reaching the girls at the same time.

As they pushed themselves off of the bottom of the pool, Emma finally released Lana's hands.

Both girls were unconscious.

'Oh, God. Oh, God. I knew we should have stopped this insanity,' Patrick gasped as he dragged Lana to the side of the pool.

'Patrick! Patrick! Patrick... Stop,' Eleanor demanded.

As he leaned over his two daughters, he turned his head, sobbing. 'I can't lose them too, Eleanor.'

'And you won't. They're going to be absolutely fine. Just step away and watch.'

'I can't, Eleanor, I can't.'

'Mr. Morgan, please,' Diarmuid said, as he gently tried to pull the older man away. 'They're going to be absolutely fine. Back to normal in no time. Please, would you give me some space?'

Defeated, Patrick stood up and stepped backwards. 'You'd better know what you're doing.'

'Patrick, mate. Are you forgetting who we are?' Declan smiled warmly.

Holding his hands up in defeat, Patrick nodded and let them get on with it, watching as Diarmuid put a hand on each of his girls' chests, where a bright light began to erupt from his fingers. Within moments, the girls both opened their eyes at the same time. Lana coughed and spluttered for a moment until she realised her head was resting on Barber's knees. She looked up at him and smiled.

Emma grinned at Diarmuid as she was slowly pulled up to her feet. 'Are you okay, sis?'

Lana nodded. 'A bit tired.'

'You scared me half to death,' said Patrick as he stepped towards them both and pulled them to him.

'Sorry, Dad. But we had to do it. We had to do something.'

'I know, girls. I know. But that doesn't make this any easier.'

'Did you discover anything?' asked Eleanor.

Both girls looked at each other with a grin. They nodded, trying hard not to cry.

'We saw her, Dad. We saw Lucy Jo. They're taking really good care of her. She's fine. She's eating her favourite cake and stuff,' Lana laughed.

'Where is she?'

'Well, we saw her on the oil rig, but they said they were going to the most south-westerly point of Portugal.'

'Sagres, they're going to Sagres,' Arabella interrupted, before rushing inside to pick up her mobile phone to start making calls.

'You did good, girls. You did real good,' Declan said. 'I told you not to worry, Patrick. You need to trust me, mate.'

'I know, I know,' Patrick said, relieved that his girls were fine as he finally let them go. Lana rushed back into Barber's arms, and Emma did the same with Diarmuid.

'Thanks for helping to bring us back,' she whispered.

He didn't say a word, but kissed her very gently on the lips and squeezed her tight.

'I'm freezing,' Lana announced.

'Oh, we've got towels and hot tea for you here,' Cassie said, rushing towards them with two large beach towels. Penny followed her, carrying two cups of tea—one green for Emma and one strong black for Lana.

'Oooh, you girls are angels.' Emma smiled.

'Yep, you could say that,' Penny laughed.

'Actually, you're quite right,' Cassie smirked. 'Well, children of angels, anyway.'

oOo

'THEY JUST SEEMED SO NORMAL, YOU KNOW?' EMMA SAID quietly.

'What exactly do you mean by normal, Emma?' Eleanor asked the girl as they sat indoors, in front of a raging log fire, half an hour later.

'They were like a regular couple. In fact, they seemed kinda nice,' replied Emma.

'I actually felt like I liked them. They were concerned for Lucy Jo's welfare, and the woman wanted to bake cakes for her and stuff. I dunno, it's just weird,' said Lana.

'Were you able to ascertain who this woman is?' asked Eleanor.

They both nodded. 'She said she was Drake's sister. And because they talked about him being a 'badass', we think they must be referring to the Drake we all know and hate,' Lana answered.

'Yes, I think so. Let me go and make some calls and see if we can find out more about her,' said Eleanor as she stood up.

'But what's going on in Sagres? When are we going?' Lana pouted.

'We've got some Watchers down there at the moment, but so far, we've got nothing. It might be possible that Sagres was just a stopover. Which would be strange, considering it's like the end of the world down there,' Eleanor said.

'Huh?' blurted Lana.

'She means that it's the most south-westerly point of the Algarve. There's nothing else in between America and us. Not really,' Arabella answered.

Gulping loudly, Lana closed her eyes and shook her head. 'Please don't tell me that they're going to take her to America. We'd never find her.'

'No, at least not from there. They'd need an airport for that or an aerodrome of some sort. I think the nearest to there is Lagos. No, if they were planning on going to America, they would probably have gone by now,' Arabella replied.

'No they wouldn't, Arabella,' Emma stated, 'they need Almerinda's sister, first.'

'Yes, that's true, that's true. Perhaps they were just using Sagres as a base because it's so far out? Perhaps they figured it would be a good hiding place—temporarily, anyway.'

'Yes, I agree, Bella. I just hope they haven't already left,' Eleanor said, putting her hand to her chest and taking a deep breath.

'Are you alright?' Arabella asked.

'Yes, yes, I'll be fine. It's just the change.'

'Ah, yes, I see. Is there anything I can do to help?'

'No, don't worry. It'll pass momentarily. Just give me a moment.' The old Eleanor returned to a seated position and leaned back on the sofa, carefully lifting her legs up until she was lying down. A deep guttural sound erupted from her lips as her body began the process of becoming young again. Her hair began to change colour from silvery white to a beautiful shade of blonde and her deep wrinkles puffed out until they were non-existent. Moments later, a beautiful young woman sat in the same place.

'Ooh, that's better.' She grinned, jumping up. 'Just going to change out of these old clothes,' she said, disappearing into another room. She returned ten minutes later wearing skinny jeans, a black turtle neck and knee-high boots... and a huge grin. 'Right, where were we? Oh yes, Drake's sister. Right, I'm going downstairs to make some phone calls and go online to do some research. Girls, I think you should rest for a while. No doubt we'll need you to go out again later, so you need to get your strength back.'

Nodding, the girls curled up on the thick blanket on the floor, yawning. They lay staring into the flames until they both drifted off to sleep.

oOo

'THERE WERE TWO SISTERS, APPARENTLY. SADLY, ONE WAS murdered when she was five years old. A twin, I understand,' Eleanor told everyone as they sat having something to eat at different spots around the open-plan room. 'The surviving twin, Kimberly, would be twenty-three now. Is this her, girls?' she asked, turning the tablet around so they could see the image on the screen of the young woman with long red hair.

'Yes! But she has really short hair now, and it's jet black,' Lana smiled.

'Kimberly's parents died a few years ago. Her father had a car accident and her mother a heart attack, just days later. Tragic, really. But from what I can understand, the parents weren't supernaturals. Which begs the question, how has Drake become a Skull? Oh, wait... Oh, I see,' Eleanor said, reading from the screen. 'He was adopted after Kimberly's sister passed away. That explains it, then. Kimberly must have started hanging out with the bad crowd with Drake. Such a shame because, according to much of this, she had such promise. Straight A student until she was about fifteen years old, and then she just spiralled out of control. That must have been when she met Drake's friends. So you said this young man she was with is Sthenelaus' son?'

'We think so,' Emma said, between mouthfuls of pasta and pesto. 'But not... what was he called? Fred? Steve?'

'Stan!' Lana exclaimed with her mouth full.

'Yes, that's it. Not Stan. They talked about Stan, he's the younger brother. The guy on the oil rig was older than Stan. They said something about being glad his dad had asked them to do this and not Stan. If Stan had done it, he might have hurt Lucy Jo,' Emma added.

'Okay, so Sthenelaus has two sons. Did you get his name?' asked Eleanor.

'Sorry, no,' Emma replied.

'Don't worry, we can try to find out.'

'So, to recap,' Patrick said, almost wearing the carpet out, pacing up and down, 'Lucy Jo was taken on Christmas Eve by this Sthenelaus character's son, the older one...'

'No, she must have initially be taken by Stan, because he was the one on Andilyse Island, remember? That Hummer jeep was sold by Stan? Remember, Lana?' said Emma.

Lana squinted her eyes and nodded. 'So he must've taken her.'

'But that doesn't add up. You said that in your vision, the person who took her was very gentle and caring. That doesn't sound like Stan,' asked Patrick.

'That's right,' Emma said, chewing on the inside of her mouth. 'He must've come to the island with his brother as well. It's the only explanation.'

'Yes, I agree,' said Patrick. 'So, both brothers came to the island, and the eldest took Lucy Jo on Christmas Eve. They then took her by helicopter to the oil rig in the North Sea, where she was looked after by the eldest son and his girlfriend, Kimberly?' He looked over at Eleanor, who nodded. 'Then they somehow arrive in the Algarve and travel to...?'

'Sagres,' filled in Arabella.

'In the meantime, they're hunting Almerinda and her sisters so that they could utilise their – powers – to change Lucy Jo's memories, to make my child think that she is the daughter of Sthenelaus?' continued Patrick.

'That about sums it up, I think, mate,' said Declan, who was warming his hands in front of the fire.

'Luckily for them, they didn't find me,' Almerinda smiled. 'But they might be getting closer to finding my sister.'

'How come your family is the only family that can change people's memories forever?' asked Ava, who was lolling on the sofa with her head on Liam's shoulder.

Almerinda shrugged. 'There were many others, but most chose to leave Europe in the Middle Ages.'

'What? You've been alive since the Middle Ages?' Rupert asked, astonished.

Laughing, Almerinda shook her head. 'No, silly.'

'Oh.' He blushed.

'I was born just a few years later.' Almerinda's eyes twinkled, and she winked.

'No way. Dude, that is awesome.'

'What's with all the Americanisms, Rupert?' Lana laughed,

throwing a cushion at him. He held up his hands to catch it, but instead, it stopped in mid-air.

'What the...?' he said, staring at it as it hovered in front of his face.

'Rupert, your powers are improving.' Eleanor clapped her hands together. 'That's wonderful.'

'But h...h...ow?

'You'll probably find that all your powers evolve and get stronger. That's what happens to most Watchers. You just need to try and control them. Like now, can you move the cushion?'

Rupert focussed on the cushion, but it plopped down on the floor in front of him.

'Don't worry, give it time,' she said.

'My powers still haven't evolved... at all,' sulked Imran.

'What can you do, Imran?' asked Almerinda.

'I can manipulate time.'

Patrick's head shot up. 'You what?'

'I can go back in time.'

'But...but... that means we can go back and stop them from taking Lucy Jo in the first place?' Patrick said, with his hands in the air.

'I'm afraid it's not that simple, Patrick,' Eleanor replied sadly. 'If the kidnap had happened anywhere near Imran, there's a chance he would be able to do that. But, as it stands, his power is not strong enough to change time for someone he doesn't really know. I wish it were different too, but alas, it's not meant to be.'

Patrick's hands dropped to his sides.

'Don't worry, Dad. We're getting closer,' reassured Emma.

'I know, sweetheart, I know.'

'Yes, that's true. We currently have people searching the whole of the area around Sagres, and we're doing everything we can to track down Almerinda's younger sister. In fact, Almerinda has indicated to me that she has reason to believe she might be living by the sea, near a place called Lagoa. We've got a group of people combing the area as we speak, while we have dinner,' Eleanor explained.

'Well, we've finished eating. I'd like to go and join the search?' suggested Patrick.

'Me too,' said Lana and Emma together.

'Okay, whoever wants to join the search should go and get ready. We'll leave in ten minutes,' said Declan, nodding at Arabella to make sure that it was okay.

She nodded. 'Perfect.'

oOo

Even though it was still reasonably early in the evening, darkness had descended, and the region was filled with twinkling lights coming from all directions, causing beautiful images to reflect off of the Arade River as they drove over a large bridge towards Lagoa.

Laughing, Arabella pointed it out. 'Hard to believe it's actually a city, it's absolutely tiny. More of a small town, more than anything,' she said. 'Having said that, it's quite a nice place. I grew up nearby.'

'Oh really?' asked Declan. 'I would've pegged you for a city girl, myself.'

'Like I said,' she laughed, pointing, 'the city of Lagoa.'

'Oh right, yeah. Good one,' he laughed, as they drove past some apartments, a petrol station and the bus station to their left.

'Down there is Praia do Carvoeiro.' She pointed off to the right. 'That's actually where I spent much of my youth. It was fun. There's a beach, lots of bars, restaurants, nightclubs and so on. It's very touristy now, though. Not that that's a problem. It's still nice.'

Declan smiled. 'Sounds perfect for a holiday.'

'It is. I'd recommend it.'

As they stopped at some traffic lights, Emma watched what appeared to be a football match, the pitch floodlit in the darkness. 'Do people like football here, then?' she asked.

'Are you kidding? They're football crazy!' Arabella grinned.

'Really? Don't get me started,' Declan laughed. 'Did you see the last World Cup? Jeeze.'

'Clearly a sore point,' Lana laughed. 'I couldn't care less about football. It's a stupid sport. Full of wusses.'

'Oi, you,' Declan warned, turning from the front seat to gently punch her on the knee.

'Aw, c'mon, Declan, you disappoint me. I figured you more of a rugby man. Rugby is a proper sport, for real men,' Diarmuid piped up, laughing.

'I forgot you used to play rugby,' Emma said, leaning her head on his shoulder.

'Yep, but that was quite a while ago. Shame we've nowhere to play at Praxos in London.'

The lights turned green, and Arabella deftly turned right, and they drove down a long winding road with just a few street lights.

'So, where are we heading?' asked Barber, who had been very quiet thus far.

'The area around Benagil and Vale D'el Rei. I'll show you where I lived when I was a child,' Arabella smiled, turning left at a little roundabout at the top of the hill.

'Do you see that little road down to the right? My house was down there.'

'Do your parents still live there, Arabella?' asked Emma.

'No, they sold it to an Englishman who tore it apart and built some ridiculously large villa instead. I think it's horrendous, myself. He ruined it. It was a beautiful old farmhouse. Oh well, never mind.'

'Where do they live now, Arabella?' she asked.

'They have a large apartment in Lagos, actually, but they travel a lot these days. They're in Thailand at the moment, helping Praxos over there.'

'There's a Praxos in Thailand? That's so cool,' Lana replied.

'Okay, here we are,' Arabella said, pulling up beside a little church.

'She lives in a church?' asked Emma.

'We have no idea where she lives, but we believe it might be around here somewhere,' Arabella said, looking around.

As if by a miracle, the church door slowly opened and a woman appeared. She looked very much like Almerinda, just a little younger, with short silver hair. She waved at them and strolled forwards.

'I understand you've been looking for me?' she said before

anyone could say a word. 'And my sister, Almerinda. She's here, too?'

Arabella shook her head. 'She's a little tired, so she stayed in the villa.'

The woman nodded. 'Well, I've packed my bags. I'm ready to come with you.'

'I'll give you a hand,' said Declan, who followed her back into the church.

'Don't you think this is a little weird?' asked Lana.

Emma nodded. 'It's a bit too... convenient. I think something's wrong.'

'They're in the church,' Lana suddenly screeched. Everyone climbed out of the two cars and ran towards it, but they were too late. They could smell the fire before they could see the flames. Soon, the building was engulfed.

'Declan!' yelled Emma and Lana together, watching in horror, sobbing.

Suddenly, the flames began to move unnaturally, as though they'd been pushed to only the sides of the crumbling building.

The girls turned, confused until they saw Elliott deep in concentration, focussing all his attention on moving the flames. The others rushed forward into the abyss, returning moments later carrying Declan's limp body.

'What about Almerinda's sister?' asked Ava.

Arabella shook her head. 'She's not there. It was a trap. The Skulls have her, I'm sure of it.'

'But they can't have gone far,' Diarmuid said, as the sound of whirring filled the night sky.

'It's a helicopter again. She's in there. I know it,' added Ava.

Everyone watched as it disappeared into the sky.

'Declan? Declan? Can you hear me?' asked Emma.

'No, he can't. It will take a while for his body to come back. Let's just get him back to Praxos.'

'Wait,' shouted a voice. 'I can help.' Imran smiled as he approached them. 'I can go back in time and stop this from happening.'

'Imran, of course, you can!' Lana exclaimed.

'How long?'

'Maybe fifteen minutes before we arrived? Tell Almerinda's sister everything.'

'Wait, no... then you'll be in danger from the Skulls. I can't allow it,' Arabella said.

'Sorry, but there's nothing you can do to stop me,' he said, and then all of a sudden, he was gone.

❧ 18 ☙

The little church was precisely how it had been when he'd first laid eyes on it from the car. Imran hid behind the wall by the road, looking every which way to make sure the Skulls weren't already there.

Confident that he was alone, he ran forward as fast as he could, pushing the door open and stepping inside the building. It wasn't an old church by any means. In fact, it looked like it had only been built a few years ago.

Sitting at the front, all alone, was the woman he was looking for. He stepped towards her, and she jumped in fright.

'Quem es tu?' she asked in Portuguese.

He shook his head. 'I'm sorry, I don't understand. Please. You must come with me. You are in danger.'

'Danger? What are you talking about, young man?'

I'm a friend of your sister's, Almerinda.'

The woman's eyes lit up. 'Almerinda, eh?'

He nodded.

'She's in trouble, is she?'

'No, you are. Please, they're coming. You must come with me. We need to get away from here.'

'Who is coming? What are you talking about? It sounds like a load of nonsense to me. Leave me alone to pray in solitude.'

'The Skulls are coming, and they want you. Please, just come with me.'

Imran became so worried about the Skulls arriving any second that he had no choice but to grab her arm and jump. He thought of the Praxos villa in Monchique and hoped he could get them both there.

But when he opened his eyes, he found himself back in the church.

The old woman gasped. 'What did you do to me?'

'I...erm... I tried to time travel, to get you away from the danger. But we're still here. Why are we still here?' he panicked.

'It's the church, you can't perform time travel from a church. You can't really perform much magic in a church. Oh dear, my boy. What kind of trouble is this? Who are you?'

'I'm a Watcher, and please, we have to get out of here. The Skulls are coming for you.' The sound of a helicopter in the distance made his heart sink. 'It's them. Please,' he begged, 'come with me. I can do it outside. We have to get away from here.'

Looking deep into his eyes for a second, she stood up and nodded. 'I believe you. Come, this way.'

They ran out of the back door, down a dirt track to the left of the church and stopped at a huge nearby tree.

'You should be okay here. Try now,' she said, taking his hands in hers.

The next minute, they were standing in the living room of the Praxos villa, while everyone sat having dinner.

'Sister?' Almerinda suddenly shrieked.

'What the...?' Declan exclaimed as everybody jumped up, wondering what on Earth was going on.

The first thing Imran did was run to Declan to give him a hug.

'Imran?

'You... you... died again, Declan,' he said, breathless.

'I did?'

Imran nodded and began to tell everyone exactly what had happened, while Almerinda and her sister sat together by the fire and did a little catching up of their own.

oOo

'SO NOW WE'VE REMOVED THE SISTERS FROM THE EQUATION, ALL we have to do is find Lucy Jo, right?'

Eleanor nodded to Lana.

'Do you think they know we've got them?' Lana asked.

'Maybe.'

'Do you think they'll try and take them from us?'

'Perhaps.'

'Are they safe enough here?' Lana asked.

'Yes, Lana.' Eleanor smiled. 'So stop worrying.'

'But... but...'

'What is it, Lana?'

'She thinks that if he can't change Lucy Jo's memories, maybe he'll decide he doesn't need her after all,' Declan answered on her behalf.

Lana bit her lip and slowly nodded. 'Maybe we've inadvertently put her into even more danger,' she breathed. 'Maybe, he'll... he'll... get rid of her.'

'Which is why our number one priority right now is to find your sister, okay?' Eleanor replied.

Lana nodded.

'Now, because of Imran's admirable actions earlier this evening, we have another lead. The helicopter' smiled Eleanor.

Declan opened the door from below and poked his head out. He didn't say a word. He just nodded to Eleanor, who said, 'Right, we might have got them.'

Lana squealed and jumped up off the sofa, knocking Barber's hot chocolate into his lap. 'Oops, sorry. That must have been hot.'

'I didn't feel a thing.'

'So, when do we leave?' Lana asked, trying to put on her coat and clear up the spilt drink at the same time.

'It's fine.' Barber smiled. 'I got it.'

'You aren't going anywhere,' Lana's father said to her.

'But... you might need me,' she said, continuing to put on her coat.

'I said no, Lana Beth. I don't want you or your sister going anywhere near this guy.'

'Well, if you don't let us come, we're only going to find our own way of getting there. You do realise that, don't you?'

Patrick rolled his eyes. 'Are they always like this at the academy?'

Eleanor smiled.

'Pretty much, mate,' Declan answered. 'Come on. Let's go.'

oOo

'WHAAAAAATTTTT?' yelled STHENELAUS. 'WHAT DO YOU MEAN, she wasn't there? They've taken her, too? Those bloody Watchers!'

Aria listened from behind the door and smiled to herself before walking away.

❧ 19 ❧

With Watchers working undercover at every airport and aerodrome, when the helicopter had landed at the Alvor airstrip earlier that evening, word had immediately spread to Eleanor about the strange people on board. Definitely Skulls. No doubt about it.

The Watchers followed their car, arriving at a small house on a development inland from the coast. Parking a few doors down, they had staked out the property until Eleanor's people had arrived on the scene.

It hadn't taken long for the Skulls to be subdued. There were only five of them, and they looked scarier than they were. And unfortunately for Sthenelaus, they also weren't the most loyal of Skulls - quite quickly revealing the location of the little girl with very little pressure involved.

Just before they left, Declan punched them all. 'That's for killing me,' he growled, before walking out the door without looking back.

'Aren't we going to do something with them? Lana asked.

'Don't worry, the Portuguese Watchers will be here any second to sort them out,' Declan smiled.

'Cool,' replied Lana. 'So next stop, Praia da Rocha? Where's that, Arabella?'

'It's along the coast. It'll take us ten minutes to get there from here.'

Hopping back into their cars, the group drove as quickly as possible until they passed a sign saying Praia da Rocha, finding mostly tall hotels.

'So where are they?' whispered Emma. 'We'll never find her in this concrete jungle.'

'Don't worry, we know exactly where,' Arabella reassured her. A few minutes later they arrived outside a huge villa. All the lights were out, and there didn't seem to be anyone home.

'Are we too late?' Lana whispered as she watched her father jump out of the car ahead of them, with Declan right behind him.

They jumped over the walls and disappeared out of sight.

'Shouldn't we be following them?'

'Yes, we will. They just wanted to check the area first. Don't worry,' said Arabella.

'You wait here. I'm going in,' Barber said as he heard the sound of dogs barking viciously.

'Dad!' yelped Lana.

'Don't worry, I've got it' Barber said, as he practically threw himself over the wall.

Seconds later, the sound of yelping filled the air and then there was nothing but eerie silence.

'Okay, let's go,' Arabella said.

Walking into the totally over the top property, Lana whistled at the tackiness of it. Gold covered everything—taps, coffee tables, oven, hob and ornaments. 'Wow, it's horrendous.'

'Very seventies,' Declan agreed.

The girls looked at him and shook their heads. 'Whatever,' whispered Lana.

'They were here,' Declan said. And not long gone, by the looks of things.

Warm half-eaten meals were strewn across the table, including a child's plate and a half-empty glass of milk.

Lana walked forward and picked it up.

Immediately she found herself standing beside her little sister, who was slowly eating the spaghetti bolognese on her plate.

'Oh, thank goodness you're safe, Lucy Jo,' Lana said, leaning forward and blowing her a kiss. 'We're really close, we're going to find you really soon and bring you home, I promise.'

Kimberly and her boyfriend were sitting chatting happily and eating their dinner, occasionally answering Lucy Jo's Eye Spy game, when Stan rushed into the room, looking panicked.

'We need to leave. Now,' he demanded. 'They're on to us. They're coming.'

'Where are we going?' Kimberly asked.

'That's on a need to know basis,' Stan barked. 'Now come on. Now!'

Kimberly slowly stood up, taking her time to drink the remains of her coke before she went to get her things.

'Will you tell your freakin' girlfriend to get a move on, Archie? It's like she's freaking' stalling.'

Archie raised his eyebrows. 'What are you trying to say, Stan?' he spat.

'I don't trust her, that's all.'

'Well I do, and that's all that matters. You hear me?'

Stan ignored him and turned away, going to grab Lucy Jo.

'Don't touch her,' Archie snarled, pushing him out of the way before very gently picking Lucy Jo up in his arms. 'You okay, honey?'

The little girl nodded and rested her head on his shoulder.

Stan shook his head in anger and ran out the front door, followed by Archie.

'You ready, babe?' he asked Kimberly.

'Yes. Oh, I forgot my bag. I'll be right out.'

Lana watched as Archie nodded and exited, then she turned her attention to Kimberly, who took a piece of paper out of her bag, followed by a pen. She scribbled something down and left it on the table. Then she looked around the room and ran. The action of slamming the door behind her made the piece of paper lift off the table and drift underneath it.

Lana walked back over to the table to take a look, but the paper was face down.

Taking a deep breath, she tried to force herself out of the vision. Seconds later, she was on the floor, scrabbling for the piece of paper.

'What? What happened, sis? Was it a vision?'

Lana nodded and stood up.

Emma smiled. 'I told you your powers are getting stronger. What happened?'

'This. This is what happened,' Lana said, placing the paper on the table for all to see.

I KNOW YOU'RE LOOKING FOR US, BUT IF WE DON'T DO THIS, HE WILL kill us. We're taking good care of her. Wish I could tell you where to find us. Just please find us... soon.

❧ 20 ❧

'Is she on our side?' asked Lana. 'I don't understand.'

Everyone stood looking at the piece of paper, nobody entirely understanding what it meant. Why did Kimberly want to be found? Was it because she was scared of Stan? Or Sthenelaus? Or Archie, even?

'Oh, I found out the other brother's name. It's Archie.'

'Archie?' asked Declan.

'Yep.'

'Does he look like Sthenelaus?'

Lana shook her head. 'Not one bit. He's really quite handsome.'

Barber raised his eyebrows.

'What? He is.' Lana shrugged.

'Can you describe him?' asked Declan.

'Sure, he has dark brown hair, quite longish—for a guy, anyway—really dark brown eyes, cute button nose and heart-shaped lips, if you know what I mean.'

Declan nodded and turned away, dialling Eleanor on his phone. 'Hey, Ellie. I've reason to believe we already know Sthen's other son. Yeah. Archie, you remember... yeah, that's right. Good, okay.'

Declan smiled.

'What, Declan? What is it?' asked Lana.

'I think you're right about Kimberly being on our side.'

'What do you mean?' asked Diarmuid.

'Because Archie is on our side.'

'Huh? If he were on our side, he wouldn't have taken Lucy Jo in the first place!' Patrick banged his fist on the dining table.

'I think he got involved in helping Lucy Jo. To keep her safe from his father and brother. Look, a few years ago, we helped a guy called Archie—he was really cool, and he was in some serious trouble. We helped him get out of it, and he's been giving us a hand on and off ever since. He told me his father was some big-time criminal who he avoided. We just never realised exactly who his dad was. But then, we never asked.'

'So you think this Archie guy is doing this from the good of his own heart? He took my daughter from my home, Declan. How can I possibly trust somebody like that?'

'I know, mate, but look at it the other way—if he hadn't been involved, Lucy Jo would be... let's just say, he's caring for her right now when she needs someone to do that. If you can't trust him, trust me. Can you do that?'

Patrick took his time but eventually nodded.

'Let's get out of here. Where do you think they went?' asked Declan as Arabella's mobile rang and they walked out of the villa, looking around in the darkness. 'We think we've got them,' Arabella breathed. 'Come on, quick.'

The girls hopped back in the car with the others, and Arabella stepped on the accelerator.

'Where we heading?' asked Declan, glancing at her as she deftly drove the car over speed bumps and negotiated roundabouts.

'They were spotted heading into Portimão. They'll probably try to hide out there, somewhere. But I have a pretty good idea which way they went.' She smiled as they sped around another huge roundabout before heading off on a smaller road with old houses to their left and an expanse of dirt to their right.

Several cars followed behind them as they whizzed down the streets of the old city. Arabella cursed, coming to a standstill. 'I'm not sure which way they would have gone.'

Picking her mobile back up again, she spoke a few words in Portuguese before the cars behind her drove off into different directions. She reversed down a one-way street and pulled over next to an underground car park.

She nodded to Declan, who jumped out of the car and ran down the ramp. 'Come on, guys, let's go on foot.'

They found a security guard standing next to a badly parked hire car, shaking his head.

Declan tried to make himself be understood but to no avail. The man just shook his head and waved his hands.

'Don't worry, Declan. I'll deal with this,' Arabella said as she turned to the man and began rabbiting off again. 'He said they just drove into the car park, stopped, had a big fight and left the car here. Apparently one of them had a knife.'

'Was it them?'

Arabella nodded.

'So we're really close, then?' Lana asked as she rifled in her bag, looking for her mobile phone.

'What are you doing?' asked Emma.

'Phoning Dad.'

'No need. He's already on his way, along with everybody else.'

Lana nodded and leaned against the car. Coming over all dizzy, she immediately found herself in the same place but surrounded by different people.

Lucy Jo was crying, and Kimberly was trying to console her as Stan shouted angrily at them all to hurry, while Archie shouted at him for yelling at them.

Lana listened, wishing she could take Lucy Jo in her arms.

'It's alright, everything's going to be fine. I promise you. Just ignore the horrid man, sweetheart,' reassured Kimberly as she hugged the child, grabbing her bag from the back seat.

'I've just about had enough of this,' said Archie. 'This is it, Stan. They've found us, maybe it's time to give ourselves up.'

'What the hell! Are you crazy?'

'No, Stan. I've just had enough. We'll never get away with it. They'll follow us everywhere, to the ends of the Earth, if they have to.'

'No,' yelled Stan as he took something from his pocket. 'They won't. They'll never find us in Canada. I won't let them. And if you're giving up, then I'm giving up on you.'

By the time Archie spotted it, it was too late. Stan jumped

towards him, pushing something long and sharp into his torso. Archie fell to the ground, holding his stomach.

'Y... you stabbed me? Your own b...rother?'

'You've never been a brother to me. I couldn't care if you lived or died,' Stan said with a wicked grin.

A scream pierced the air, and Stan turned to see Kimberly staring at him, her eyes wide in shock. She put Lucy Jo down slowly and pushed her behind her, shielding the child from him with her body.

Stan smiled and aimed the knife at her. Shaking her head, she said, 'You'll never get the girl, Stanley. They're coming, right now, and they're going to stop you.'

'Perhaps,' he replied, 'but not before I take great pleasure in plunging this knife into your body,' he growled.

She stepped backwards, taking the little girl's hand. 'If you feel me fall, little one. You run, you run as fast as you can, you hear me?' Kimberly whispered.

Lana watched her little sister nod, her face paling at the sight of Archie on the ground.

Thinking he was dead, Lana jumped when he suddenly lurched forward, pulling himself along the floor with his strong arms, towards Stan. Although he wasn't quick enough to reach him, he was able to distract him for a second. Just long enough to allow Kimberly to turn and run.

'Nice try... brother,' Stan shouted, kicking Archie in the face so that he fell back between two parked cars. 'You're not going to get away from me,' he shouted, turning and scanning the area for movement.

Lana realised she was holding her breath as she tiptoed through the cars, trying to find Kimberly and Lucy Jo, but they'd disappeared. Feeling herself fading back out of the vision, she cried, 'No, no, no, I've got to find them, I've got to find them.'

'Lana, Lana? Are you okay? We found Archie,' Emma whispered.

'Come on, babe. Wake up,' said Barber as he gently patted her cheek.

'I need to find them,' she yelled, opening her eyes wide. 'Is he dead? Stan stabbed him and kicked him in the head.'

'He's alive, just about. What happened?' Emma asked.

'We need to find them, they're on foot. Kimberly's got Lucy Jo. She's trying to save her from Stan. They must be close. We need to go and find them now.'

'It's okay, all the others are combing the streets. They'll find them, babe,' Barber said as he lifted her up off the ground until she was steady enough to stand.

But before she did anything else, Lana gave a detailed description of Kimberly and what the young woman was wearing. 'You need to tell the others,' she said to one of the Watchers, who was hanging around waiting for instruction. He nodded and ran off to the rest of the group.

'Where's Dad?' asked Lana.

'He's with them.'

Lana nodded.

'Are you okay, sis?' Emma asked as she began to lead them out the same way they'd come in.

'Yeah, I'm fine. Look we can't go that way. We need to go this way.'

'Huh?' said Emma.

'We should go the same direction Kimberly was heading,' Lana said, pulling them both through several parked cars until they reached some stairs. 'Up there,' she motioned.

They climbed the stairs until they came out in an outdoor square, where they scanned the area. Some of their classmates hovered around, waiting to be told what to do.

'Do you know which way they went, sis?' Emma asked.

'I'm not sure. I need another vision to help me. But nothing's coming,' Lana cried. 'Wait, Kimberly knows we're behind them. Maybe she left some kind of clue—breadcrumbs. Look around, everyone, and see if you can find something.'

Thoroughly scanning the area, they were soon joined by Diarmuid, Liam, Rupert and Elliott. All of them scoured the ground, the surrounding buildings and cars until Rupert yelled, 'Over there.'

Following his gaze, Lana ran over to a large bin. Tears filled her eyes.

Rupert nodded. 'There's something blue and white in there. I can see through it, remember?'

Barber lifted the large lid, turning his face away from the stench of rotting food before he leaned in and pulled out a blue and white scarf.

Lana gasped. 'That's Kimberly's. She was wearing it in my vision.'

'But what does that mean? Where did she go?' asked Emma as they looked around.

Holding onto the scarf, Lana started to go dizzy again. 'It's happening again,' she yelled, before crumpling to the floor.

Opening her eyes, she watched Kimberly and Lucy Jo hiding between the bin and the wall. They both held their breath as Stan slowly walked around the square, his beady eyes searching for them. He stopped for a moment and went to look down the side of another building. Kimberly breathed out for a second and slowly took off her scarf, lifting the lid without making a sound, and dropped it inside. She turned to Lucy Jo and held a finger over her lips, whispering something Lana couldn't hear.

Lucy Jo's eyes were full of tears, but she managed to stay silent. She just nodded and gripped Kimberly's hand even tighter. Slowly they stood, carefully watching for Stan. And then they turned and ran down an alley. Lana could feel herself drifting again. 'No! Which way? Which way?' She whispered to herself. Before her eyes went black, she saw them turn right at the end.

The moment she opened her eyes, she grabbed hold of Barber.

'Just keep me steady,' she whispered. 'This way,' she yelled to everyone.

Instead of steadying her, Barber picked her up, and she pointed him in the right direction.

At the end of the next street, he put her down.

'Which way?' Lana muttered to herself. 'Which way? I don't know which way!' Crying, she turned to Barber and sobbed into his chest.

'It's okay. Just wait for a second,' Barber said, looking around as the others arrived.

'What's up?' asked Liam.

'Just give me a sec,' Barber said, as he turned his face from one side to the other.

'Can you... Can you... smell them or something?' Emma asked out of breath.

He nodded. 'I got her scent from the scarf. It's not very strong, but I think... I think she went this way,' he said, lifting Lana in his arms and running left and then right. The others struggled to keep up; even Liam, who possessed the gift of speed.

Soon they found themselves standing at the riverfront, with a huge square between them and the water.

'There!' Barber shouted.

Lana looked across and saw a small bridge over the river. Running across it was Kimberly. Lucy Jo was holding on to her back, and Stan was closing in on them. They could even see the glint of the knife from where they stood.

'No!' yelled Emma and Lana.

At the sound, Kimberly stopped for a second and looked towards them. Then she looked backwards; Stan was just a few metres away. He stopped when she stopped and smiled at her, but he failed to notice that she was moving towards the edge. Before anyone else knew what was happening, Emma ran as fast as she could towards the water, diving in and swimming towards the bridge.

'What? What's happening?' cried Lana.

Seconds later, Stan stood alone and confused as Kimberly, and Lucy Jo jumped into the water below.

Emma watched as they crashed into the water ahead of her. She swam as fast as she could, reaching them in seconds. 'It's okay, I've got you. I've got you, Lucy Jo,' cried Emma as she held her little sister close to her chest, allowing a warm glow to envelop them and protect her from the cold.

'Emma? Is that you?' the little girl asked. 'What happened? Where have you been?'

Emma smiled and kissed her on the forehead before she realised Kimberly was nowhere to be seen. 'Kimberly?' she shouted. 'Kimberly!'

But the young woman failed to emerge from the dark waters of the River Arade.

Suddenly there were several large splashes into the water, and Emma watched as Patrick, Declan, Barber and Diarmuid all swam towards her.

'Lucy Jo. Lucy Jo, oh my god, my girl. Is she okay, Emma? Is she? Is she safe? Is she hurt? Oh God, Oh God,' Patrick murmured over and over.

'It's okay, Dad. She's fine, she's fine,' Emma cried.

Emma could hear Lana sobbing from the waterside. 'Take her, Dad. I need to find Kimberly.'

Swimming down into the murkiness, Emma could barely see a thing, not even with her glow. She scoured everywhere beneath her, but there was no sign of the woman who had rescued her little sister. A sob escaped her lips, but as she was about to give up, she spotted something out of the corner of her eye.

Swimming closer, Emma reached out, her movements causing even more sand and dirt to drift upwards. The water cleared for a second, and she spotted Kimberly, her foot somehow caught on what looked like an old anchor.

Emma unhooked Kimberly's shoe and grabbed her, speeding upwards through the water until she could propel them both out onto dry land.

'Diarmuid!' she shouted, 'Diarmuid!'

Diarmuid ran over and nodded at her as Kimberly was carefully laid on her back. While Declan performed mouth to mouth, Diarmuid placed his healing hands on her chest, his light and warm touch hopefully bringing her back from the depths.

'She was under a long time.' Lana swallowed.

'Daddy? Daddy, don't let her die. She was my friend,' cried Lucy Jo, who had managed to escape from Patrick's grip and run towards them.

'No, Lucy Jo, you shouldn't see this.' Lana tried to hold her back.

'No, Lana,' she cried. 'She was my friend.' Lucy Jo collapsed to the floor and cried her little heart out.

'L...u...cy... J...o?'

The little girl lifted her head up slowly. 'Kim?' she said. 'You're alive!' she squealed, jumping and running towards her.

Lana smiled and picked up her sister. 'Calm down. She's very weak. Let's not get too excited. Okay?'

Lucy Jo nodded and then put her arms around Lana and squeezed tight. 'I missed you.'

Tears began to roll down Lana's face. 'I missed you too, I missed you too.'

❧ 21 ☙

'Do you think she's going to be okay?' Lana asked Emma as they stood looking out the window of the Praxos villa.

'I don't know. I hope so.'

They stood watching the young woman, who was wrapped in a blanket on a sun lounger, staring out at the magnificent view beyond. She'd barely said a word since they'd brought her back.

'I'm going to speak to her. I'll take her some tea.' Emma quietly placed a cup of green tea beside Kimberly and sat down on the chair next to her.

Kimberly smiled. 'Thank you.'

'That's okay. How are you feeling?'

She waited a moment before saying anything. 'Alright, I guess. Still a bit weak, I suppose.'

'Why did you do it?'

Kimberly looked at the floor. 'You wouldn't understand.'

'Try me.'

But she just let out a deep sigh. 'How's Archie?'

'He's still sleeping, but the doctor says he's going to be just fine. He was lucky that Stan missed all his vital organs. It'll probably be a while until he's back to normal, though.'

Kimberly nodded.

'Kimberly, you can trust us. You know that, right?'

The young woman turned to look at Emma. 'Yes, I do. I just... I don't know. I feel so helpless now.'

'Why? You helped us get Lucy Jo back.'

'I also helped take her in the first place.'

'Yes, but only to protect her. We understand that.'

'You don't understand why I...'

'Why you what?'

Kimberly sighed again and reached out for her tea. Taking a sip, she held her breath for a second.

'Careful, it's hot.'

'Yeah.'

'You can talk to me, Kimberly.'

'Please, call me Kim.'

'Kim. You can talk to me. You can talk to all of us here.'

She nodded. 'I know. I'm sorry, I...'

Emma waited patiently, saying nothing.

'The reason I'm with Archie, it's not what you think.'

'No?'

Kim shook her head. 'Revenge.'

'Revenge?' asked Emma.

Kim nodded. 'When I was five years old, my sister was killed. She was my twin.'

'I'm so sorry, Kim.'

'She was murdered.'

'God, that's awful.'

'And my parents died a few years ago, too.'

'Oh no.'

'But it's all connected.'

'What do you mean?'

'I believe that that... that family killed them all.'

Emma gasped. 'When you say 'that family', who do you mean?'

'Sophokles, the Sophokles family.'

'Sthenelaus? Archie? Stan?'

'I know Archie had nothing to do with it, now. But yes,' she nodded, 'that's why I started dating him. I wanted to try and get into his family so I could get revenge. But then I...I... fell in love with him.'

'Oh, Kim,' Emma whispered.

A lone tear rolled down Kim's cheek as she nodded. 'And then we got all caught up with you and your family and well, you know the rest.'

'Does Archie know?'

'What? About why we're together? Of course not. How can I tell him that?'

Emma sat back and looked out at the view. 'It's a beautiful view, isn't it?'

Kim nodded.

'Maybe Archie deserves to know, to see the bigger picture,' Emma said, using her arms to point ahead of her. 'From what I understand about him, Kim is that he is nothing like his family. That he would rather have nothing to do with them.'

'I think you're right. But how would he take it? Knowing that I got close to him so that I could kill his father?'

Emma gasped.

'Yes, that was my plan. I wanted to kill him.'

'Do you still want to?'

'Every single day.'

'But could you?'

Kim shrugged.

'I don't think so. I've seen you with Lucy Jo. You have too much love in here,' Emma said, pressing her hand against her heart. 'A person like that can't kill, Kim.'

Kim began to cry, her body shuddering under the weight of her burden.

'Oh Kim,' Emma said, moving over to hold her.

After a few moments, Kim lifted her head up. 'Thank you,' she whispered.

They sat in silence for a while longer before Emma moved back onto her chair and they drank their tea.

'You're a Watcher, aren't you?'

Emma glanced sideways. 'What do you know about Watchers?'

'A lot. Drake told me about you.'

'Drake, your brother?'

She pulled a face. 'He's not my brother. My parents adopted him. I think they adopted him for a reason.'

'What do you mean?'

'My parents spent years trying to find out who murdered my sister. That's when they found out about the supernatural world, and they knew their only way in was to adopt one. Drake should have been a Watcher, but he went down the wrong road and became a Skull. I know all about you guys.'

Emma raised her eyebrows.

'But don't worry, your secret is safe with me.'

'So that's why you wrote the note, back at that tacky villa?'

She nodded. 'I knew you wouldn't be far behind. It was super tacky, wasn't it?'

Emma grinned. 'It was horrendous!' She laughed, before whispering, 'Thank you for keeping Lucy Jo safe.'

'She's a special little girl. I'm just really, really glad that she doesn't remember half of it.'

'We're lucky to have Almerinda and her sister with us.'

'They're amazing, those two. Can you imagine what would have happened if Sthenelaus had found them first, though?'

'Let's not even think about that.' Emma grimaced.

'Is Archie a Skull too, then, Kim?'

Kim thought about it for a while and shrugged. 'No. The Skulls are all evil, and Archie isn't evil. Yeah, he has a temper sometimes, but he's a good guy.'

'Does he have a tattoo?'

'Yeah, but there's no skull if that's what you're asking.'

'Is there an eye?'

'It's kind of a weird one really, there's nothing much, just a few wavy lines around an empty space.'

'That's weird. Maybe he's somewhere in the middle. Does he have any powers?'

'I've never seen them, but I heard Stan mention something about him being able to hover—not fly, just hover—or something like that. But we don't really talk about it. He doesn't like to talk about his family, and I guess that's all connected, isn't it?'

Emma nodded. 'I guess so.'

The door opened, and Lana appeared. 'Hey, Kimberly.'

'Kim, please,' she smiled.

'Kim, Archie's awake. He's asking for you.' Lana smiled.

Kim's eyes grew wide. 'What am I going to say?' She turned to

Emma.

'The truth?'

'Oh God, I think I'm going to be sick.'

Emma stood and helped her up. 'You'll be fine. Do you want me to come with you?'

Kim shook her head. 'No, I can do this on my own. I guess I have to. I owe it to him, right?'

Emma nodded.

oOo

ABOUT TWENTY MINUTES AFTER KIM WALKED INTO THE ROOM where Archie was resting, the whole building seemed to shake for a few moments.

'Is it an earthquake?' asked Lana as she hurried to the nearest table and crouched underneath it.

'Nope, not an earthquake,' said Theodore who had arrived shortly after Kim had gone to see Archie.

'How do you know?' she asked when he leaned forward to help her to her feet again.

'No seismic activity—not today, anyway,' he said, touching his head.

'Oh, okay,' Lana replied, confused.

'Thanks for coming, Theo. I believe Archie will need some kind of pain relief. We'll wait until Kim has had a chance to talk to him though,' said Eleanor.

Theodore nodded and sat down.

'If it wasn't an earthquake, then what was it?' Lana asked.

Theo turned to look at her and shrugged. 'Somebody's powers, I guess.'

'There's a Watcher here that can do that?' she asked Eleanor, intrigued.

Eleanor shook her head. 'Not one of ours.'

Suddenly Kim rushed down the corridor and into the living room. 'Erm... Eleanor?'

'Yes, Kimberly. Is everything alright?'

'Erm, I'm not sure. I think Archie just made the earth move.'

Lana chuckled.

'No, I didn't mean...' Kimberly blushed.

'Just ignore her,' Eleanor said, shaking her head. 'What happened, dear?'

'I was telling him the truth about me.' She turned to look for Emma, who was sitting at the dining table with Diarmuid. Emma smiled reassuringly. 'Then he went a little red in the face, and it felt like an earthquake, and when his colour went back to normal, it stopped.'

'Oh, in that case, I'd better come and have a look. Theo, please come too.'

'Emma? Have you got a minute?' asked Kim.

'Sure,' Emma said, as she got up and walked towards her.

'I told him. Apart from the whole earthquake thing, I think he took it pretty well. Will you come in and see him? He wants to speak to you.'

'To me?'

Kim nodded.

As they walked into the room, they found Eleanor leaning over Archie, inspecting his eyes. She was talking to him very quietly. He nodded a few times, looking embarrassed, and sat up. She helped him lean forward slightly before she walked around the other side of the bed.

The girls followed her and Kim gasped. 'Archie!'

'What? What is it?' he asked.

'It's your tattoo. It's changed.'

'What do you mean, changed?'

'It's got a big eye on it. Oh and look... there are some words. Bono Malum Superate. What does that mean? 'Kim asked her eyes as wide as saucers.

Eleanor grinned and told him to lie back down before Theo took Archie's hands in his.

'Erm, what's he doing?' Archie asked warily.

Eleanor smiled. 'He's just administering some pain relief. Trust me, you'll feel much better when he's finished.'

'Eleanor, what does it mean?' Kim asked again.

Smiling, she said, 'Bono Malum Superate – Overcome Evil with Good. Welcome to the Watchers, Archie.'

❧ 2 2 ❧

With everything that had happened, there was much-needed rest and relaxation, so Arabella invited everyone to spend the rest of their Christmas holidays at the Praxos villa in Monchique. And that included Audrey and Greg, who had finally been told the truth about the girls and the academy in London. Even Scott had been invited but was devastated when his mother had declined due to a family wedding.

After a particularly tearful reunion with little Lucy Jo, both Audrey and Greg had spent several minutes hugging Emma and Lana.

'I'm sorry we didn't get a chance to talk about all of this before, but I just want you to know that I always knew you were special. Since that day you arrived on our doorstep, I just knew there was something... something different about you both,' Audrey said proudly.

'Are you... erm, are you okay with it, Mum?' asked Lana.

Audrey took a moment to answer and then slowly nodded. 'It's taking some time to sink in, and I know that I will never be able to accept that you will often be put in danger, but there's little I can do about that. I love you both dearly, and the fact that you're a little different from the rest of us means nothing. You're still my girls,' she said, hugging them even tighter. 'I'm just sorry you weren't able to share it with us before all this happened.'

'I'm sorry too, Mum,' Emma whispered. 'But you know now.'

Audrey nodded just before Greg grinned. 'Me too,' he sang. 'My sisters have got special powers,' he said beaming.

The girls laughed and ruffled his hair.

'You know what? I think you've grown since we last saw you.'

'Aw c'mon, I'm thirteen, not six,' he said, pushing away from her. 'So, are you going to show me, or what?'

'Show you what?' Lana asked, her lips turning upwards. 'There's nothing to show.'

'Aw c'mon, please. I wanna see.'

'Come on, Greg, get in the car. Your sisters can't do anything out in public. You must understand that. It's very important that what they can do is kept a secret. Do you understand?' Patrick asked as he pushed him into the vehicle before shutting the door behind him.

Nodding, Greg turned to look at Emma, staring for a moment.

'What?' she asked.

'Nothing.'

She laughed and let her head fall to one side, staring back. 'Really?'

'I'm just looking to see if you look any different.'

'What? You mean now that you know the truth?'

He nodded.

'And?'

Shrugging his shoulders, he said, 'You look exactly the same.'

oOo

DELIGHTED TO HAVE THE FAMILY BACK TOGETHER AGAIN, AND everyone safe and sound, the girls began to enjoy themselves at the party the following afternoon. It was to celebrate so many things: the return of Lucy Jo; the 'arrival' of the new Watcher. Archie; Almerinda's reunion with her long lost sister; the girls no longer having to hide their true selves from their family. There was much to celebrate, and they were thrilled with the arrival of Sonia, who had finally mastered the art of walking with crutches.

'Sonia!' squealed Emma from the indoor swimming pool, where

she'd spent the past hour with Diarmuid and some of her other classmates, just being silly in the water.

'Hello, everyone,' Sonia whispered, smiling.

As Emma jumped out of the water, Greg stood open-mouthed. 'I wish I could do that. That is wicked.'

She ruffled his hair as she walked past, grabbing a towel and wrapping it around herself, before stopping in front of the younger girl. 'How are you? How's your leg?'

'Better, now that I can walk with these.' Sonia smiled. 'I'm very happy you found your sister. You must be so relieved.'

'I can't describe the feeling—we're so happy, Sonia. Come on, let's get a drink and sit down.'

Sonia nodded and followed until they found a bench in the garden, looking out over the rest of the Algarve.

'Aren't you cold?' she asked, shivering a little in her coat.

Emma wrapped the towel around her a little more tightly but shook her head. 'I can warm myself easily enough.'

Sonia raised her eyebrows and Emma shrugged. 'Just one of my... abilities. Speaking of which, how is yours going?'

Sonia raised her eyebrows again.

'The invisibility thing? Are you getting any closer to being able to control it?'

'Oh, that? Yes, I've had lessons with my father every day, and I'm much better now,' she smiled.

'That's fantastic. Where is your dad? Is he coming?' she said, looking around at all the people pottering around.

'Yes, he dropped me off first. He's just gone to pick up his sister.'

'He has a sister?'

'Yes, my auntie is wonderful. I love her very much.'

Emma smiled. 'Is she a Watcher too?'

Sonia grinned. 'A very special one.'

'Cool.'

'You'll like her. She should be here soon.'

'I'm sure I will. What about your stepmother? Isn't she coming?'

Sonia rolled her eyes.

'You don't like her very much, do you?'

'She's okay, I guess. She's just a bit...' she shrugged, 'normal.'

Emma laughed. 'Normal?'

Sonia bit her bottom lip and nodded.

'Is that why you're not keen on her?'

She shrugged again.

'We all need some normal in our lives, to balance out all this craziness.'

'Yes, I guess so. I just wish...'

'That your mother was still here?'

Sonia nodded.

'I understand.'

'My stepmother is nice... She treats us well, she's an amazing cook, and I think she loves me but...'

'I'm sure she does. You see that woman over there, with the long light brown wavy hair?' Emma asked, pointing.

Sonia nodded.

'That's Audrey Morgan. She's my mum—not my real mum, obviously. She and Patrick, who you've already met, adopted Lana and me when we were babies. That crazy kid over there?' she pointed, 'That's Greg—he's my brother—and there's Lucy Jo, who he won't leave alone.'

Sonia grinned. 'They look like a really cool family.'

'They are totally cool, and they are totally normal. I don't know what we would be like without them. You understand?'

Sonia looked a little ashamed and nodded. 'Totally.'

Emma put her arm around her and squeezed.

'You're like a psychologist or something,' Sonia laughed.

'If that's a compliment, I'll take it.'

'Hey,' said a voice from behind them, making them both jump.

Laughing, Emma replied, 'Hey yourself, Kim. Everything alright?'

Kim nodded with a grin. 'It's better than alright, actually.'

Emma scooted over a little, to allow Kim to sit down, before introducing her to Sonia.

'Hi,' Kim said. 'I heard about you breaking your leg down there,' she pointed down the hill in front of them. 'How are you feeling?'

'Much better, thank you. And you? My dad told me all about

you and... Archie?'

Kim nodded and smiled. 'I guess you could say it's been a crazy week, but things are good now. I'm so glad Lucy Jo is back with her family and Archie has finally become what he was always meant to be.'

'But what about you, Kim? How are you? Really?' Emma asked.

Kim smiled and turned to Sonia. 'I heard your comment about her being like a psychologist, and I have to agree.'

The three of them laughed while Emma rolled her eyes.

'No, but seriously, I'm good. Since Archie's change, I don't know... I feel like a huge weight has been lifted from my shoulders.'

'No more talk of revenge, then?' asked Emma.

Kim sat quietly for a couple of seconds before shaking her head. 'No. I don't think I've even thought about it. All I care about now is Archie. We've decided to put the past behind us and move on. Eleanor has asked us to come to Praxos in London and learn together.'

'Really? But you're not a Watcher?' Emma exclaimed without thinking first. 'Oh, sorry, I didn't mean to sound so... mean.'

Kim smiled. 'It's okay. That was actually my exact reaction too. But apparently, there are a few normal people who work with Praxos. I guess I'm honoured to have been asked.'

'Wow, that's really cool,' Sonia said, and then her eyes lit up at the sight of her dad and his sister.

'See,' Emma added, 'normal people can be cool too, Sonia. Maybe you should think about that and your stepmother.'

'Yes, perhaps I should,' Sonia said, struggling to stand up.

'Oh, let me help,' said Kim, hopping up and giving her a hand.

'Thank you. Come with me, both of you. Come and meet my auntie.'

As they turned to head towards the villa, Kim gasped and almost fell backwards.

'You okay, Kim?' Emma asked.

But the young woman shook her head and pointed.

'What? Why are you pointing at my auntie, Kim?'

'It's... it's...'

'Hi, girls,' said the most beautiful woman with long, silvery-blonde hair. 'I'm Aria.'

❧ 23 ❧

'No, no...' murmured Kim.

'Please be calm,' said Aria softly, as her niece exchanged looks with Emma.

'What's going on?' asked Sonia.

'You... you...'

Aria stepped forward to place a hand on Kim's arm, but the woman turned, stumbling, and ran into the house, searching for Archie.

'What's going on?' asked Eleanor as she approached them with a walking stick in one hand and a glass of port in the other. 'Oh hello, you must be Aria, Luis' sister. It's lovely to finally meet you. I've heard much about you.'

Aria smiled warmly and waited for Eleanor to put her drink down on a nearby table before returning to shake her hand.

'Likewise. It's a pleasure to meet you, Eleanor.'

Emma and Sonia both stood silently, trying to figure out what was going on with Kim when suddenly Archie appeared in the doorway. His face like thunder, he slowly approached the women. With every step, the earth beneath his feet seemed to shudder until the whole building shook.

'Archie,' Eleanor shouted. 'You must stop this at once.'

But he had angry eyes only for Aria. 'You,' he boomed, pointing to her.

The whole party had stopped, not a single person looked elsewhere.

'Please, I can explain,' Aria said, shielding her face from him.

'Explain? Explain what?' Eleanor asked. 'Archie, please stop, you're going to destroy the house. Kim, please tell him to stop.'

Kim approached him from behind and gently put her hand on his arm, whispering something into his ear.

Immediately the ground stopped shaking, and he just stood, staring, accusing Aria of something that nobody else seemed to have a clue about. 'This woman is married to my father.'

There were gasps of horror; people fled indoors assuming that the Skulls were close by, but Aria held up her arms and tried to calm everyone down. 'Please, you have nothing to fear,' she said.

Luis stood beside her and nodded. 'It's true, you have nothing to fear. This is my sister. She is one of you. She is a Watcher. Please, just listen to what she has to say.'

Hearing the words come from Luis' lips made what he was saying easier for them to accept, so they stood silently, waiting to listen to what she had to say.

'I am Aria, I am a Watcher, like most of you. And Archie speaks the truth. I am married to Sthenelaus.'

'Good God, Aria, what on Earth were you thinking?' Eleanor said, her knees buckling. Declan rushed to her side and helped her into a chair. 'Continue,' she demanded.

'Several years ago, while I was studying abroad, I met a wonderful man, who was also a Watcher. We fell in love instantly and spent the most wonderful year travelling around the world. When we returned, he had to go back to London to sort out his affairs. Our plan was for him to move here, where we would marry and have a family of our own,' she stopped and smiled before continuing. 'But something happened. Something that put an end to our dream.'

'What? What happened?' asked Lana.

'He was taken.'

'Taken? By whom?' asked Eleanor.

'By Sthenelaus.'

More gasps filled the air.

'Do you believe her?' Kim whispered to Emma, who slowly nodded.

'Look at her face, the truth is written all over it. This woman has been hurting for a very long time.'

Kimberly looked a little ashamed and nodded.

'So you married him? Why? Why would you do that?' Lana almost shrieked.

Aria rubbed her forehead. 'It was the only way in, the only way I could find out the truth.'

'But why didn't you come to me, Aria?' Eleanor asked. 'That's why we're here.'

But Aria shook her head. 'No. I needed to get as close as possible to him. I needed him to trust me. It wasn't just for my John, it was for everyone else who has ever suffered at the hands of the Sophokles family.' She stopped, her eyes searching Archie's. 'I'm sorry, but I didn't know the truth about you either, Archie, until I discovered that he had forced you to kidnap that poor little girl.'

'But why didn't you tell us then? You could have helped us?' Patrick interjected, pointing at her. 'You could have avoided all this pain.'

'I'm sorry, truly I am, but I didn't know about it until she had already been taken. It was only when I discovered Kimberly's past that I decided that I must tell you, which is why I came here today. Kimberly, I'm sorry I frightened you. If I'd known the truth about you earlier—if I'd known that you had entered the family for the same reasons I had—things would have been different. I hope you can forgive me.'

Kim stepped forward, eyeing her. 'Do you know what happened to your John?'

Tears filled Aria's eyes, and she shook her head. 'So far, I have been unable to uncover the truth.'

'Then together we must do just that,' Archie whispered, pulling Kim towards him and holding out a hand to Aria.

She stepped forward and took it. He squeezed her fingers and smiled as a huge, collective sigh of relief seemed to be released from all around.

oOo

'HOW CAN A BROTHER AND SISTER LOOK SO DIFFERENT FROM each other?' Lana asked as she carefully combed her wet hair in front of the mirror.

Emma approached her and placed her head on her sister's shoulder and pulled a face.

'We're twins—you're black, and I'm white. Need I say more?'

Lana laughed, tapping her on the head with her comb. 'You know what I mean. Luis is like, well, really quite ugly, in a sense, and Aria is just well, probably one of the most beautiful women I've ever seen. He's really dark, erm—everything—and she's all pale-skinned, silvery hair and light eyes. It's just weird.'

'They're Watchers, sis. Just like us,' she said, dropping onto her bed and picking up her book.

'Yeah, I guess. Don't you think it's weird, though?'

'What? The fact that they look different? Not really.'

'No, I mean this whole weird connection thing. You know, the fact that Kim started going out with Archie so she could get revenge on his dad. And Aria actually marrying his dad so she could find out what happened to her real fiancé. And then the fact that Aria is Luis' sister, who lives in Portugal. I mean, it just seems so, oh, I don't know... just weird.'

'It's a small world we live in,' Emma murmured.

'Hm? Yeah, I guess so. Especially a small supernatural world. What's that six connections thingy?'

'Huh?'

'You know - the six degrees of separation?'

'Yeah.'

'Maybe it's got something to do with that?'

'Maybe.'

'Are you even listening?'

'Uhuh.'

'Whatever.'

A knock on the door startled Lana, who dropped her comb on the floor. 'Come in,' she shouted as she stooped to pick it up.

'Lana? Emma?'

'Hey, Lucy Jo, what are you doing in here? I thought you'd gone to bed ages ago?' Emma asked, putting her book down and tapping the side of the bed beside her.

'I couldn't sleep. I asked Dad if I could come to sleep in your room, and he said it was okay. Is it okay?'

'Of course it is. Dad actually let you out of his sight?'

A chuckle could be heard on the other side of the door before the sound of footsteps walking away echoed down the corridor.

Lucy Jo raised her eyebrows and smiled.

'I guess that answers my question,' Emma grinned before pulling her sister close and holding her tight.

'Hey, sis,' Lana said, throwing herself on the bed next to them. 'How are you feeling?'

'I'm alright. Are you?'

Lana grinned. 'Of course I am. I am now, anyway. Now that we've got you back safe.'

'I missed you. Both of you,' snivelled the little girl, wiping her nose with the back of her hand.

'Ewww, Lucy Jo. That's something Greg would do,' Lana winced with a grin.

The little girl grinned and shook her head. 'I don't mind anymore.'

'Don't mind what?' asked Emma.

'Being like Greg.'

'What do you mean?' Emma smiled.

'Before, I didn't want to be like him at all, but then I realised how much I missed him, so I figured I wouldn't mind, you know, being like him.'

'Lucy Jo, that's the sweetest thing. Maybe you should tell him.'

Lucy Jo shook her head. 'No way.'

The girls laughed.

'But I wish I could be like you even more,' Lucy Jo continued. "With all those special powers. Do you think I might get them when I'm older?'

Sharing a glance, Emma squeezed her again and shook her head. 'Believe me, Lucy Jo. You are very special as you are, you don't need anything extra to make you even more special, because that just wouldn't be possible.'

Content with her answer, the little girl climbed under the

covers. 'I want you to sleep on this side of me, Emma, and you to sleep on this side, Lana,' she said, patting both sides of the bed.

'I'm just glad the beds are huge in this place,' Lana laughed. 'Okay, I'll be right there. I just need to finish doing my hair. You wouldn't want to sleep next to me with wet hair now, would you? Oh, I nearly forgot,' she said, opening her top drawer. 'I have something of yours.'

'You do?'

Lana nodded, turning around to reveal her favourite bracelet.

'My bracelet!' Lucy Jo exclaimed. 'I thought it was gone for good.'

'No, it's safe and sound, just like you.'

Lucy Jo smiled as Lana put it on for her, before sliding down until her head rested on the pillow.

'Emma, please tell me a story while I fall asleep.'

Grinning, Emma proceeded to tell her all about Sleeping Beauty—well, her own version, anyway.

❧ 24 ❧

Eleanor and the other Mentors sat talking to Aria until well into the night, eager to find out more about the evil Sthenelaus.

Aria was able to give them more information than they ever thought possible, including his plans to take Lucy Jo and the rest of his family to the back of beyond, in Canada, somewhere.

'So he never actually mentioned where in Canada he planned on settling down?' asked Eleanor.

Aria shook her head. 'For some reason, he was trying to refrain from telling me about Canada.'

'Do you think he was on to you?' asked Declan.

'I don't think so. I think maybe he wanted to surprise me with it.'

'So what about the other son, Stan? What happened to him?'

'You mean... you don't have him?'

Eleanor slowly shook her head. 'He disappeared from the bridge the moment Kim jumped. We assumed he ran home to tell his father what had happened.'

Aria shook her head. 'He made a phone call to Sthenelaus while I was with him, telling him that Archie was dead and that the little girl was gone. That's all he said.'

'And then what happened?' asked Eleanor.

'Sthenelaus was absolutely furious. He threw things around the office for a while, until his other wife arrived to calm him down.'

'His other wife? He has another wife?' Eleanor shook her head.

Aria smirked. 'Typical evil guy behaviour, right? Yeah, I know. Her name's Madge, she married him when they were both really young. It was an arranged marriage, but one that suits them both.'

'Tell us more about this... Madge,' Eleanor leaned forward eagerly.

'She's from a powerful Greek Skulls family herself. She's probably about as crazy as he is.'

'How did she take it when he married you?'

'Honestly? She seemed perfectly fine about it. As if it were normal to have two wives.'

'Do you, erm, get on with her?'

'Let's just say... I have my ways to make people accept me.'

Eleanor raised her eyebrows as Arabella opened the door carrying a large tray with tea for everyone.

'I can calm people down and, well, mesmerise them, for want of a better word. Thank you, Arabella. That's very kind.'

'And you often did this with Sthenelaus?' Eleanor asked, rather quietly.

Aria blushed and looked down. 'Yes, all the time. But if you're asking about, well... erm, we were never intimate. I was able to avoid that by using my power.' She smiled, relief covering her face.

'I see,' smiled Eleanor, winking cheekily. 'Thank goodness. So technically your marriage is null and void because it was never consummated?'

'I guess you could say that, but he wouldn't understand because he doesn't realise that it wasn't... consummated.'

'So as far as he's concerned, everything is alright between the two of you?'

Aria nodded, taking a sip of her tea.

'Do you think he suspects anything?' Eleanor asked.

Aria shook her head.

'How did you manage to marry him without him knowing who you really are?' Eleanor asked, leaning back in her seat.

Aria looked at her hands. 'This power of mine is pretty impressive,' she smiled.

Eleanor nodded. 'It certainly is. But why didn't you just use it to ask him what happened to John?'

'It doesn't work like that, unfortunately. Otherwise, I could have avoided all of this. I can encourage people to do what I want them to do. I can't always encourage them to speak the truth,' she looked down. 'If only I could...'

'I understand. So where is Sthenelaus now? And where does he think you are?'

'He has a health problem, which, when he becomes stressed, gets a lot worse. It's a kind of cough that won't go away. Madge usually takes him somewhere to soothe him. Well, after destroying the room, it got pretty bad, so he went with her.'

'Where do they go?'

'Turkish baths are usually their first choice, so I'm not sure where that would be over here.'

'What do you mean by over here? Is he here? In the Algarve?'

Aria nodded. 'Well, he came here a couple of weeks ago for business, that's what he told me, anyway. But since Lucy Jo was taken, we've actually been staying in Seville.'

'Seville?' asked Eleanor, leaning forward.

Aria nodded. 'He wanted to be close, but not too close, he said.'

'Exactly how far is Seville from here?' she asked eagerly.

'A couple of hours' drive if you use the motorway.'

'Can you show us where you've been staying?'

'You mean to go there? But, he's dangerous Eleanor, you might get hurt,'

'Aria, you've spent, what, a few years living with this man as his wife?'

Aria nodded blushing.

'If he's not expecting us, now is the time to strike. But before we do, tell me more about this illness of his. Declan, please let everyone know that we're heading to Seville in an hour. I'd take the helicopter, but we need more people to assist. Please organise the cars. Thank you.'

Declan stood up, nodding, draining the last of his tea from his cup before he left the room.

oOo

'WHAT'S GOING ON?' YAWNED LANA, WAKING AT THE commotion outside. Getting up and padding over to the door, she opened it, peering out; in the hallway, lots of people were preparing to leave.

'What is it, Lana?' asked Emma from beneath the covers.

'Get up and get dressed. Quickly. Something's going on, and I don't want to miss it... Eleanor?' Lana asked as the young woman ran past the door. 'What's happening?'

'Oh, we didn't want to wake you. We thought you'd want to spend some time with your family.'

'Eleanor?'

She sighed and stepped into their room, where Emma was busy tying the laces of her Converse.

'You should be sleeping,' Eleanor said before Lana put her finger to her lips and pointed to Lucy Jo, who was still fast asleep. Eleanor nodded and continued in a whisper. 'We're going to Seville. We have reason to believe that Sthenelaus is there.'

'We're coming too.' Lana said instantly.

'No, Lana, I think you should sit this one out and stay with your family.'

'No, please, Eleanor, we want to help, and you know that my visions can help. Please let us come.'

'I don't think that's a good idea.'

'What's going on?' asked a sleepy Patrick, who appeared in the doorway, tying the belt of his dressing gown.

'Dad, they're going to try and catch Sthenelaus.'

'Why didn't you wake me? Wait for me, I'm coming.'

Eleanor sighed.

'I was trying to avoid this, Patrick. I think you should stay here.'

Patrick gave Eleanor a look, and she backed down immediately, holding up her hands in defeat. 'Fine,' she said. 'Your girls are trying to come along too. I'll leave that to your discretion.'

'Dad, please, we can help. You know we can. You've seen how we work. We could help. We're coming, okay?' Lana continued.

He just sighed and walked back to his room to change. 'I'll be out in a sec. Go get ready.'

oOo

WAKING UP IN THE CAR WITH DROOL DRIBBLING DOWN HER chin, Lana quickly wiped it away and stole a glance at Barber, to make sure he hadn't seen. He had, and he was smirking. She elbowed him in the side and stuck her tongue out before smiling.

'Thanks for coming,' she whispered.

'I'll always be here to look out for you, Lana. You should know that by now,' he whispered back.

Leaning her head against his shoulder, she gazed out at the sky as the sun threatened to show itself to the world. The motorway was monotonous—there was nothing but tarmac for miles ahead— but at least it meant they'd arrive in Seville sooner. Hopefully, Sthenelaus would still be there.

Lana shivered at the thought of finally coming face to face with such evil. She'd seen him before, of course, but this time they'd be prepared to take him down, for good.

She had no idea what the plan was, as there had been such a rush to leave Praxos. Audrey had tiptoed into the girls' room and gently lifted Lucy Jo, carrying her back to her own bedroom, where Greg was sleeping in the spare bed. She placed her little girl next to him and stood watching them both; Lana had hugged her mother then, kissing her on the cheek before they left her under the watchful eye of Theodore, a few other mentors, and most of her classmates. Eleanor had only allowed Lana, Emma, Diarmuid and Barber (who wasn't technically a Watcher and so he could pretty much do whatever he wanted) to join them.

Lana glanced down at her watch. That had been a couple of hours ago.

'Are we almost there?' she asked no-one in particular.

Declan nodded. 'That's Seville, over there,' he pointed. 'We'll be there in a few minutes,' he said, driving in convoy behind Arabella's car.

'Do you know what the plan is yet?' Lana asked, as Emma slowly lifted her contorted neck and rubbed it sleepily.

'Are we there?' Emma murmured in a state of semi-sleep.

'Yeah, almost,' Lana answered. 'Here, have a drink,' she offered her a half-drunk bottle of coke.

Turning her nose up, Emma shook her head. 'Anyone got any water?'

Diarmuid rifled around in the back and handed her a bottle.

'Thanks.'

'It's very quiet,' Lana murmured as they drove through little streets lined on either side with pretty old buildings.

'It's just after five in the morning, what do you expect?' replied Declan with a smirk.

'Oh yeah, I suppose.'

'There are a few people about, though.' Diarmuid said, pointing to a small group who had clearly been drinking.

'Probably just left a night club or something,' Declan added.

'Where are we going, anyway?' Emma asked as she watched one of the drunken men stumble in the gutter. The other went to help but ended up falling on top of him.

Shaking her head, she looked at Declan, waiting for an answer.

'Apparently, this guy has got some kind of illness, and his only reprieve is at Turkish baths or something like that. Apparently, there's a large one, here in the centre. Aria believes he might be here... he usually has to stay for a day or so for it to make any difference.'

'His cough,' said Lana.

'Huh?'

'He has a nasty cough. I remember seeing him coughing like nobody's business in some of the visions. When he has an attack, it's horrible. It's like he's gonna die or something.'

'Yeah, wish he would. It would certainly solve a lot of problems, don't you think?' Diarmuid added.

'I don't know what his illness is, but I don't know if it's deadly,' Declan replied.

'Well, let's just hope that he's having a terrible attack right now and that he's where we think he is,' Emma said as they eventually came to a standstill. They watched as the others began climbing out of the cars.

Arabella approached their vehicle. Rolling down his window, Declan leaned out to listen to her. 'I think we should go in first. Wait here. We'll come and let you know if he's there.'

'Just look for him, Arabella. Don't go in all guns blazin', mate.'

'Don't worry, we won't. Be right back.'

Declan sat back, tapping his fingers on the dashboard.

'Are we really just going to let them go in first? Shouldn't we go too?' asked Lana. 'I don't want to miss that son of a b—'

'Lana!' Emma scolded.

'Really, Em, it's like having Mum here,' Lana moaned.

Barber and Diarmuid exchanged glances with a knowing smile.

'What?' Lana exclaimed.

'Nothing,' said Barber.

'You're just so predictable,' answered Diarmuid.

Both girls raised their eyebrows but said nothing.

'Come on, I can't just sit here,' Lana attempted to open the door, but Declan turned immediately.

'Oh no, you don't. Just sit tight and wait.'

'Please,' she sighed. 'Come on, I know you want to go in too. Let's just go.'

'Stop it, Lana. We wait. Now sit still and do as you're told.'

'Dad's going in,' she said as she watched Patrick climb out of one of the other cars and disappear inside. 'And he's without backup, Declan. I'm going to help him.'

Declan watched Patrick and shook his head. 'Okay, okay, let's go. Just stay behind me. And above all, be careful.'

Grinning, Lana climbed out and let the others out after her. They walked into the building – straight in through the main entrance – without anybody stopping them.

'Wow, it's hot in here,' whispered Emma as they walked down a beautiful Moroccan corridor and out into a covered courtyard. 'It smells nice, though.'

Aria appeared in one of the doorways to the side. She hushed them and nodded. 'He's here.'

Declan nodded. 'Arabella and Patrick?'

'Through there,' she pointed. 'The others, too.'

Suddenly, the sound of splashing water could be heard, following by intense coughing and then silence. Declan rushed past Aria, pushing the others out of the way.

Patrick stood in the water, soaked from head to foot. In his arms was an unconscious Sthenelaus, wearing nothing but a big pair of Y-fronts.

'Lovely,' Lana said, screwing her face up in disgust. 'That's a picture I'm not going to be able to get out of my head. Gross.'

'This was way too easy,' Declan said as he helped pull Sthenelaus out.

'He was in the water, unconscious,' Patrick said, wiping his brow and climbing out.

'Do you think it's a trap?' asked Emma as they just stood and watched the other Mentors handcuff him and carry him out of the building.

'I don't know. I don't think so... I mean, he was unconscious,' he whispered, looking around. 'I honestly think he thought he was safe. If it weren't for Aria, we'd never have known about him coming to this place.'

'But why was he unconscious? He might have drowned in there.' Emma pointed. 'Not like that would have been a bad thing.'

Declan shook his head. 'Honestly? I haven't a clue.'

Aria had been standing in the shadows, not keen at that point to reveal herself to her 'husband' until he'd been taken away.

'Aria?' asked Lana. 'Are you okay?'

Nodding, she turned. 'Did you find Madge, too?'

Patrick shook his head. 'He was alone in the water.'

'Then she must be close by,' Aria gulped nervously.

'Let's split up,' Declan suggested as they formed groups and headed off to look for his other wife, but after an hour of searching every part of the building, Madge was still nowhere to be found.

Regrouping outside of the Seville Thermal Bath House, they decided to leave her behind and take Sthenelaus back to Praxos in London, where he would eventually stand trial for his crimes.

Climbing back into the vehicles, the convoy set off, but as they did, Emma could have sworn she heard the sounds of a woman screaming out. It sounded like she was shouting 'Sthenelaus!' It made her shiver.

'You okay?' asked Diarmuid.

'Did you hear that?'

'What?'

'Never mind, maybe it was just my imagination,' Emma said, leaning her head against the cold window.

'That was totally weird, like totally surreal.' Lana said what everyone was thinking.

'It was, wasn't it?' Barber replied, patting her knee gently.

'I mean, he's meant to be a leader of the Skulls, yet he was so weak, he had no powers, and we found him just like that... I don't get it. What's going on?'

'I don't know, but at least we have him now. He can't do any more harm. Not anymore. We'll see to that,' Declan said. 'Now, why don't you all try and get some sleep? We'll be travelling another few hours before we get back to Monchique.'

❧ 25 ❧

One Week Later

'I can't believe we're back at the Academy. It doesn't seem like we had a proper Christmas holiday at all,' moaned Lana as they climbed the stairs out of the building to meet Declan for their first class of the year.

'That's because we didn't. Not really,' Emma said, adjusting her warm winter coat and hat against the bitter wind.

'Where are we going, anyway? We don't usually get to go out during class.'

Before Emma could answer her sister, they were joined by the rest of their classmates as they approached Declan, who stood at the gate.

'Morning, guys. I hope you're all appropriately suited and booted for today's class. The first class of the year with me, Declan Alexander, and my able assistant...' he said, flourishing his hands for added effect before someone stepped out from behind him. 'Aria Sophokles.'

Aria grinned and then smacked him on his arm. 'Don't call me that,' she almost shouted.

'Well, that's your name, isn't it?' He laughed as everybody giggled at them before welcoming Aria to London.

'What are you doing here?' asked Lana.

'I work here now—at least for a little while, anyway,' she smiled.

Declan cleared his throat. 'As I was saying, today we're going on a field trip. We'll be doing a fair bit of walking in the cold, so if you're not wearing the appropriate footwear...' He stopped and glanced at Lana.

'What?' she cried. 'These are okay, aren't they?' she said, looking down at her knee-high boots with kitten heels.

'Lana Beth Morgan, go and change your shoes,' Declan sighed.

The others all chuckled as she reluctantly turned and stomped away, almost slipping on the ice beneath her feet in the process.

'Typical girl.' Rupert grinned when Emma glared at him. 'I only speak the truth.'

'Yeah, yeah, I know,' she laughed.

Some fifteen minutes later, the group had arrived at their destination. Camden Town.

'Camden? Why are we in Camden?' asked Emma. 'This is my favourite shopping street in all of London,' she said, trying hard to keep her eyes from straying towards the multitude of weird and wonderful gothic, steampunk and alternative shop windows.

'I'm afraid we're not here to shop, Emma. You'll have to wait for the weekend for that.'

She frowned but chuckled as Declan led them away from the shop fronts and down beneath a secluded bridge.

'I want you in pairs, please,' Aria announced, and the couples each stood apart when they had finally decided. Naturally, Lana and Emma had wanted to be together, leaving Diarmuid to partner with one of the boys. He was used to it; he didn't mind.

Declan began handing out flyers.

Looking down, Emma laughed. 'This is a class? But this is fun?' she said as Lana pulled the piece of paper from her hand and read the instructions.

'We're doing a treasure hunt? How cool is that?' she guffawed.

'Well, we figured you didn't get much of a Christmas holiday, so we decided to have some fun during your first week back,' Declan grinned.

'We have a whole week of fun?' asked Emma.

Both Declan and Aria nodded.

'Cool.' Emma grinned.

'So now you're in your teams, here are the clues. Go have fun. We'll be around whenever you need us. If you get lost or lose us, just give us a buzz. You've all got mobile phones. Now, no cheating. Enjoy!' he yelled as everyone scrambled away from the two adults, all laughing and whooping as they ran under the bridge and across the other side before finally stopping and realising they needed to read the paper to find out their first clue.

Declan and Aria laughed as they watched the teenagers all scatter in different directions.

'I think this might take a while,' he smiled, 'considering they're all looking for the same thing.'

Aria laughed as she leaned on the wall and looked down.

'So how are you doing?' He asked her.

'Okay, I guess.'

'C'mon, spill it.'

She sighed and stood upright again, turning so her back leaned against the bridge. 'It's been over a week now, and we still haven't managed to get any information out of him. Not even with Penny's ability to make people speak the truth.'

'He's not just anybody, Aria. He's Sthenelaus, one of the most powerful Skulls around.'

'Do you really think that?'

He shrugged and rubbed his hands together for warmth. 'Honestly?'

She nodded. 'Of course.'

He shook his head. 'Not anymore. I don't know what happened, but he's like a shadow of his former self. Although he's obviously still capable of resisting our powers, he's just a guy with an illness. An illness that appears to have taken all his own powers. I've never seen anything like it, and I can't get my head around it.'

'I know, that's exactly how I feel now. But I don't quite under-stand how quickly he deteriorated. He wasn't like that a few days before.'

'No?'

'No. He was quite strong. Yes, he kept having the coughing fits, but then he'd be fine after a day or two in the Turkish baths.'

'I wish I knew what was happening, and I wish I could find out the truth for you. It can't be easy, not knowing.'

Aria sighed. 'It's been years, I guess I'm getting used to it.'

Declan patted her on the shoulder. 'Don't worry, mate. We'll get to the bottom of this.'

'I hope so. Come on, let's get a coffee while they work this one out.'

Declan grinned. 'Good idea.'

oOo

Down below in Camden Town
a hospital is what you'll find
But once where horses soothed
Now belongs to the shopping kind
Find a locket with hair so pale
and a lady with eyes of night
There you'll find your next clue
And a prize for the first of delight

'Come on, Emma, we've got to find this clue. Stop looking at all this weird stuff. We're not here to shop. I can't believe I just said that.'

Emma raised an eyebrow and grinned. 'It's usually me that's saying that to you.'

Lana linked arms with her sister as they reread the clue. 'Do you think we're in the right place?' she asked.

Emma nodded. 'Definitely, this place was an old horse hospital back in Victorian times,' she said as they looked around them, realising none of their classmates was anywhere to be seen.

'How do you know that?'

'Are you kidding me? Like I said before, this is one of my favourite places in London.'

'If you're so smart, then where's the next clue?' Lana asked, smiling and pulling her sister towards the old tunnels.

'I'm not sure, although I do recollect seeing a woman who likes to wear way out contact lenses. Maybe it's her?'

'Where? Come on, show me.'

Emma let go of her sister and ran in the opposite direction. 'This way, I think.'

Walking quickly past a multitude of weird stallholders and shoppers, Emma stopped suddenly at the entrance to a small boutique. Inside sat a woman making jewellery. She looked up when they stepped inside and smiled.

Lana gasped and then giggled.

The woman was clearly wearing contacts, but they had nothing to do with night – instead, her eyes looked rather like a lizard's.'

'Can I help you lovelies?' she asked, in a broad London accent.

'Erm, no thanks. Just browsing.' Lana smiled shyly as they backed out. 'Any other ideas?'

Emma shrugged. 'It's quite difficult, considering everyone here is very, erm...'

'Unique?' Lana suggested linking arms again.

'Oh, I just had an idea,' Emma said. 'I bought a locket once from somewhere. Maybe...'

'Yeah, let's go. Which way?'

They walked quickly again, still noting that they were the first of their classmates to figure out that they should be in the Stables shopping area.

'Hello again,' said a young man dressed entirely in Steampunk clothes.

'Hi.' Emma blushed. 'You remember me?'

'I remember everyone,' he replied. 'Looking for another locket?'

Emma nodded.

'Yes, one with hair so pale,' Lana quizzed.

The man frowned for a second, but it was clear he was hiding a smile.

'It's here, Em. It's here somewhere.'

The man stepped back to reveal an older lady sitting in the corner, she looked up with a toothy grin and revealed black eyes. Emma gasped and clapped her hands, moving closer.

'Wow,' said Lana. 'That's amazing.'

They both stood watching the woman whose eyes looked like twinkling stars in a dark night.

'They are the most amazing contacts I've ever seen,' Emma whispered.

'Can I buy some?' asked Lana, temporarily forgetting why they were there.

'I'm afraid these aren't for sale, love,' she said, laughing. 'These ain't contact lenses,' she winked.

'Oh, you're super...' Emma nudged Lana and shook her head. Her sister stopped talking.

'The locket,' Emma said. 'We need to find the locket.'

Suddenly Lana started laughing. Following her gaze, Emma chuckled too. In the woman's lap was a large white cat, around whose neck was an unusual locket.

'I think we found the clue,' Emma said.

'May I?' she asked the woman, who was grinning.

'You may, my love. Don't worry, she's a gentle one.'

Leaning forward, Emma gently stroked the cat's back before opening the locket. Inside was a picture of the young man they'd spoken to moments before.

'Oh,' Emma exclaimed. Turning to him, she smiled. 'Do you have our next clue?'

The man nodded and bowed, revealing several envelopes hidden in the very top of his hat.

Lana grinned and took one. 'Why thank you, kind sir.'

'My pleasure. Your prize,' he said, turning away from them for a moment. When he turned back, he held out his hands and nodded to them both.

Lana and Emma each held out their hands, cringing with expectation.

But when he released his own hands, they felt a tickle before a beautiful white dove appeared in both girls' hands. They sat for a moment before flying up and away.

Both girls squealed with delight as they watched the doves fly through the stalls and out into the daylight.

The man tipped his head and walked away.

'That was awesome,' Emma grinned as they opened their envelope to reveal their next clue.

'Are we first, then?' Lana asked.

'Of course. We got the prize of delight, remember.'

'Oh yeah. Cool. What's next then?'

A JOURNEY DOWN UNDER
With the warmth on your skin and
the wind on your face
Look for a place of worship
Down by the water
You'll find your next clue
In the hands of someone's daughter

'WHAT THE HECK DOES THAT MEAN? THIS IS SO HARD, EM,' LANA said, pushing her hair behind her ear.

'We can figure it out. Right, so we need to travel somewhere. By bus?'

'You don't really get warm skin and wind on your face on the bus though, do you. Oh, it's the underground, it's the underground,' she answered. 'Come on, let's go to the nearest station.'

Both of them squealed like little girls before running up out of the Stables and down the road. They passed Liam and Ava, who were looking a little lost.

'So long, suckers,' Lana shouted from across the road.

'Aw, c'mon, give us a clue!' he shouted back.

'You're almost in the right place,' Emma yelled back.

He gave them the thumbs up as they continued running until they came to Camden tube station. Getting their passes out of their handbags, they went through the barriers and stood facing a large map.

'Okay, where do we need to go?' Lana said, more to herself then Emma.

'Hmmm, we're looking for a place of worship. There must be tonnes in London. St. Paul's?'

'No, it needs to be near the water,' Emma replied, her finger in her mouth as she concentrated.

'It might not be a regular church, though, sis. It might be where

Muslims go to pray and stuff. What are they called? Erm, mosques? Are there any mosques around?'

'I wouldn't know what to look for. Do you think it would really be a mosque? Surely it would be something a little easier to find, don't you think?'

'Yeah, I guess. Erm... I can't see anything, can you?'

'Oh, oh I've got it!' Lana squealed as she placed her finger on the map.

'Temple? Oh, Lana, you're a genius!'

'I know,' she said, rubbing her fingers on her coat. 'Let's go! I think we might win this thing.'

'Don't talk too soon, sis. We've only been at it for what, less than an hour?'

Lana laughed. 'Yeah, I know, but we're good.'

Running down the escalator, both girls enjoyed the warm air coming from below and laughed together as they sit on a bench to wait for the next train, which was due in a matter of minutes.

Emma's mobile phone, beeped.

'Let me guess... Diarmuid, right? Looking for a clue?'

Emma shook her head. 'No, he's actually not far behind. They've just got the next clue. Don't worry, I'm not going to tell him anything.' She grinned as she sent him a text and put her phone back in her bag.

'What's Barber up to today?'

'Same thing he's been up to all week. Trying to get the truth out of Sthenelaus.'

'How's that going, by the way?'

'Not great. The guy is so ill, he can barely talk.'

'Weird, isn't it?'

Lana nodded as she looked at all the people buzzing around them. 'I'm just glad we got him. So many people can sleep easier, knowing he can't hurt them anymore.'

'Now they just have to worry about Stan.'

'God, I'd actually forgotten about that creep.'

Jumping up at the sound of the tube coming around the bend in the tunnel, Emma grabbed her sister's arm, so they didn't get split up in all the commotion. The seats were pretty full, so they stood, Lana trying to avoid touching any surfaces.

Emma pulled a face at her.

'What?' she whispered. 'They're full of other people's germs.'

'You're wearing gloves.'

Lana poked out her tongue, but when she noticed people watching her, she quickly put it back in and turned away, glancing at a man standing by the door at the far end of the carriage.

'Hey, is that...?

'Huh?' said Emma, following her gaze. 'Who?'

But when Lana turned back, he was gone. She shook her head.

'It's nothing, I think I'm just imagining things,' she shrugged and smiled.

'This is Temple. The next station is Embankment,' said the recorded voice.

The cold hit them as they exited the underground, making them both breathless for a second before they headed off to find a zebra crossing to get to the riverside.

Soon, they were wandering up and down the street looking for 'someone's daughter'.

'It could be anyone,' moaned Lana, after ten minutes of drawing a blank. 'What do we do?'

'We need to think about this,' Emma said, as they leaned against the wall and looked out across the Thames. They both watched the boats for a moment before their eyes landed on one that looked familiar one just metres away from where they stood.

'Is that Declan's boat?' asked Emma as she grabbed Lana and pulled her along the pier.

Gingerly climbing aboard, Lana almost lost her balance as Emma hopped on with confidence. 'Jeeze, Em, I nearly fell in the water!'

'No you didn't. Come on, let's see if the clue is here. Someone's daughter? Who could that be?'

Pushing open the door to the houseboat where they'd spent their first few weeks in London the year before, both girls collapsed with laughter at the sight of a cardboard cutout of Daisy. Stuck to her hands were several envelopes.

'That is brilliant. I wonder whose idea that was,' Lana laughed. 'I bet it was Beau's.'

. . .

RISE HIGHER AND HIGHER UP IN THE SKY
   A view from above using a special eye
   There you'll find clue number three
   And something to eat and a cup of tea!

'OH, THIS ONE IS WAY TOO EASY,' SAID LANA WHILE EMMA nodded.

'Come on, let's run,' she said, pulling her sister off of the boat and heading towards the London Eye.

As they sprinted down the road, they spotted some of their classmates looking somewhat confused across the other side of the street. Laughing, the girls ignored them and continued on their way to the famous wheel.

Approaching, they spotted Declan and Aria, in animated conversation sitting on the wall beside the wheel. Both grinned at the sight of them.

'So you made it this far.' He smiled as Aria poured them both a drink from a large flask and handed it to them.

'Yup!' Emma smiled. 'We particularly liked Daisy's cutout.'

Declan chuckled. 'That was Beau's idea.'

'We thought so. So what's next?' Lana asked.

'Drink your tea, eat your sandwich and hop into a capsule. We'll hand you your next clue when you've made one revolution,' he grinned.

'Hurry up, Em. Eat fast!'

Emma nodded, and both girls munched down their food and gulped down the hot tea before jumping into the capsule.

'It's so slow,' Lana moaned after a couple of minutes. 'I wanna get going.'

'Just enjoy it. We're still in the lead, and everyone else has got to do the same task.'

'Yeah, I guess.'

Looking down below them, there was still no sign of the other teenagers, so Lana smiled and sat down, peering around at the view beyond.

'It's pretty special, isn't it, sis?' asked Emma.

'Huh? What?'

'London.'

'Oh yeah.'

Some tourists were wandering around their capsule, taking photos of the various landmarks that could be seen from their vantage point. A woman brushed by Emma as she stood up to get a better view of St. Paul's Cathedral.

'We should go there, Lana. We've never been before.'

'Huh? The cathedral? Why would we go there?'

'Because it's beautiful,' the woman interrupted.

Lana and Emma both looked at her and cringed at her face. She was about fifty years old, with small beady droopy eyes and a nose that was far too big. Her thin lips were stretched into a smile that made her look more like the Joker than anything else.

Lana shivered as she reached for her sister's hand.

'Yes, I've heard that it is,' Emma replied with an attempted smile.

'Did you know that it was the tallest building in London up until about thirty years ago?' the woman asked, stepping closer.

Both girls shook their heads, Lana pulling Emma backwards.

'No, we had no idea,' Lana spoke loudly. 'Thanks for that info,' she said, with a fake smile, pulling them away towards the door. 'Did you feel that?' she asked.

Emma nodded. 'Evil. Pure evil.'

'We should get off.'

'I wish we could,' Lana agreed.

'It's just a few more minutes,' Emma whispered, looking over her shoulder at the frightening woman who stood looking away from them.

Counting down the minutes until they could step off, both girls held each other's hand tightly, waiting patiently without saying a word.

Not soon enough, they'd reached ground level.

Lana let out a sigh of relief as they hopped off and ran as quickly as they could towards Declan and Aria, who were standing chatting to a small group of their classmates.

'Declan!' Lana shouted.

Lifting his head, his expression changed almost immediately, and he stepped forward. 'You alright?' he asked.

'Yes, but it was weird,' Emma breathed as the three of them turned to scan the crowd.

'What, what was weird?' asked Rupert.

'There was an evil woman in the capsule with us.'

'What did she do?'

'Nothing, really.'

'So how did you know she was evil?' he asked.

'We could feel it.'

'Oh, right, okay.'

'She was freakishly ugly, though,' Lana said, scrunching her face up in disgust.

'Sorry, Lana. What did you just say?' asked Aria, who had overheard the conversation.

'She was freakishly ugly.'

Aria's face turned white.

'What? What's wrong?'

'Can you describe her?'

'Beady brown eyes that seemed to droop down into her cheeks, and a huge nose,' Emma described.

'But she had the most perfectly done hair,' Lana added. 'And beautifully manicured fingernails.'

'Oh, dear,' Aria whispered. 'It sounds like Madge.'

'Right, this treasure hunt is officially over,' Declan announced.

'Oh no,' Lana pouted. 'It was fun.'

'Sorry, guys, but if Madge is out there, stalking any one of you, then it's too perilous. Until we know how dangerous this woman is, we need to get the rest of the kids together and back to Praxos ASAP.'

'Really? But she's just one woman? What harm can she do?' Lana pulled a face.

Declan turned to face Lana and raised his eyebrows. 'She's a Skull, kiddo. And, like I said, we don't know just how dangerous she is. And we don't know who she's working with, either. I know you're all keen to help, and we appreciate that, but we mustn't forget that you are all just sixteen years old. Let's re-group, find her, and then maybe we can continue the treasure hunt afterwards, got it?'

'Yeah, Declan. We got it,' Lana groaned.

🏵 26 🏵

Climbing onto the private bus that had been organised to take them safely back to Praxos, Lana took one last look around to see if she could spot Madge Sophokles, but the woman seemed to have vanished.

'How did she know that we'd be on the London Eye?' Emma asked, as Diarmuid slung his arm over her shoulder and shrugged.

'You know, earlier I thought I saw Stan,' Lana leaned forward and whispered to Emma.

'What?' she cried. 'Why didn't you say anything?'

Lana put her fingers to her lips and grimaced. 'I thought it was just my imagination.'

'You've got to tell Declan.'

'He already knows.'

'Huh?'

Looking towards the front of the bus, Declan was staring at her, his eyebrows raised as he walked towards them.

'See?'

'Yep,' Emma replied.

'You should have told me the moment you thought you saw him.'

'I didn't think it was real, Declan. Sorry.'

'If you see anything else remotely suspicious, tell me, okay?'

Lana nodded and slid down in the seat as Declan turned around and returned to the front.

A couple of minutes into their journey, Lana yelled at the top of her voice, 'Declan, I see him, I see him.'

Sure enough, Stan Sophokles was standing on the other side of the road with a grin on his face.

'Keep driving,' Declan instructed.

'What?' Lana squealed. 'We should go and get him.'

Shaking his head, Declan stood staring back at him, deep in concentration.

'What's he doing?' whispered Emma.

'I think he's trying to read his mind,' Diarmuid replied.

But then another bus passed between them and when it had gone, so had Stan.

Declan cursed under his breath and said something to the driver, who nodded. The bus began to slow, and the front door opened. Without stopping, Declan jumped off and ran back towards where Stan had been.

'No,' shouted Lana. 'We can help.'

But the door closed and the bus sped up.

Aria stood and walked towards them. 'Don't worry, Declan will be fine.'

'But why can't we go too?' Lana complained.

Aria shook her head. 'He gave explicit instructions that you are all returned to the academy as quickly as possible. Let the adults deal with this.'

When Aria walked back to her seat, Lana turned towards Diarmuid and Emma with her mouth open. 'Let the adults deal with this? Who does she think she is? We're not children. Jeeze.'

'She's also not English, Lana. She probably didn't mean it like that.'

Lana raised her eyebrows and crossed her arms, sitting back in her seat. 'Yeah, whatever.'

oOo

DECLAN ARRIVED BACK JUST A FEW MINUTES AFTER THEY DID

and he didn't look happy. Looking at him expectantly, he shook his head and headed straight to Eleanor's office.

'What should we do?' asked Emma before he disappeared out of sight.

'Erm, just go chill out in the white room for a bit,' he yelled.

The class did as they were told, taking the elevator down to the main Praxos hall before heading towards their so-called chill-out room, where giant white beanbags were scattered around the carpeted floor.

Flopping down into one of them, Emma sighed. 'So, what happens now?'

Nobody answered, they all just shrugged.

'There must be something we can do. I hate just sitting around, doing nothing.'

'I know, babe,' Diarmuid said, handing her a small bottle of water.

'Thanks.'

'Maybe we should sneak out and try to find them ourselves?' suggested Lana.

'Eleanor and Declan would go mad if we did that again,' Emma half-smiled.

'Do you have a better idea?' Lana asked.

'Not really.'

'Exactly.'

'How about trying to have a vision?' Liam suggested from across the room.

'I need something that belongs to them to do that, or at least touch something that they've touched.'

'Unless we're underwater, together,' Emma whispered.

'Where do we go for that? I'm not going into the Thames again. No way... that's so gross.'

A few of the others sniggered.

'Public swimming pool?'

'Too many people around,' Diarmuid replied.

'And just as gross,' Lana added.

'I wish there was a Praxos pool,' sighed Emma.

'Actually, there is,' said a voice from the doorway.

Everybody's head turned to find Wilbur, standing holding a large tray full of snacks and drinks.

'Wilbur, you're the coolest,' Liam said, hopping up and rushing over to grab a chocolate bar.

'What do you mean there's a Praxos pool, Wilbur?' Emma asked.

After placing the tray on one of the large tables next to the wall, he turned and smiled. 'We've got our own swimming pool you could use to try and, erm, have a vision.'

'Where is it? Is it here? Why didn't we know about it before?'

Wilbur chuckled. 'Because it didn't exist before. Eleanor had it built during your Christmas holidays, not that you had much of one and...'

'And it was meant to be a surprise,' said another voice as Eleanor appeared. 'Your last treasure hunt clue today was going to lead you to it. Unfortunately, certain Skulls prevented that from happening. So, why don't you all follow me and I'll show you where it is.'

Delighted voices filled the great hall as they walked through it and headed down into one of the darker tunnels past the archives. Soon they came to a large oval wooden door. Eleanor turned the handle and pushed it open to reveal a room that looked like something from an aquarium. Directly in front and above was a massive glass pool, illuminated from beneath. It was stunning.

'How do we get in?' squealed Emma.

'There are steps at the far end, over there,' Eleanor stated. 'And changing rooms down there,' she pointed to the right. 'You'll find all the necessary swimwear and towels in there, too.'

'Eleanor, this is just magical,' Lana grinned.

'It is, isn't it? I wanted it to be special for you all. I hope you enjoy it. However,' she added before anyone could disappear. 'This wasn't built purely for fun, we will be using this room for training too, and sometimes it may have to be utilised for alternative practises. But more on that later. I understand you and Lana wish to attempt further visions, Emma?'

Emma nodded. 'We just want to help find Madge and Stan so we can all stop worrying.'

Eleanor smiled. 'Thank you. We want the same thing, so please use the pool, but be careful. I'll have one of the Mentors come down to keep an eye on you. Good luck,' she said as she disappeared out the door.

Lana and Emma both squealed with delight as they followed the others towards the changing rooms.

oOo

Aria sat beneath the large pool of water, watching as some of the teenagers swam by, waving at her. She waved back, smiling before she noticed the two sisters slowly descend into the depths. Intrigued by their close bond, she thought of her brother Luis and smiled.

The girls turned to face her and gave her a thumbs-up before they held hands and closed their eyes.

'It's pretty cool, isn't it?' said a shy voice to her side.

'It certainly is. You're, erm, Nisha, right?'

Nisha nodded and sat down.

'You're not swimming?'

'I'm not much of a swimmer, really.'

'You'll be safe in there with the rest of them.'

'What I meant to say is, I can't really swim.'

'Oh.' Aria smiled. 'Well, now that there is a pool here, you can be taught. It's not too difficult, you know.'

'I guess so.'

They sat in silence for a couple of minutes before Nisha opened her mouth to speak, then bit her lip and closed it again, shaking her head.

'Is everything alright, Nisha?'

'Erm, do you know what my ability is?'

Aria shook her head.

'I can see and speak to dead people.'

'Oh?' It took a moment for Nisha's meaning to sink in, and Aria slowly turned to face the teenager. 'Is there something you need to tell me?'

Nisha dropped her head and looked sad.

Taking a large breath, Aria's eyes grew large. 'Is it... is it... John?'

Nisha nodded.

'Oh God,' she gulped. 'Is he... here?'

Nisha shook her head, 'He came to me last night, and the night before, while I was sleeping.'

Tears began to fall down Aria's cheeks. 'When? How?' she cried.

'Well, that's kind of the confusing bit. I'm not sure exactly. He doesn't seem like the other ghosts I've seen before.'

'In what way?'

'I'm not sure, I'm still pretty new to this. I'm so sorry, I didn't mean to upset you, but he wanted me to tell you...'

'What, Nisha? What did he want to tell me?'

'He said something about being trapped, that he can't get out, he can't let go.'

'I don't understand.'

'I'm sorry, I don't either.'

'Oh Nisha, don't be upset. Thank you for telling me. Is there any way you can reach out to him?'

Nisha shook her head. 'I've tried since this morning, but nothing happens. It's like he can only reach out to me, and maybe only at night. I don't know what to do.'

'Maybe I should be with you tonight, and you can try again then. Is that okay with you?'

Nisha nodded.

oOo

AFTER THEIR THIRD FAILED ATTEMPT, EMMA OPENED HER EYES and pulled Lana's hand, gesturing that they should get some air. Lana nodded, and they swam to the surface. All their classmates were sitting on the edge of the pool with their feet dangling in the water.

'Well? Anything?' asked Diarmuid.

Shaking their heads, Lana and Emma pulled themselves out of the water and began drying themselves with oversized towels.

'I don't get it. Why did it work in Portugal and not here?' she said, flopping down on a chair beside the pool.

Emma sighed. 'I wish I knew. Maybe we were closer then? I dunno. I've no idea how this works.'

'This sucks,' groaned Lana.

Aria and Nisha walked around, and up the steps, so they stood in front of the class. 'No luck?'

Everyone shook their heads.

'I wonder... Why didn't I think of this earlier? I wonder if this would help?' she said, taking off her wristwatch and walking over to Emma. 'This was a gift from, from Sthenelaus. I've no idea why I'm still wearing it.' Aria cringed.

Lana's eyes widened. 'That's gotta work,' she said, jumping back into the water and splashing everyone.

'But, it'll get ruined,' Emma said, without thinking.

'I really, seriously, don't care.' Aria smiled. 'I should have thrown it away before now, anyway.'

Scrutinising the watch carefully, Emma's brow furrowed. 'What's this?' she said.

Diarmuid leaned forward and gasped. 'No freaking way!' he yelled and grabbed the watch, throwing it into the water.

'Diarmuid! What are you doing?' asked Emma.

Nobody said a word for a few seconds. They just watched the wristwatch sink to the bottom of the deep end.

'Diarmuid?' asked Lana.

'That's how they knew everything. She obviously suspected you, Aria.'

'What are you talking about, babe?' asked Emma.

'That wasn't just a watch. It was a listening device.'

Aria's hands flew to her mouth. 'Oh my goodness. I must tell Eleanor immediately.' She turned and ran down the stairs, opening the door and disappearing. The others listened to her footsteps growing further away.

'Oh man... this is bad. This is really bad,' Liam said. 'You girls need to use that watch and have a vision like... pronto.'

Emma nodded her head, turned and kissed Diarmuid on the lips, and dived back into the water. Lana took a deep breath and followed her sister to the bottom of the pool.

❧ 27 ❧

Emma looked at Lana and nodded. Her sister did the same, and they both closed their eyes, gripping each other's hands tightly around Aria's watch.

They could hear the vague sound of voices coming from outside the pool, the sound was almost mesmerising, and they soon found themselves drifting slowly into another vision.

Lana's eyes opened wide. 'Emma? You here? Can you hear me?'

Suddenly Emma was standing beside her.

'We're on the capsule again?'

Lana nodded, searching for the ugly woman.

'There, look. It's us. That's like... too weird.' Lana gasped at the sight of themselves.

'I know, right? Isn't that her there?' Emma whispered, walking closer. 'She's just brushed up against me. Did she just put something in my pocket? Oh my god. It's not just the watch. We need to get out of this vision now and tell them.'

Lana agreed.

'We can come back to it straight away, okay?'

Lana nodded. 'How do we get back, though? I've never managed to figure that out.'

'I'm not sure. Let's just close our eyes and concentrate on the water. The sounds of the guys talking outside, yeah?'

'Uh-huh.'

Soon, the girls found themselves back in the pool. Lana immediately released her sister's hand and pushed herself up from the bottom. 'Guys? Guys! You need to go tell Eleanor immediately—' Lana paused. 'Huh? Where is everyone? Why is it so dark?'

Emma appeared beside her and swam towards the edge of the pool. 'What's going on?' she whispered.

'I... I don't know, but I don't like it.'

The sound of laughter erupted from all around them, echoing off of every surface.

'Oh God, sis. I know that laugh. I've heard it before.'

'It's Madge, isn't it?' Lana whispered.

Emma nodded. 'What should we do?'

'I spy with my little eye, something beginning with s...' Madge sang.

'Where is she?' asked Lana.

'I don't know. But it sounds like she's everywhere.'

'What do you want?' shouted Lana.

'Answer my question, and I will tell you...'

'What question?'

'I spy with my little eye, something beginning with s...' she repeated.

'S? What begins with S in here?' whispered Emma.

'You can't seriously be willing to play her game?'

'We have to, or we'll never get out of here.'

Lana nodded. 'Swim,' she yelled.

'Wrong,' Madge's voice sang, and then a scream echoed throughout the room.

Emma gasped. 'Who was that? What is she doing?'

'It sounded like Aria. I think she's hurting her.'

'Get it wrong again, and I'll slice her again,' sang the voice.

'S, think of something beginning with S, sis,' whispered Emma.

'I can't see anything, it's too dark with all the lights out.'

Emma closed her eyes and concentrated hard until her body began to glow, a light slowly emanating from her core.

'That's better,' whispered Lana.

'Oh my, the girl glows,' sang the voice. 'What a pretty picture.' She cackled again, and the quiet was pierced by another scream.

'Diarmuid!' cried Emma. 'Leave him alone, you witch,' she shouted.

'Now, now, there's no need for that, little girl.'

'S think of something beginning with S, Lana! What is it?'

'Swimming pool!'

'That was too easy,' Madge sang. 'But I'll give it to you. But first, here's a little gift.'

A loud splash made both girls jump.

'What is it?' Emma yelled.

'Not what, who. It's Sammy. She's bleeding. I think she's unconscious.'

Emma and Lana pushed themselves away from the side of the pool and swam down to Sammy's side, pulling her up.

'Is she breathing?' Emma asked.

'Yeah. She's got a deep cut on her arm. Emma, you've got to try and heal her, like Diarmuid does.'

'What? But I can't?'

'Emma you can, babe. You can.'

Diarmuid cried out in agony, and as the sound echoed between the walls, the smell of burning flesh filled the air.

'No!' cried Emma.

'Just help Sammy, now. Just do what she says, okay, but for now focus on Sammy. Em, you can do this,' Lana whispered.

Emma sobbed loudly before she tried to push Sammy's body out of the water.

'He'll be okay, hon. Diarmuid can look after himself. Just concentrate on Sammy right now. Just focus.'

Closing her eyes, Emma concentrated on her core warmth, forcing it upwards. She breathed deeply and let the light and the heat seep up through her chest and down her arms.

Lana watched, barely breathing, as eventually, the energy filtered out through her fingertips. The warmth of her healing touch brought Sammy back round.

'What's happening?' Sammy whispered. 'Awww, my arm.'

'Shhhhh, Sammy, you're gonna be fine,' Lana whispered.

'Holy Hell... we were jumped. There's quite a few of them.'

'Shhhhhhhh now, child, that's enough of that,' sang Madge. 'No more telling lies.'

'Oh no,' Emma cried.

'What?' Sammy asked.

'She's going to hurt someone again,' Emma cried.

The sound of cackling laughter filled the air again, followed by groans of pain.

'Who was that?' whispered Lana.

'Maybe Ava?' Sammy said, biting her lip.

'Oh God, Ava,' Emma cried.

'Tell us what you want, you old crone,' yelled Lana.

'What do I want? Well, have you got all day, love?'

'My God, she's totally insane,' whispered Sammy.

'Sthenelaus isn't here, you witch,' Lana shouted.

'Sthenelaus? You think I want him? Oh, goodness me, have you still not managed to identify his illness?' She sighed audibly. 'I thought you Watchers were meant to be smart.'

'What are you talking about?' Lana asked.

'I don't want my useless husband. Aria can have him, for all I care. He should have been dead by now. The poison should have killed him months ago, but no, he keeps fighting and fighting and fighting. I was very close to getting rid of him in Seville until you turned up.'

'But you screamed for him in Seville?'

The echoes of laughter were followed by her screaming out his name, just like Emma had heard in Spain. 'I studied theatre, you know, as a child. I was rather good.'

'If you don't want him, what do you want from us?' asked Sammy.

'I want you to suffer,' Madge said simply.

'But why?'

'You're Watchers. We're Skulls. It's what we do.'

'But that can't be it?' Emma shouted. 'Why go to all this effort? Just to hurt us?'

'Well, of course there's more to it, stupid little girl. I had plans, you know. Big plans – to rule. And he took it away from me. That stupid, incompetent ugly, despicable man. A sorry excuse for a man.'

'She can talk,' whispered Lana under her breath.

'He wanted you all to himself. To be the big tamale, that's what he used to say. Pathetic. He couldn't even keep his own son in check. Sorry, Stan, darling, but it's true.'

'That's okay, Mother,' said another voice in the darkness. 'When can we kill them?'

The three girls in the pool gasped.

'All in good time, my boy. All in good time. Are you enjoying yourself, son?'

The younger Skull laughed. 'Of course, Mother,' he said before they heard the sounds of him choking one of their friends.

'Please stop, please,' begged Emma.

'We need a plan,' Lana whispered. 'We have to do something.'

'I know. But what? We're stuck in a swimming pool. We could be surrounded, for all we know.'

Laughter surrounded them again. 'Oh dear, girls. You really should just come out of that water. We can hear everything that you say. And you are quite right. You are surrounded.'

'We're not coming out until we know what you're going to do to us?'

'If you don't come out, we'll just have to send someone in to get you. It won't be difficult. You're not the only one who can swim like a fish, Emma Jane Morgan. In fact, I have a rather special Skull with me who is more akin to a... shark.'

Suddenly there was a huge splash, and the girls screamed.

'Get out! Get out now, sis!' Lana yelled.

Both girls struggled to climb out of the water, pulling Sammy at the same time. But it was too late, the Skull had already reached them.

Lana screamed as she felt something brush against her hand as she pulled it out of the water.

'Emma, that's a real shark, there's a real shark in the water,' Lana cried, hyperventilating.

'Sammy!' screamed Emma as their friend disappeared below the water.

Both girls cried.

'I'm going in, I have to,' Lana said, standing up and preparing to dive in after them.

'No, sis, don't. Please don't. It's a shark, it'll kill you.'

'If we don't do this, Sammy is going to die, Emma. She's going to die. Give us some light.'

'No, I'm the one who can swim better. I'll do it.'

Panicking, trying to focus on the light from within, Emma slowed her breathing down, closed her eyes and thought about the warmth. Soon enough, light shone from her core and emanated down her arms and legs. The pool shone brightly, revealing a shark in the centre. But it wasn't tearing Sammy to bits like they'd imagined. It was gently carrying her through the water. Sammy was whispering something to it, something the girls couldn't understand. The beast had become tame with her words and her touch.

Moments later, it pushed her up and out of the water.

The girls breathed a massive sigh of relief.

'Are you alright?' Lana asked as Emma continued to sob, her light slowly fading.

'It's okay. I'm fine,' she said as the shark disappeared back under the water. 'I'm just so relieved I can communicate with animals,' she whispered as quietly as possible.

'We've got to get out of here,' Lana lowered her voice even further. 'Emma, give us some light and let's try and make a run for it. Make it big, sis, and make it bright.'

Emma nodded, rubbing the tears from her cheeks.

Again, Emma closed her eyes and concentrated hard, focussing on that inner light and warmth until it shone from the centre of her body, the light getting brighter and brighter until Lana had to shield her own eyes before they adjusted.

Looking around, Lana saw nothing—not a single Skull, apart from the shark in the pool. Not a single Watcher except for her, Emma and Sammy.

'I don't understand,' she muttered. 'There's no-one here.'

'They must have gone when the shark jumped in,' Sammy said.

'Come on, let's go,' Lana said, pulling Emma along down the steps and under the pool until they reached the large oval door.

Pushing it open, they were greeted by total chaos. Skulls were fighting Watchers all along the corridor. Some were injured and lying on the floor, and others fought on, bleeding and tired.

Emma gasped. 'Diarmuid!' she yelled, watching him fighting a

Skull with particularly long talons and sharp teeth. He had long gashes down each arm.

Emma rushed forward to help, leaping onto the creature's back and pounding him with her fists until he staggered backwards. Diarmuid responded with the most forceful punch he could muster, and the beast fell unconscious to the ground.

Putting his hands on his knees, Diarmuid leaned forward and took a deep breath.

'Are you okay?' she asked. 'Your arms, they're a mess.'

'Look out, babe. There's more... they seem to be coming out the woodwork.'

She turned to see a man changing into a wolf, snapping at her feet, but before she could react, Liam grabbed it by its tail and swung it hard against the wall. The beast yelped and slumped forward.

Proud of his accomplishment, Liam let his guard down for a second, allowing a second creature to pounce on him. Its fangs protruded from a long ugly brown, hairy face and sharp claws sprung from its hands.

'Liam!' Emma yelled as it dragged him a little further down the hallway. But Liam was one of the strongest Watchers in their class, and he managed to punch it in the face, forcing it to release its hold on his leg. Throwing himself at the beast, Liam pounded and pounded its body until it no longer moved. Seconds later though, two more appeared, backing him against the wall.

Every one of the Watchers was being cornered, including Lana and Emma, as several Skulls more than seven feet tall overpowered them.

Moments later, Madge walked through the hallway, grinning wildly.

'You really shouldn't have retaliated like that. It's really not very nice, and you will pay... Oh my, you will pay. But where are all the grown-ups? Leaving their children to fight for them? Not very fair, is it?'

Everybody kept their mouths shut, knowing that many of the Mentors were still trying to break Sthenelaus in another location and were probably unaware that Praxos had been infiltrated.

Lana looked around, noticing Aria lying unmoving on the ground, just outside the swimming pool door.

Madge followed her gaze.

'Stupid girl. She should have stayed by Sthen's side, and then all of this would never have happened,' she tutted. 'Good for me that she didn't, though.'

'Is she... is she... dead?' asked Moira

'Who cares?' replied Madge with a cruel smile.

'What do you want from us?' Lana yelled.

'I'd quite like Eleanor, actually. Where is she? Has she run away and left you all to die?'

'Never!' shouted Rupert. 'Eleanor would never do that.'

'But she's not here. Very few adults are here, my boy. What does that tell you? That they couldn't care less about you, that's what. Perhaps you should come and join the Skulls. I could use the likes of you. I'm quite impressed with your abilities. But of course, you're not quite as strong as my Skulls.'

'Maybe not yet. But we will be,' shouted Rupert.

'Of course, but I could help make you stronger. Join me if you wish... or face death. The choice is yours, children.'

'We will never join you, you evil bitch,' yelled Rupert, who was nursing a huge black eye and swollen lip. 'We would rather die than join the Skulls.'

The rest of the gang cheered in agreement.

'Well then, death it is... But not quite yet. I'd rather like Eleanor and her friends to witness your excruciating deaths,' Madge cackled.

'I think not, Madge,' came a familiar voice from the darkness.

'Eleanor,' whispered the Watchers.

'You will not lay another finger on my students, and they will most certainly not be joining you.'

'Eleanor Hayden-Jones, it's about time you showed up. We've been waiting rather a long time, and look at the state of your so-called students. They're a little beaten up. Oh dear.'

'That's enough of your evil, Madge Sophokles. I presume you're here for your husband?'

Madge responded with the most shocking laughter yet. 'You must be joking. You Watchers really are very dim, aren't you?'

Eleanor said nothing.

'Like I've already told these children, I couldn't care less about what happens to Sthen. He's a deadweight. I've been trying to kill him off for years, but that damn poison didn't quite do the job.'

'You've been poisoning him?'

'Oh yes,' she laughed. 'What do you think causes the cough?'

Eleanor shook her head, carefully checking out her students at the same time, assessing how bad the situation was.

'How did you find and get into Praxos?' Eleanor asked.

'Incredibly easily. I placed a tracking device on Aria, over there. Poor dear thought it was a genuine gift from her' husband', she did. I've been tracking her for years. Oh, and then I placed a wire in the pocket of that girl over there. Emma Jane Morgan, I believe. I always thought Praxos was a closely guarded place, but now I know that it is not. This,' she pointed around her, 'was far too easy. You really ought to change your security measures around here, Eleanor. Oh, I guess that won't be possible, considering you're going to be dead rather soon.'

'I don't think so, Madge. You might think you have the upper hand here, but you are—quite literally—surrounded, you know? There is nowhere for you to go. You should just surrender now, and you won't be harmed.'

Madge's laughter was beginning to irritate the hell out of Lana, and she winced every time she heard it.

'Oh dear, Eleanor. You're quite wrong. You see, that chap over there,' she pointed to a very tall thin man with pointy ears and unusually long arms. 'He has rather a unique ability. Found him quite recently, actually. Much to my delight, he wanted to join us, and not you. He can create wormholes with his bare hands, allowing us to simply walk away from this place, and you'll never find us. We are quite clever, us Skulls, you know? No? I think you're probably well aware of our powers, considering you've been killing our kind for hundreds—thousands—of years. But no more. We will rid this world of every last one of you, and the Skulls will rule this place,' she chuckled.

Suddenly, there was a massive clap of thunder, and the walls began to shake.

Madge looked around with a smile.

'Your games don't scare me.'

'Well, they should, Mother.'

'Archie?' she asked, looking, for the first time, a little confused.

He stepped forward out of the darkness, a little out of breath.

'That's right, Mother. It's me. And I'm a Watcher now.'

Madge gasped and took a little step backwards. 'A Watcher? But that's impossible. Not my son.'

'No, Mother. It isn't.'

'But why? You're my son, my own flesh and blood. Why would you do such a thing?'

'Growing up, I tried and tried to be the son you always wanted, but I'm not evil, Mother. I never will be, and I cannot allow you, Father, or Stan, to continue this ridiculous escapade. You must stop now.'

Madge's chuckles made the hairs on the back of Emma's neck stand on end, it was unnatural. 'Well, well, well. I guess I only have one son left, now. That's a shame. I was rather looking forward to a future with Stan, you and Kimberly, oh and the little girl I recently acquired.'

'The little girl you acquired but lost,' Archie replied. 'Don't you realise that she is now safe and sound, back with her family. Where she belongs?'

'Oh, Archie. I'm not talking about, what was her name? Lucy something or other. I'm talking about the baby girl we took from the hospital this morning. She's a newborn, so she won't ever know the truth. We haven't got to worry about memory spells or anything like that,' she laughed. 'But I guess it'll just be me, her and Stan, in our new home—far, far away from here.'

'Mother, you are despicable. Where is the baby?'

Madge just shook her head. 'I've just about had enough of talking. I think it's time we finished this. Stan, you know what to do.'

But before Stan could move a muscle, Declan rushed forward with about thirty Watchers, ready to fight. Unfortunately, though, Madge was prepared. A single nod to the tall skinny guy and he lifted his arms, creating a large circular hole in the ground. Most of the Skulls jumped in and were sucked through what looked like swirling water. Madge had managed to grab hold of Lana while Stan had his grip firmly on Emma. Both were holding daggers to the girls' throats, and all four of them were hanging precariously over the edge of the wormhole.

'One more step and they both die,' she sniggered.

'No,' Eleanor said. 'Please. Take me instead.'

Madge glanced at her youngest son and smirked. 'I told you it would work.'

She nodded to Eleanor, who stepped forward.

'No, Eleanor,' the girls cried. 'You can't!'

But she continued to walk forward.

'No sudden movements, you lot,' Madge said to Declan and the other Watchers, who could do nothing but watch helplessly.

'It's alright, Declan. This is the right thing to do. Just let me go.'

When Eleanor was close enough, Stan loosened his grip on Emma, but not before slicing her arm with his knife.

'No,' Eleanor yelled as Stan took hold of her and pushed Emma away. Emma stumbled, shocked at what was happening.

Now holding Eleanor in his grip, Stan sniggered. Madge laughed and let go of Lana, who fell forward towards her bleeding sister.

At the same time, Madge turned to look at Declan. Her eyebrows rose before she turned back and plunged the dagger into Eleanor's chest. And then, a split second later, all three of them had disappeared into the wormhole.

'Nooo!' Declan yelled as he ran forward, preparing to follow the group into the strange hole in the ground, but the second Madge had jumped in, it had vanished.

He landed on the ground and punched it as hard as possible, splitting his knuckles and making his fist bleed.

The only sounds were the quiet sobs of the remaining Watchers and Mentors, who stood helplessly around their students.

❧ 2 8 ❧

'I just don't understand how this could have happened,' Declan said later. 'We have strict security measures throughout Praxos. How did they get in?'

'The wormhole. It's the only way,' Wilbur said, placing his hand on Declan's back.

'I can't believe she's gone,' Lana whispered as she wept into Barber's shoulder. He rubbed her back gently.

'I'm sorry I wasn't here, my angel. I should have been here.'

'You weren't to know. Praxos is supposed to be safe,' Lana said.

Emma opened the door and walked in with a bandage around her arm.

'Hey,' Lana said, walking up to her and hugging her. 'How are you doing?'

'Okay,' she murmured, sitting next to Declan, who put his arm around her and pulled her in close.

'You sure?' he asked.

Emma shook her head and broke down in tears again.

'I'll go and make some more sweet tea,' Wilbur suggested, and slowly walked out of the room.

'How is everyone else doing?' Declan whispered to Emma.

'Some okay, some not so okay. Aria's in a pretty bad way. They're preparing to fly her over to Praxos hospital, along with a couple of others. What about you, Declan? Are you alright?'

He hung his head low and nodded.

'I'm sorry we couldn't save her.' Emma looked at the ground.

'We don't know that she's dead, Emma,' he replied.

'She stabbed her in the heart. There's no way she could live through that.'

'Yes, usually – but this is Eleanor we're talking about. Eleanor Hayden-Jones, who has lived for centuries.'

'Yes, but I bet she's never been stabbed through the heart with a Skull's dagger,' Lana interrupted, as she sat down on the floor in front of the roaring fire. A fire that would typically have warmed her, but she still shivered.

'How will we ever know? How will we find them? They could be anywhere on Earth right now?' Emma cried.

'We'll find them. If it's the last thing I ever do, we will find them,' Declan answered.

The girls smiled. They'd always loved his unbending dedication to Praxos, and especially to Eleanor.

The door was pushed open and a face they hadn't seen for a while appeared. She was so pale, in shock. 'Declan. Oh My God, Declan,' Saleena said, rushing to his side.

He stood and opened his arms wide. 'Sal, I'm so glad you're here.'

'I had to come. The moment I heard what had happened, I got the very next plane. Are you okay?' she asked, and they hugged for the longest time before she turned to look at the girls.

'Emma, Lana. Oh God, I'm so sorry, I'm so very sorry. Are you alright?' she asked as Declan stepped back and allowed her to hug them.

'Saleena, it was horrendous, horrendous,' Lana muttered. 'She's dead. She killed her.'

'Now, now. We don't know that. Let's not focus on that yet. She might be alive – Eleanor is an amazingly strong woman, you remember that?'

The girls nodded before letting go and returning to the sofa to sit down.

Wilbur returned with hot sweet tea for everyone before he stood up and said, 'Look, this has been a terribly long, horribly tough day for us all. Why don't we call it a night and try and get some sleep?'

Declan nodded and stood up, 'I think you're right, Wilbur, mate. Come on, folks. Let's get to bed. If you want to visit your friends in the infirmary first, that's fine, but please don't stay for too long. They need their rest too. And if you hear a lot of noise shortly, don't worry, it's just the helicopter arriving to take some of them to Praxos hospital,' he added sadly.

Lana and Emma both nodded, giving Declan and Saleena a long hug before they stepped out of the room with Barber and Diarmuid.

'Look, I'll leave you to say goodnight to your friends. Try and get some sleep, okay?' said Barber as he kissed his girlfriend gently on the lips.

'Where are you going?' she asked as she held on to one of his hands, not letting go for a moment.

'I'm going to walk around the grounds with Wilbur and a few of the others and make sure everything is safely locked up.'

'Okay, be careful,' she added, as he squeezed her hand before turning to walk away.

Diarmuid pulled Emma close, wincing as he brushed his injured arm against her body.

'Are you sure you're okay?' she whispered.

He nodded. 'I'll be fine. Get some rest, try and sleep.'

'I'll try. See you in the morning.'

Diarmuid ran to catch up with Barber. He wasn't quite ready to call it a night either. Emma watched him and sighed, and Lana rested her hand on her sister's shoulder. 'Come on, let's go and see the others, first.'

The two of them turned and headed down towards the lift, stepping in and then waiting for it to reach the lowest level. Lana shivered as they passed the spot where Eleanor had been stabbed and pushed into the wormhole.

Emma noticed but said nothing.

Gingerly opening the door to the infirmary, both girls gasped at the sight of so many injured people. Several nurses walked around each bed, tending to their patients quietly. One of them noticed them and beckoned them over.

'Hello, girls,' she smiled to look less upset. 'Can I help you?'

'We just wanted to see how our friends are doing before we go to bed. Is that alright?' Emma asked.

The nurse nodded. 'You're Diarmuid's girlfriend, aren't you?'

Emma nodded.

'Sorry,' the nurse said. 'We haven't had the chance to meet before, I usually work up at the hospital. I'm only drafted in when there's an emergency. I'm Agnes,' she held out her hand.

'How do you know Diarmuid?' Emma replied, shaking her hand as Lana wandered off.

Agnes smiled. 'He came in earlier to try to heal the wounded. He's got quite a talent, that boy.'

Smiling, Emma nodded. 'I know.'

'He told me about you while he was healing some of them.'

'Oh?'

'Yes, he believes you share the same talent, you know?'

'I wish,' Emma said.

The nurse put her hand on Emma's arm. 'You do. I can tell. Perhaps you'd like to volunteer for a little while. We could always use soothing hands.'

'I... I'd like that Agnes, but first, do you mind if I go and see my classmates?'

'Of course, go ahead.'

Emma followed Lana to the nearest bed, where Ava sat propped up by pillows, drinking something that clearly tasted horrible.

'Hey, Ava, how are you feeling?' asked Lana.

'Lost, confused, in pain,' she whispered, lowering the cup from her lips. 'Sorry, I just feel terrible about all this.'

'I know.'

'I just don't understand. How were they able to subdue us the way they did? It was horrible. I was trying so hard to put thoughts into your mind to tell you what was happening out of the water, but I couldn't get through to anyone. I've never felt so helpless in my life,' she cried. 'And then to be choked half to death... It was so horrible,' she cried, carefully rubbing her neck. 'They were so evil, I've never felt such evil before.'

The sisters just nodded, not knowing what to say. When Ava

yawned and coughed, she shook her head and handed Lana the cup. 'Sorry, I'm so tired.'

'That's okay, Ava. Lie down,' Emma whispered, helping her move the pillows before tucking her in. 'Try and get some sleep.'

Ava nodded and closed her eyes.

Waiting a moment until Ava's breathing had slowed, the girls stepped away and walked over to the next bed, where Liam lay staring into space.

'Liam?' asked Lana. 'You okay?'

'Huh? Sorry, I didn't see you.'

'You okay?' she repeated.

He closed his eyes for a moment, his nostrils flaring, and shook his head. A tear rolled down his cheek, and he turned away from them, rubbing it away. 'I'm... I'm fine.'

'No, you're not. None of us are. It's been absolute hell, Liam. You're allowed to be upset,' Emma reassured him.

'I thought I was stronger than that,' he murmured.

'Oh, Liam,' Lana said, sitting down on his bed. 'You're one of the strongest people here. We were taken by surprise. You can't win every fight.'

'I couldn't do anything. Ava was being strangled—strangled, right across from me—and I couldn't do a single thing. They had this power like nothing I've ever seen.' He gulped.

'It's okay, Li. Really. We were ill-prepared, that's all,' Lana replied. 'We never expected they'd be able to come into our home, our place of safety. We were caught off-guard. We'll get them. We will. Just you wait.'

'She's right, you know,' said a voice from a bed across the room.

'Nisha, I didn't know you were injured too,' Emma said, walking to her bedside and then gasping at the sight of her bandaged head. 'What happened?'

The young Indian girl sat up slightly. Her eyes were completely covered. 'They put something in my eyes. I can't see, Emma. Nothing. Everything is black.'

Emma put her hand to her mouth, trying not to cry but a loud sob escaped. 'I'm sorry,' she cried.

Nisha held out her hand. Emma walked forward and held it tight.

'I wish... I wish... Imran was okay. If he was, then maybe he could turn back time, and we could prepare for this properly.'

'What happened to Imran?' Emma choked.

'Didn't you hear?'

Emma shook her head before realising Nisha couldn't see her. 'No, is he... okay?'

Nisha shook her head. 'He was the first one they grabbed. He tried to fight, God did he try to fight. I saw, Emma. I saw him trying to go back in time, but they did something to him. They bound him, somehow. He was paralysed. He's in a coma.'

Lana gasped behind Emma. 'A coma. Is he here?'

'I think they took him out just before you came. He's going to the hospital with Aria and a couple of the Mentors.'

'Oh God,' Lana sobbed, trying hard not to be sick. Her breathing became more rapid, and she felt like she was getting hotter and hotter.

'Now, now,' said Agnes, as she approached and rubbed her back gently. 'Breathe deeply through your nose. It's just a little panic attack, that's all. There, there. Come and sit down for a moment.'

As Agnes led Lana away to a nearby seat, Emma took off her jumper and walked closer to Nisha.

'Nisha, would you mind if I tried to, erm, heal you?'

Nisha smiled. 'Go ahead. Diarmuid tried earlier, too. He made me feel a whole lot better, but my eyesight didn't return. Maybe you could change that,' she said.

Placing her hands over the bandages, careful not to exert too much pressure, Emma concentrated on her inner light, focussing the warmth on her friend's eyes.

'I can feel it,' Nisha whispered. 'It's very soothing. Just like Diarmuid.'

Emma smiled, but after five minutes, nothing more had happened. She dropped her hands down and let out a sigh. 'I can't do it.'

'Don't worry, Emma. I'm sure I'll be able to see soon enough. Maybe you're too tired. You've—we've—all been through so much today.'

Emma nodded. 'Have you, erm...'

'What?'

'Have you spoken to any ghosts since the attack?'

Nisha waited for a moment. 'Are you asking me if I've seen Eleanor?'

Emma bit her top lip and nodded. 'Yeah, I guess I am.'

Nisha shook her head. 'She might not be dead.'

'I hope not.'

'I'm going to try and sleep now. Maybe you should too?'

'No, I want to try healing again, with some of the others.'

Nisha nodded. 'Good luck.'

'Thanks. Night.'

Nisha muttered goodnight, leaving Emma to try to heal someone else. She looked around and focussed on Liam again.

'Liam?'

He nodded. 'You can try,' he said as he carefully pulled back the sheet to reveal both legs covered from thighs to ankles in thick white bandages.

'Werewolves?' she asked.

He nodded, wincing as he tried to move them.

'Don't try to move,' she said. 'Couldn't Diarmuid help?'

'Yeah, he eased the pain, but it came back about an hour ago.'

'Haven't you been given any painkillers?'

'Yeah, but apparently werewolf injuries are tough to treat.'

'Oh, maybe I shouldn't...'

'Please, Emma. Please try,' he said.

So she stepped forward and hovered her hands over his legs.

He smiled when the warmth seemed to seep into his bones.

'It feels just like when Diarmuid did it. You obviously share the same healing power.'

'I don't think so, he's so much stronger and more capable than I am.'

'Don't sell yourself short. You're just as good, maybe even better,' he said, trying to smile even through the heartache he was feeling.

'Thanks, Liam,' she whispered. 'That means a lot. How does that feel?'

'Honestly?'

She chuckled. 'Of course.'

'The pain is way less than it was.'

Emma grinned and nodded. I'll come back again when you need me,' she said as she very carefully placed the sheet back over him. 'Try and sleep.'

He nodded and closed his eyes. As she walked away, he whispered, 'Thanks, Emma. We're lucky to have you.'

Tears immediately welled in her eyes, and she couldn't help but think of Eleanor.

❧ 29 ❧

News travelled fast, especially the bad kind, and when Emma and Lana heard, they both broke down and cried for hours. Imran hadn't made it. He'd died in the helicopter, on the way to the hospital.

'Oh God, Emma. Why, why is this happening to us?' Lana wailed, in her sister's arms, as they sat on her bed the following morning.

'I don't know... I wish I knew, sis. I wish we could turn back time and make everything as it should be.' When she realised what she'd said, Emma chastised herself and cried even harder. 'Oh, Imran. I'm so sorry.'

'Emma?'

'What?'

'We need to go see Nisha,' Lana whispered.

'Oh—Nisha! They were finally going out together. Oh, God. Oh, poor Nisha. I don't know how she's going to take this.'

'I'm sure Declan has probably already told her. Let's get dressed and go see her.'

Emma nodded and grabbed her nearest clothes. Even Lana just put on a pair of sweatpants and jumper. She didn't even bother with her hair.

The infirmary was full of the sounds of sobbing as they pushed open the door. They went straight to Nisha's bed. Leaning back against the pillows, she was smiling.

'Nisha?'

'Emma?'

'Yes, it's Lana and me. We came as soon as we heard. We're so sorry. Are you... okay?'

'I wasn't okay. I felt it when it happened... you know? I just knew. It was like my heart had been ripped out of my chest, but then... then...'

'What? What happened?' interrupted Lana.

'Then he came to me. Imran came to me.'

'Oh Nisha,' Emma broke down again and rushed forward, sitting on the side of the bed. Nisha held out her hand until she found her friend's.

'He's okay. He told me not to be sad. He said...' She sniffed loudly. 'He said he never felt like he really fitted in with the real world, like he wasn't meant to be here for long. He knew that. He wanted me to know that he finally felt right, like he belonged, like he is where he should be now.'

Lana and Emma both let out loud gasps, as the rest of the patients listened to what Nisha was saying.

'He asked me to tell you—all of you—not to mourn him. But to think of him and smile. Remember his silly baseball caps and cheesy jokes. Don't cry for him. He doesn't want you to. Even though I can't help it,' she stuttered, sniffing again. 'I know he doesn't want me to cry, but I will, just for a little while. I'll never forget him.'

'Will he come back, Nisha. Will he?'

Nisha smiled and shook her head. 'Maybe someday. He said he was going to be with the other angels and that he would only return if we ever really needed him. But he didn't think so, because he knows that we are all so strong and we will... sur-sur-survive this.'

'Oh Nisha,' Emma whispered. 'We'll be strong for him. We promise.'

'Absolutely,' said Liam from across the room.

'We will,' said Ava quietly, 'for Imran.'

Everybody else in the room nodded and agreed.

'We'll celebrate him,' said Declan from the door, roughly brushing a tear from his cheek.

'Declan,' Lana cried, rushing to him. 'Have you any news?'

But he just slowly shook his head. 'Nothing. Sorry, guys, still nothing.'

'What are we going to do?' she asked.

Declan put his hand on Lana's shoulder and looked deep into her eyes, 'We're going to carry on, that's what we're going to do. That's what Ellie—Eleanor—would want us to do.'

'Yeah, I guess so,' Lana said, tears rolling down her cheeks.

'We'll carry on, Declan. For Eleanor and for Imran,' she choked, and he pulled her into a hug.

oOo

Do not stand at my grave and cry,
    I am not there, I did not die,
    I am the thousand winds that blow,
    I am the diamond glint on snow,
    When you awaken in the morning hush,
    I am the swift uplifting rush,
    Of quiet birds in circled flight,
    I am bright stars that shine at night,
    I am the sunlight on ripened grain,
    I am the gentle autumn rain.
    Do not stand at my grave and weep,
    I am not there, I do not sleep.
    Tempus Edax Rerum, for you Imran.

Declan finished by closing his notebook and looking around at the many Watchers and Mentors who had arrived to say farewell to Imran Chaudri, a boy they'd taken into their hearts even though he had been a dear friend for just a year.

He smiled at the sight. A sea of silly baseball caps surrounded him.

Nisha stood by his side, holding his arm, wearing a large pair of dark sunglasses. She smiled as he finished.

'Imran would have liked that very much,' her voice wobbled.

Declan patted her hand and led her away from the grave, off the lush green grass and onto the nearby paving stones.

'Be careful, the path is a little rickety here and there,' he said.

'It's okay. As long as you keep hold of me, I'll be fine.'

Lana and Emma stayed a few more minutes, Barber and Diarmuid by their sides, holding them and preventing them from falling into deeper despair.

Lana looked up at the sky and smiled before turning her attention back to her boyfriend. 'That really was something, you know?'

He nodded.

'I think he would have liked it, don't you, sis?' Lana asked.

Emma smiled. 'Definitely. There was a good crowd too. Considering he never felt like he fitted in, he was so well-loved,' she wept, her voice quivering under the strain of trying so hard not to cry. It was what Imran had wanted, after all.

The four of them looked around, preparing to follow the crowd when someone in the distance with long wavy blonde hair caught their attention. As she slowly walked towards the group gathered for the funeral, Barber let out a deep gasp.

'Barber? What's wrong?' Lana cried.

'It's her,' he said.

'Who?'

He pointed towards her.

'My... Guardian Angel.'

'Your Guardian Angel? What are you talking about?'

'The woman who rescued me, all those years ago, when Sthenelaus stabbed me through the heart and left me for dead.'

It was Lana's turn to gasp.

The woman smiled as she approached Declan.

'Can I help you?' he asked.

Lana and Emma both grabbed their boyfriends' hands and walked forward.

'Actually, I was hoping I might be able to help you.'

'Sorry I don't understand. Do I know you?'

The woman shook her head. 'No, but I know you, Declan.'

He raised his eyebrows and turned to Nisha. 'Nisha, Saleena will help you back, okay?' he gently took her arm and put it on Saleena's.

Nisha nodded and was led away with most of the others. The only people left standing in the graveyard were the strange woman, Declan, the two sisters and their boyfriends.

'How do you know me?' he eventually asked.

'I've been following you and the Watchers for years.'

'Following?'

The woman nodded. 'Sometimes helping, whenever I could,' she briefly glanced at Barber and nodded.

He nodded back.

'Perhaps we should talk indoors?' suggested the woman.

'Look, we've just lost two of our loved ones. I'm not in the mood for games, darlin'. Who are you, and what are you doing here?'

'Declan,' Barber said, stepping forward. 'This is the woman who rescued me from Sthenelaus all those years ago.'

Declan raised his eyebrows. 'In that case, follow me.'

oOo

'THANK YOU,' THE MYSTERIOUS WOMAN SAID TO WILBUR AS HE passed her a cup of black tea with a slice of lemon on the side.

Declan opened the door and walked in.

'Sorry, I had some important business to attend to. Now, who are you?' he asked as he sat opposite her.

Lana and Emma hadn't left her side; neither had Barber and Diarmuid.

'My name is Marlene,' she said, taking a sip of tea. 'I'm Eleanor's daughter.'

Everybody gasped, even Declan. 'No, that isn't possible, love.'

'I can understand that you don't want to believe that, but it's true.'

'If it's true, then why did you never show yourself to her?'

'Oh, I wanted to, how I wanted to, but I wasn't permitted. They placed some kind of curse on me that prevented me from showing myself to her.'

'And now?'

Marlene looked pained.

'And now she's gone,' Emma whispered.

Marlene nodded.

'Do you know if she's... if she's...? Lana began.

'Dead?' Marlene asked.

Lana nodded.

'To be honest, I'm not sure. All I know is that I've never been able to get past the Praxos gates, but this morning when I tried, I walked straight in.'

'But how did you know to try in the first place? Declan asked.

'I know an awful lot of people, and I hear the news, the gossip. I heard about her, and I knew I had to try.'

'Marlene, how can we believe you?' he asked. 'After everything that's happened over the past few days... you could be a Skull, for all we know.'

Marlene looked a little hurt but nodded. 'I understand,' she said, placing her cup and saucer on the coffee table in the middle of the sofas before standing and lifting her blouse to reveal the true Watcher's mark: a winged-eye with the words Seculo Seculorum.

'Seculo Seculorum? What's that mean?' asked Diarmuid.

'Forever and ever,' Declan answered, smiling.

'In that case, welcome to Praxos Marlene. I'm sorry I doubted you.'

'You believe me now?'

Declan nodded. 'Ellie once told me she'd had a dream about a young woman with the words Seculo Seculorum on her back. She was certain it was you. I guess she was right.'

Marlene nodded, and tears began to build up in her eyes. 'I've wanted to come here for so long. I can't describe how good this feels right now. This is where I belong. I just wish that my mother was here, too.'

Declan nodded. 'I know. We've been trying to work out where Madge disappeared to, but so far, nothing. Not a single thing. The only lead we have is that she may have gone to Canada.'

Marlene nodded. 'I take it you'll be planning a trip there?'

Declan looked around at everybody and slowly nodded his head.

'Declan? You didn't tell us that? Why? We're coming with you. You're not leaving us behind. No way, not when Eleanor's involved,' Emma and Lana both began talking at once.

'Whoa, whoa, wait a minute,' he said gesturing with his hands to try and calm them down. 'It's being organised at the moment. We're just waiting for confirmation from Patrick.'

Lana squealed. 'You mean you were planning on taking us along?'

Declan nodded. 'As much as it pains me to say so, yes. We need you. Your class is the strongest class of Watchers we've ever seen. We have no choice.'

Emma turned to Diarmuid and squeezed his hand so tightly he actually winced. But it didn't stop him from grinning.

After a few minutes of thinking about Eleanor, Marlene, and a possible trip to Canada, Lana turned her attention back to Marlene. She scrutinised her for a few minutes, making Declan laugh out loud.

'What are you doing?'

'It's okay, Declan,' Marlene smiled. 'I think maybe she recognises me.'

'You do seem a little familiar, but I can't put my finger on it.'

'Perhaps that's because you never actually saw me. Not properly anyway.'

'I'm not sure.... when?'

'When you first came to London, looking for Praxos. You were bullied by a couple of pretty mean guys. I threw you some rope.'

'That was you?' Lana laughed.

Marlene laughed.

'Thanks,' Emma said with a grin.

'You're most welcome.'

'You sound a lot like her, you know?'

'Really?'

Emma nodded.

'Thank you, that's really quite special to hear.'

'You look a little alike too,' Lana added. 'When Eleanor's young, that is, not old,' she chuckled.

'Thank you.' Marlene smiled.

'So what happens now, Declan?' Lana asked.

'We finalise plans, and then we head to Canada.'

'But what about classes?'

'Oh, your classes will continue alright.'

Lana groaned.

'But we'll be concentrating on fighting, self-defence and anything else you might need against the Skulls.'

'Cool,' Diarmuid said.

'But what about Nisha?' Emma whispered.

Declan's face dropped. 'I'm afraid Nisha will have to stay here. We can't take her. Unless her eyesight returns, it's too dangerous.'

'She's going to be devastated,' Emma said, standing up and pulling Diarmuid up too.

'Where are you going?' asked Lana.

'To do some more healing. If we can fix her before we leave, then she can come too.'

Marlene and Declan smiled.

'Your friends are fortunate to have you,' Marlene said.

'I think we're all lucky to have each other,' Emma replied, as they disappeared through the door.

❧ 30 ❧

News had reached them of the mysterious disappearance of a baby, kidnapped from a hospital in Chelmsford, but bizarrely the baby had been returned just a day later. Other than that, Declan could not find any trace of any further kidnappings of a similar nature in Britain, so he had no choice but to visit the hospital in question and take the girls with him, in the hope that a vision might shed some light on the matter.

With a couple of police officers (who worked with Praxos), Declan, Emma and Lana were led to the room where the child had been taken. Nodding for them to remain outside, Declan entered with the sisters in tow.

'You know the drill, girls. We need to find out if this case is connected to Madge, in any way, and it seems like the only way we can do that is to rely on your visions. So, whenever you're ready.'

Lana nodded and held out her hand towards her sister.

Taking it, Emma smiled. 'I really don't know what use I'm going to be. I can only have them in the water.'

'Up until now. It might happen, so we must try,' Lana reassured, squeezing her hand.

'Okay.'

Closing their eyes, the girls focussed hard, but all that continued to appear in Emma's mind was the day of the attack on

Praxos. No matter how hard she tried to rid her mind of the memories, the stronger they became, culminating in the stabbing of Eleanor.

Emma let out a deep sigh and opened her eyes. 'I'm sorry, I can't do it. All I can think of is...'

'Eleanor,' Lana answered.

'Yeah.'

'I can feel your thoughts, sis. Maybe you should go and get a drink. I'll stay here and try on my own.'

Emma nodded. 'Okay, I could really do with some water. Can I get you anything?'

'A coffee would be great,' Lana said as she turned and sat on the empty bed.

'A coffee for me too, thanks, Em,' said Declan.

Emma walked out of the room, searching for a coffee machine. 'Excuse me,' she said to an orderly who was walking past, reaching out her hand to stop him. 'Can you tell me where I can find some coffee?'

'Just down the corridor to your left,' said the young man.

'Thanks.'

'No problem.'

Walking further down the corridor, Emma began to feel a little woozy. She held out her arms and steadied herself against the wall.

'Are you alright, miss?' said one of the police officers who was keeping an eye on her.

'Just a little... dizzy.'

'Perhaps you should sit for a minute. Here, I'll get you some water.'

'Than...'

Before the words came out of her mouth, Emma slumped back in her seat. What seemed like nothing more than a second later, she opened her eyes to find the policeman had disappeared. Her dizziness had vanished, so she stood up, turning back to the room. As she approached, she thought she must have the wrong room as there was someone else inside. Turning back, she caught sight of the window. It was dark outside.

'Huh? What's going on?' she thought. 'Am I having a vision? Wow, no water!'

So when the nurse came out, she hurried through the door and found a beautiful newborn baby, fast asleep in a cot beside a bed where her exhausted mother slept peacefully.

Suddenly, a familiar face appeared out of thin air: the Skull who could create wormholes. Emma gasped at the sight, wanting to run and hide until she realised he couldn't see her.

She watched as another pair of long spindly arms appeared out of nowhere, and before long Madge stood in front of her. Emma wanted to smack her in the face, but she knew it was pointless. She wouldn't feel a thing.

Madge grinned at the sight of the baby as she leaned into the cot and grabbed her. Seconds later, they were gone, leaving the poor mother alone in her bed.

'Emma?' asked a voice. 'Emma?'

'Lana?'

Lana was standing in the corner of the same room. 'You saw that, too, huh?'

Emma nodded.

'So you can have visions without water... and without me.' Lana smiled.

'I guess so. But we're still in the same vision now. I don't understand.'

Lana shrugged. 'I know. This is totally weird. Shall we try and vision hop?' she grinned.

Nodding, Emma walked forward and held out both hands, which Lana gripped.

They closed their eyes and focussed on what they'd just seen. Soon, they found themselves in the same room, but a Skull carrying the baby came in through the wormhole. He looked around before placing it back in the cot.

'Shall we try and jump into the wormhole?' asked Lana.

Emma nodded. 'I doubt it will work, though.'

But it did work, and as the Skull turned around, the girls followed closely behind him, finding themselves back on the oil rig in the North Sea.

'Why are they here?' whispered Emma.

'It's probably just temporary, because of the baby.'

'But they took the baby back. Why?'

Again, Lana shrugged and motioned to follow the Skull as he walked through a long corridor until he arrived at the furthest door. He tapped on it and waited.

'Yes?'

'It's me. I'm back.'

'Come in.'

They followed him into the small room where Madge stood waiting.

'Well?'

'It's done.'

'She's returned to the hospital?'

He nodded. 'Can I ask why, Mrs Sophokles?'

'Don't call me that. Just call me Madge, for Christ's sake.'

'Sorry, Madge.'

'Why what?'

'Why you didn't keep the baby?'

The evil woman just shrugged. 'She wasn't needed anymore. Pointless keeping her.'

'You could have just thrown her overboard, you know.'

Madge raised an eyebrow. 'I might be evil, my boy, but I'm not that evil. Besides, I quite liked the little blighter. I think she deserved to live with her family. For now, at least.'

Emma and Lana exchanged confused glances.

'Are we all set for Canada?' she asked.

'Ready when you are... Madge.'

She grinned. 'Excellent. I presume everyone's waiting on the helipad?'

He nodded.

'And the bodies?'

'They're there too.'

Lana gasped. 'We've got to follow them.'

oOo

WAITING AT THE HELIPAD WERE SEVERAL SKULLS, ALL HUDDLED up together, cigarette smoke winding its way all around them. At their feet were two tightly wrapped bodies, their faces just poking out.

Lana gasped at the sight of Eleanor, her face almost blue and her deathly eyes wide open, staring into nothingness.

'She's dead, Lana. Eleanor isn't there anymore.'

'Wait, we don't know that.'

'Look at her, Lana. She's nothing but a corpse.'

'Who's that?' asked Lana as they glanced at the other body beside her.

'I've never seen him before.'

'Well, just try and remember his face so we can tell Declan. He might know who it is. Now, we need to find out where they're going.'

'I think they're going through a wormhole again. We should try and follow them again?'

Emma nodded, watching as the young Skull performed his party trick, creating a strange water-like hole in front of them. Skull after Skull jumped in; Madge and Stan were next to last, taking both bodies with them. Just before the wormhole closed up, the girls ran forward. But it wasn't like the time before, where they'd just followed them in, this time they were bashed about as if in a whirlpool.

'Emma,' yelled Lana, 'hold on!'

'I can see it, Lana. I can see where they are. Look,' shouted Emma pointing outwards.

Lana's gaze followed hers as they tumbled about before eventually being thrown out back into the hospital.

Emma opened her eyes and found herself still sitting on the chair outside of the room, the police officer standing beside her with a glass of water.

'Oh, have a good nap, love? You looked like you needed it, which is why I didn't wake you.'

Emma slowly stood up, her balance a little off, and stumbled.

'Oh, careful. Here, let me help you,'

Emma smiled. 'Thanks.'

They walked slowly back to the hospital room, where Lana was just coming round. Declan sat beside her, grimacing.

'We had separate visions that connected together,' Emma said. 'I think we should get back to Praxos and finalise the travel plans.'

'Oh, was it a successful vision?'

'Oh, Declan. Definitely,' said both girls at once.

$$\approx \quad 3\,1 \quad \approx$$

'It's him,' whispered Aria. 'It's John. She's got him. After all this time, he must still be alive,' she cried.

'But he didn't look alive, Aria,' Lana replied. 'I'm sorry, but he looked like a... a... corpse.'

'But if he was dead, why would she want his body? And Eleanor's, too? There's much more to this, and I refuse to believe that he's dead.' Aria winced as she tried to get out of bed.

'No, Aria, you're much too weak,' said Agnes. 'You need to rest up a few more days. I still can't believe you demanded to be returned here, instead of staying at the hospital.' She tutted.

Aria nodded and fell back into the bed.

'Lana, please do me a favour,' she asked. 'Please ask Nisha to come. I must speak to her.'

'Of course.'

Lana disappeared out of the room, leaving Emma and Diarmuid to continue healing the patients. A few minutes later, when the door opened, Aria smiled, expecting to see Lana with Nisha on her arm. Instead, it was someone entirely unexpected.

'Theo!' exclaimed Emma.

Theodore seemed to glow as he walked into the infirmary. 'Emma, lassie. Good to see you. Healing, I see? I knew you could do it. Good for you. Right, who's first?' he asked, looking around.

His eyes met Aria's, and he immediately set about making her feel better. 'You'll be right as rain in no time, lassie.'

Aria smiled. 'It's good to see you, Theo. Thanks for coming. I take it you've heard the news?'

'Mentors and Guardians the world over have heard the news, lassie. It's shocking, downright shocking.'

'There's a chance she might be alive,' she whispered before she told him about the sisters' vision.

'Aye, that sounds positive.' He smiled. 'Now, will you relax and let me heal you?'

Aria smiled. 'Don't let me sleep, though. I need to speak to Nisha before I sleep.'

'Aye, Aria, you needn't worry. Nisha is on her way now,' he said with a grin.

The door flew open, and Nisha stood there without her sunglasses on.

'Nisha?' screeched Emma. 'You... you can see!'

'Shhhhhhhhh, we've got patients sleeping in here,' chastised Agnes.

'Sorry,' Emma whispered as she tiptoed forward and looked her friend in the eyes. 'What happened?'

Nisha said nothing, she simply pointed to Theo.

Emma hugged her and laughed. 'I'm so happy for you.'

'Thank you. Me too. It's such a relief to be able to see again. It's really tough, being blind.'

'I can't even imagine it,' Lana said, walking in behind her.

'Theo's a genius,' Nisha stated before she went to sit beside him. 'You wanted to see me, Aria?'

Very nearly drifting off to sleep, Aria was having trouble keeping her eyes open during Theo's intense healing session, but she was determined to speak to Nisha.

'Nisha? I need to recap the conversation you had with John.'

'Oh, okay. Which part?'

'All of it.'

'Has something happened?'

Aria smiled. 'I think he's alive—at least partly alive—and I think Eleanor's being kept in the same condition.'

'You do?'

Aria nodded. 'Emma and Lana can explain, but for now, I need you to tell me everything, exactly what you remember, okay?'

Nisha nodded. 'I'll try,' she said, and so she did, trying to remember every part of the conversation she'd had with the man she'd thought must surely be dead.

oOo

EMMA AND LANA'S DESCRIPTION OF THE PLACE MADGE HAD jumped into sounded a lot like Canada; spectacular snow-covered mountains as a backdrop and deep azure blue lakes. Declan was almost sure of it.

'But why Canada?' he pondered, not really expecting an answer from anyone.

'It's vast. They could hide in so many places over there. That must be the plan. Have you tried Sthenelaus? Maybe he'll be willing to tell you if you tell him the truth about Madge?' Emma suggested.

'We thought of that, but he's been unconscious for about a week now. He's no use to anyone.'

'Have you tried using Theo to heal him?'

'Yes, but it's not working.'

'What about using Theo, Diarmuid and Emma, all at the same time?' Lana suggested.

'Actually, that's not a bad idea.'

'Of all the people we could use our powers on, it has to be that dirtbag?' Emma said, sinking into the sofa.

'Yeah, but if it takes us to Eleanor, it's worth a shot, right?' asked Lana.

'Absolutely.' Emma grinned. 'When can we give it a try?'

'We'll head over as soon as possible,' Declan answered, disappearing from the room. 'Be ready in fifteen minutes,' he yelled.

Emma pushed herself out of the comfy sofa and stood up. 'That was a short rest. Come on, I'll go get Diarmuid. Are you coming too?' She turned to Lana.

'Are you kidding? I wouldn't miss it for the world.'

oOo

STHENELAUS WAS BEING HELD IN A SECURE LOCATION A FEW miles away from Praxos HQ; apparently, the building used to belong to MI6 but had been given to Praxos as a gift from the prime minister after they'd saved him from a particularly nasty assassination attempt. An attempt that had been kept from the press, of course.

When the small group of Watchers and Mentors arrived, Declan was surprised to see Giovanni waiting for them outside. 'Giovanni, what are you doing here?'

'I had to come, Declan. I've been tearing my hair out trying to find out what happened to her, to Ellie. I can't bear not knowing. I was hoping he might reveal something.'

Declan nodded. 'I understand mate, I really do. We feel like you do. We're doing everything physically possible to find her. You know that, right?'

Giovanni nodded, taking a puff on his cigarette. 'I understand you're going to Canada? I want to be there when you find her. I want to go with you.'

Declan nodded and smiled. 'Giovanni, we'd be honoured to have you join us.'

The man threw the cigarette on the floor, standing on it and twisting his foot. 'Thank you. I'll wait to hear from you then.'

'Soon,' Declan replied as they parted ways.

The group finally arrived at Sthenelaus' cell, and Emma was surprised to see that it looked more like a hospital room than a cell for someone so evil, but he was on death's door, so it made sense. She turned her nose up at the sight of him, wishing she didn't have to do what she was about to, but it was necessary to find their loved ones.

'I think we ought to restrain him in case he suddenly comes to,' Declan suggested.

The two men who were responsible for watching over Sthenelaus walked forward and cuffed him to the bed. His legs were chained as well, just in case.

Theo stood behind Sthenelaus' head, Emma stood to his right and Diarmuid to his left.

'You ready?' Theo mumbled.

Both of them nodded, and they placed their hands above the man who had caused so much pain and heartache for so many people over the years.

Emma had to try and push the thought from her head to focus on getting Eleanor back. 'It's the only way, it's the only way,' she kept whispering to herself under her breath.

Soon, the thought disappeared, and all she could think about were the healing powers around her. The warmth from all three of them began to create a low light in the centre of Sthenelaus' body, which moved up and down his chest, over his heart and lungs, and up to his face.

Slowly, they moved their hands, following the light, concentrating on nothing but the warmth and light and making him better, so he could talk.

After about fifteen minutes, Theo released his hands and gently tapped both of them on the shoulder. Brought suddenly out of their meditation, Diarmuid and Emma looked at each other and smiled, before they glanced down at their patient. His eyelids flickered like he was dreaming, before suddenly opening.

Emma and Diarmuid stepped backwards suddenly. Declan stepped forward.

'Hello, Sthenelaus,' he said.

'Wh...where am I? Aren't I dead?'

Declan shook his head, 'You would have been, had it not been for our healers.'

'You should have let me die. It was time.'

'No,' Declan growled.

A tiny speck of fear glistened in Sthenelaus' eyes before it disappeared.

'We want answers, and you're going to give them to us.' Declan said.

'I don't think so.'

'Look, do you know the real reason you're here, half-dead?'

'I'm sick,' he said.

'No, Sthen. Not sick. Someone was poisoning you. On and off, for years.'

'No, I would have known.'

But Declan shook his head. 'No, you wouldn't. She's smarter than you ever knew.'

'She?'

'You really don't know, do you? It was your wife, Sthen. Your wife wanted you dead.'

'Aria?' asked Sthenelaus.

Declan laughed. 'Yes she probably wanted you dead too, but I'm not talking about her. I'm talking about your other wife. She's been poisoning you for years.'

'Madge?'

Declan nodded. 'Afraid so.'

'No, you're wrong. She wouldn't.'

'She would, and she has been. Hence your so-called condition. All because of the poison she's been feeding you. She even planned for us to find you.'

'No,' Sthenelaus croaked.

'Uh-huh,' Declan nodded.

'Why?' he cried.

'Beats me. Maybe she hates you? Wants all the Skulls to work for her. Wants to rule herself, yadda yadda yadda, blah blah blah.'

'It's true,' Emma whispered.

Sthenelaus' eyes moved and focussed on her. He tried to lift his hands, banging the metal cuffs against the metal bed, making Emma jump nervously.

'No point in being frightened of me now, little girl. I'm just an old man. My powers faded some time go.'

'They didn't fade,' said Lana from beside the door, 'they were taken from you. By Madge.'

His eyes looked around the room until they stopped on her face. 'Ah yes, I remember you.'

Lana looked ready to strike him at any moment. 'You son of a—'

'Lana, no,' Emma said. 'It's pointless.'

Sthenelaus' eyes returned to meet hers. 'You're a healer?'

Slowly, she nodded.

'You healed me?'

She nodded again. 'Just a little.'

'But not completely?'

Emma shook her head.

'Thank you.'

Knitting her eyebrows together, Emma stole a glance at Declan, who shrugged.

'I just want to die in peace, now.'

'Not before you tell us...'

'Tell you what, little girl?'

'Where we can find Madge.'

His eyebrows rose, and he coughed. 'You want me to help you?'

Emma nodded. 'Will you?'

He looked at the faces all around the room. 'Perhaps, under one condition.'

'You're in no state to be making demands, old man,' said Declan.

'I want you all to leave this room, except you,' he said, his eyes focussing on Emma's.

She stepped back and shook her head.

'I will only tell her,' he said. 'Take it or leave it.'

After giving it some thought and seeing Declan eventually give a reassuring nod, she said 'It's okay. I'll do it.'

'Oh and one other thing... No cuffs.'

Declan laughed out loud. 'You must be crazier than I thought. No way.'

'Well, then, what I know will go with me to my grave.'

'Declan,' Emma whispered, 'I'll do it. It's okay.'

'Emma, no. He's dangerous. He is—was—the leader of the Skulls.'

'Declan, he's just an old man who's dying. What harm can he do?'

'She's right, Declan. If it's the only way we can get Eleanor back, then we must try,' Lana whispered.

Sthenelaus watched the conversation, his eyes moving from one person to the next.

After a couple of minutes, Declan nodded. 'We'll be right outside. Are you sure?'

'I'll be fine,' Emma whispered.

oOo

'YOU'RE A VERY BRAVE LITTLE GIRL TO AGREE TO THIS.'

'I've got nothing to lose,' Emma said. 'You're dying, there's not much you can do to me now.'

'I am and will always be a... Skull,' he said, trying to sit up. 'You don't know what underlying power I have. Please, help me sit,' he said.

Emma contemplated his request for a second before she stepped forward and put her hands on his arms, pulling him very gently until he sat upright, leaning to one side.

'Not many people, let alone Watchers, would have done that for me, little girl. Thank you.'

Emma nodded.

He patted the bed next to him. 'Sit down for a moment.' When she hesitated, he smiled. 'Don't worry, I can't hurt you. Not anymore. Just sit, and I will tell you what you need to know, under one condition.'

'I thought the condition was for me to be alone with you.'

Again, he smiled. 'I just have one request of you.'

She looked at him and dropped her head to the side, 'What?'

'I want you to use those healing powers of yours and reverse them.' Sthenelaus lowered his voice to a whisper. 'I want you to kill me.'

Emma suddenly stood up.

Lana banged on the other side of the glass.

Turning to face the window, Emma mouthed, 'It's okay. I'm fine.'

She turned back to Sthenelaus. 'Why? Why me? I don't kill people.'

'It's not like you'd be murdering me. Look at it more like assisted suicide.'

Emma was horrified. 'I can't. I won't.'

'My dear, this is the only way I'll give you what you want. What you need. Help me or lose Madge for good.'

After a couple of moments, Emma slowly nodded.

He grinned and fell back down into the bed. 'Very well,' he said quietly. 'Start the process, and I'll tell you everything.'

Emma nodded and turned away from the others at the window. Holding his hand, she focussed on pulling the healing from him, sucking out the goodness she, Theo and Diarmuid had given him earlier.

As his breath started to become more shallow, he began to talk. After twenty minutes, she knew all she needed to know and Sthenelaus was no more.

❧ 32 ❧

Emma left the room and didn't say a word to anyone, despite them all trying to find out what had happened. When they arrived back at Praxos, she wrote down what Declan needed to know for their trip and then she went to her room and sobbed for hours.

When Lana followed her, Emma asked her to leave. She wouldn't even speak to Diarmuid or any of the others who tried to get through to her. There was one person who she would have liked to talk to, but that person wasn't there. Eleanor. She really needed Eleanor.

That night, she dreamed of Sthenelaus; the life seeping out of his body. The life she'd taken. She felt her body shuddering with sobs, even in sleep. She knew Lana had climbed onto the bed with her and had tried to comfort her, but nothing would take the pain away. She'd killed a person. Willingly. She would never be able to take that back, and she hated herself for it.

As she dreamed, she imagined Eleanor sitting beside her, stroking her hair. 'There, there, my dear Emma Jane. Don't be sad.'

Emma sat up. 'Eleanor?'

'I'm here, I'm right here.'

'I killed a man, Eleanor,' she whimpered.

'No, child. You didn't kill anyone. He was an evil beast who was already dying. You didn't kill him, you merely sped it up a little.

This is precisely what he wanted. He wanted to get to you. It was his dying wish, to take a little of the innocence from a dear, sweet Watcher with a heart of gold. No matter what he made you think or feel, you did what was right. I would have done exactly the same thing. And so would Declan, or Lana, or even Diarmuid. It needed to be done so you could find me.'

'Are you still alive, Eleanor?'

'Barely, my dear. If you get to me in time, I should survive. But John is close to death. He has been in this condition, on and off, for many years. You must hurry. Tell Declan to hurry.'

'We will, Eleanor. We will. Do you know where you are?'

'Canada, Emma. We're in Canada. Sthenelaus told you where to find me, didn't he?''

'Roughly, but he said Madge would certainly not stay there for long. Can you be any more specific?'

'In the mountains somewhere, lots of snow. Alberta, perhaps? I'm not sure. I must go now. Sleep, Emma Jane. Rest. I have confidence in you,' Eleanor smiled, stroking her face.

'Oh, Eleanor?' Emma whispered.

'Yes, dear?'

'Your daughter has returned. Marlene is here.'

Eleanor's face filled with light and joy for a split second before she faded back into the darkness.

'Eleanor? Eleanor? Eleanor?'

'Emma? Wake up, wake up.'

'Huh? Lana?'

'You were sobbing and talking in your sleep. Are you alright?'

Emma slowly opened her eyes and hugged her sister. 'I'm fine, sis. I'm going to be just fine,' she smiled.

THE END

Read on for an excerpt from We Stand Against Evil

33

WE STAND AGAINST EVIL

AN EXCERPT

'I've just got this horrible feeling that we're travelling to the wrong place,' sighed Lana rather too loudly as she gazed out of the aeroplane's window, seeing nothing but thick, fluffy clouds beneath them and blue sky above.

'Eleanor told me she was in Canada, Sis. She's not usually wrong,' Emma said, fidgeting with her long dark hair.

'Yeah I know,' she replied quietly, sitting back in the seat before continuing, 'But I just have this really weird feeling deep in my stomach and these kinds of feelings aren't normally wrong. Are they?'

'I guess not. Look, just go and tell Declan,' Emma muttered under her breath before closing her eyes and turning away from her sister.

'Are you alright, Emma?' Lana asked.

'Yeah, why wouldn't I be?' she answered with her eyes still closed.

'You're just not yourself, you know?'

'Yeah, whatever, I'm going to sleep. Go and talk to Declan.'

Lana raised her eyebrows and fumbled with her seatbelt, eventually undoing it. Standing up, she scanned the seats around her until she spotted Declan who was talking quietly to Aria and Marlene.

'Hey Lana,' Aria smiled. 'Are you okay?'

Nodding, Lana leaned against the seat, 'A bit worried about Emma though.'

'What do you mean?' asked Declan as they all glanced over to look at her sister.

'She's not herself. I mean really not herself. She sounds more like me and that's never a good thing, is it?'

Declan raised his eyebrows, 'She'll be okay. She's still adjusting to what happened. It's not easy getting over killing someone,' Declan added in a whisper, glancing around at the strangers surrounding them.

Marlene nodded, grimacing slightly as she continued to watch the goth girl in the seat up ahead of them. 'Would you like me to talk to her?'

'She said she's going to sleep, but maybe later?'

Marlene nodded.

'There's something else though,' Lana added.

'What's up?' Declan asked, concerned.

'I just keep getting this feeling that we're going to the wrong place.'

'What do you mean? One of your gifted feelings?'

Lana nodded.

'You don't think Eleanor is in Canada?' Aria asked.

'I'm not sure. I just have this weird feeling about Scotland.'

'Scotland?' Declan said loudly. 'That's weird. Eleanor definitely said Canada.'

'I know, which is why I'm so confused. My feelings are usually right. I don't get it.'

'Well, we're flying to Calgary right now, there's not much we can do to change that.'

Lana nodded and sighed, 'I don't understand why we couldn't have used the private jet again and then we could have just turned it around.'

Declan dropped his head to one side, 'We've already talked about this Lana. Eleanor left strict instructions about what we should do in the event of anything happening to her, especially when it concerns the Skulls. We have to keep things under the radar which means we have no choice but to use limited resources.

We don't know how much Madge knows so by flying economy under false aliases, we've got a better chance of finding her.'

'Not if we're flying to the wrong country,' Lana exclaimed, crossing her arms like a naughty child.

'Look, I know you're angry about so many things but we have to do this properly. It's what Eleanor wanted.'

'What? That all of our friends should stay in England?'

'Oh c'mon, Lana. We've been over this too. Most of the Watchers in your class were not given permission by their families to fly all the way over to Canada, anyway.'

'And Barber? He's an adult,' she pouted.

Marlene smiled and placed her hand on top of the teenager's.

'Barber is needed in London to help protect the students. As a Watcher yourself, surely you must understand that?'

Lana sighed, 'Yes of course I do. Sorry, I'm just worried.'

Declan smiled, 'We know.

But,' he lowered his voice to a whisper, 'your boyfriend is a pretty strong vampire. He can take care of himself,' he sniggered before adding, 'Everything is going to be fine, Lana.'

His wrinkled forehead, however, said something else entirely.

oOo

'Hey,' Lana said, watching her sister slowly open her eyes as the plane finally came to a smooth halt on the tarmac.

'Hey, she yawned. 'Are we here?'

Lana nodded, 'Calgary airport.'

'What did Declan say?'

'The usual.'

'And your feeling about Scotland?'

Lana shrugged, 'We're in Alberta now. Not much we can do about it. Here,' she said, handing Emma her thick purple winter coat from the overhead locker.

'Thanks. It looks pretty cold out there.'

They both looked out of the window and saw a blanket of snow on either side of the runway, twinkling in the bright sunlight.

'Yeah, loads of snow,' Lana sighed, before adding. 'I feel so awful.'

'Don't you feel very well?' asked Emma.

'I feel fine. I just feel awful about this whole situation.'

'I don't follow you, Lana,' said Emma.

'We are the only ones that came to find her. It's not right. We should have the entire Watcher population out here searching for her.'

Emma groaned and plonked herself back on the seat while they waited for the other travellers to start leaving the aircraft.

'They have their reasons, we have to respect them.'

'We don't have to bloody like them though,' Lana said loudly, glancing backwards at Declan and the others, before delving into her handbag to find her lipstick.

Emma looked at her and pouted. 'You're right, we don't.'

'I just don't get it.'

'What?' asked Emma, getting a little exasperated.

'Why us? Why did they only choose the two of us to come with them? And why Aria and Marlene? Why not some of the others? Why couldn't Barber come? There's loads of other Watchers and Guardians to look after things in London and the rest of England for that matter? And why... why not your

Diarmuid?'

'Diarmuid's mum said no. Simple as that.'

'It wasn't just his mum, Em, and you know it. They didn't let a lot of kids stop their studies to come and help.'

'It was mostly their parents though, really,' Emma replied. 'Their parents are worried as hell.'

'And ours weren't?' stated Lana. 'Mum and Dad didn't want us to come either but we made it quite clear there was no way in hell we weren't coming. The others could've done the same. They could have taken a stand, right?'

Emma lifted her eyebrows, 'It's not as simple as that, Sis. The other parents aren't as close to Declan like ours are. Declan saved Dad's life before, remember? They're like best mates. I reckon that's the main reason they let us come, because they know that Declan would lay down his life to save us. Plus, they know what Praxos means to us. They know what Eleanor means to us.'

'Maybe,' Lana sighed. 'Why us though?'

'Because Eleanor left strict instructions that if anything should happen, she wanted both of you to help us,' Declan said as he approached them from behind, making them both jump.

'Really?' Emma's eyes lit up.

Declan nodded, 'Girls, you must realise by now that you've both got something special going on. You're stronger than the majority of the Watchers that we know, adults included. Eleanor believes in you. She believes you will set us free.'

'Set us free?' Lana whispered. 'What does that mean?'

Declan shrugged ever so slightly, 'We're not entirely sure ourselves. Eleanor wrote it in a letter that Wilbur was keeping safe, only to be opened in the event of something happening to her.'

'What else did it say, Declan?' whispered Emma.

All the seats in front of them were now empty and a small queue was developing behind them.

'Oh sorry mate,' Declan said, moving out the way of a tall Chinese man who had cleared his throat, clearly trying to get their attention. He nodded respectfully as he passed.

'Look, I'll tell you more later. Let's just get off this plane first and sort ourselves out. Just...,' he pushed his hair back off his face, '...just... stop worrying. It's gonna be okay.'

Lana glanced at Emma and they both smiled, albeit with tight lips.

'Now c'mon, let's get out of here.'

❧ 34 ❧

WE STAND AGAINST EVIL

'Wow, it really is beautiful,' sighed Lana. 'I wish we were here under different circumstances, though,' she said, shivering as she zipped her coat right up to her chin.

'So this is Banff?' Emma said as she stepped out of the car and looked around at the warmly dressed people milling around. 'It's pretty.'

'Yes it is,' Aria smiled. 'It's a wonderful place for a holiday. Shame that's not why we're here though. This was one of the places John and I were planning to visit one day.' Her voice cracked and she cleared her throat. Looking away, she bit her lip before turning back to them. '

Come

on, let's head inside. Declan's already grabbed the bags,' she smiled as the girls followed her indoors.

'Well this is cozy,' Marlene said as she put the kettle on to make some tea and busied herself in the small open plan kitchen.

'So what happens now, Declan?' asked Lana. 'Is there a plan? Can you tell us more about the letter?'

'Come and sit down girls,' he ushered them onto the large old leather couch that faced the kitchen and then sat down on the armchair beside them.

'There's not an awful lot that you need to concern yourselves with right now girls. But if you must know, she left me instructions on running Praxos in London in the event of her dea..,' he stopped for a second, '... of something happening to her. But she did say that if something happened and she went missing, she was adamant that you both, the Morgan sisters, were to come and help find her. In the letter she told me how important you both are to Praxos - but I already knew that of course,' he looked up and smiled. 'And that she wanted you to work with us to find her.'

'But what about this whole setting us free business?' asked Lana.

Declan looked up at Aria and Marlene, 'We don't really understand what she means but she underlined it in her letter, so it's obviously something important.'

Everyone was silent for a moment before Lana piped up, 'So what now? What's our next move?'

Declan stood up. Leaning against the fireplace, he sighed.

'What's the matter, Declan?' Emma asked, knowing something wasn't quite right.

'Well, here's the thing,' he eventually replied, turning to face them. 'We don't have any clues at the moment. All of our research seems to have come against a brick wall.'

Emma's eyes open wide, 'You mean all we're going on are our visions?'

Declan slowly nodded.

'But why?' Lana asked loudly.

'Let me guess,' Emma said somewhat bitterly. 'Because Eleanor told you to?'

'Pretty much. Look Emma, your vision with Eleanor was a strong one. You actually talked to her and she told you to come here. We're simply following that lead.'

'And then what?'

'Then we wait.'

'But waiting might be too late,' Emma yelled. 'She said they didn't have much time. She said to hurry.'

'Which is why we flew here immediately,' Marlene answered as she placed a few cups of tea on the coffee table in front of them.

'But what if that was wrong?' Lana said, exasperated. 'I told you it didn't feel right. I told you I think there's something going on with Scotland. What if she's there? What if John's there?'

Aria leaned against the inner archway that led to the bedrooms beyond, crossing her arms.

'We have to go on what Eleanor told Emma, Lana. It makes more sense. Why would Madge go to Scotland? Eleanor specifically said Canada and that's where we are now. We need you to work together to get down to detail. We need you to tell us what's next. We're counting on you.'

Emma burst into tears and ran out of the room.

'See?' Lana said. 'She just killed a man and now you're putting all this pressure on her to stop two more people from dying. Declan, this is...this is... this is crazy,' Lana seethed, standing up abruptly.

But when she got to where Aria stood, she stopped and let out a deep breath. Closing her eyes, she dropped her head backwards and took another deep breath before turning around.

'I'm sorry,' she whispered.

Declan smiled, his nostrils flaring slightly while he rubbed his chin, 'It's okay. I get it. I really do, mate and I'm sorry that this is all on you and your sister. It isn't fair but you are all we've got right now. Everyone and everything else has turned up nothing. I wish it was different, Lana, I really do but I believe in you both. Big time. I know you can do this,' he nodded. 'But you have to believe in yourselves too.'

'I'll go and speak to Emma,' she said, turning.

'No need. She heard me,' Declan smiled.

Emma gingerly appeared from the hallway wiping the tears from her eyes.

'I'm going to need some water.'

'I'll pour you a drink,' said Marlene, standing up.

Declan smiled and shook his head, 'She doesn't want a drink, Marlene. She wants to swim.'

oOo

'IT'S TOTALLY FROZEN OVER. ARE YOU SURE THIS IS A GOOD idea?' Marlene asked as they approached the nearby lake.

Lana and Declan smiled, 'Emma can thaw pretty much anything.'

'Oh right,' she said, looking a little confused.

'It would be quicker if Diarmuid was here to help me though,' Emma said as they found a spot that was totally isolated from the tourists that swamped the town.

'Is there anything we can do to help? Aria asked.

Emma shook her head, removing her clothes so she stood in just her swimsuit, before closing her eyes and concentrating hard on the task at hand.

'Do you want me to come in with you?' asked Lana who stood shivering next to Declan and the two women.

'Let me try alone first.'

Emma's body heat began to increase substantially until, eventually, she grinned as the ice below her gave way and she plunged into the icy lake.

The moment her body hit the water, Emma's heart soared. She was sure she was in the right place, she hoped so anyway.

'I hope she doesn't freeze down there,' Marlene said, a deep crease appearing down the middle of her forehead.

'You look so much like Eleanor when you do that,' Lana smiled. 'The old Eleanor.'

'Hey,' Marlene grinned, 'thanks very much.'

Chuckling, the group stepped backwards and waited patiently while Emma disappeared and swam deep beneath the frozen lake.

Although dark, Emma was amazed at the clarity of the water. She was able to light all around her using her unique ability to warm and lighten things up. Nestling on the bottom of the lake, she sat cross-legged and smiled to herself, waiting for inspiration to come.

Looking around, she was suddenly hit by a feeling of intense sadness and dread. It hit her in the stomach as if she'd been punched.

'Something's happened,' Declan said from the water's edge.

'Is she okay?' asked both Marlene and Aria at exactly the same time.

'She's fine,' Lana whispered. 'It's just a vision. I can feel it. Just... wait,' she breathed.

Beneath the surface, Emma was struggling to maintain calm within herself. The feeling had almost winded her, but she forced herself to take a couple of moments to understand what was happening. There didn't seem to be any actual visions, just feelings that were difficult to comprehend.

Closing her eyes again, Emma thought of nothing but Eleanor, yet her mind kept shifting to Madge and then to Sthenelaus. It was too much for her to take and she yelled at the top of her voice, letting water enter her lungs. She had to get out. Pushing herself from the bottom of the lake, Emma looked upward for the hole she'd made in the ice. Spotting it, she propelled herself out until she was laying on the ice, coughing.

Lana was first by her side, followed by Declan who gently picked her up and cradled her in his muscular arms.

'You're alright, shhhhh. Just breathe,' he said calmly. 'Take a few moments to let the breath come back to its natural state. Breathe. That's it.'

'She's shivering like crazy,' said Marlene as she and Aria wrapped blankets around her for comfort, as she was placed into the back of the car.

'Let's get her straight back to the house,' he said.

oOo

Lana shook her head as she walked back into the living room.

'Nothing at all?' Aria asked.

She shook her head again, 'All she said she got was a feeling of intense sadness and dread. She didn't see anything.'

'Poor thing,' Marlene said. 'Is she okay?'

Shrugging her shoulders, Lana sat down on the couch. 'She said she just needed half an hour on her own. But she's having a hot shower first.'

Everyone sat back. Nobody said a word.

In the shower, Emma curled up on the tiles and sobbed. She'd never felt such sadness before and it was overwhelming her, taking over her very being and she hated every second of it. She wanted to sleep, just sleep. So closing her eyes, she let the warmth of the water take her there.

'I just feel so awful that I haven't had any visions either,' Lana said quietly as she leaned forward on to her knees.

'Well, apart from the Scotland thing,' Aria added.

'Yeah but that wasn't really a vision, it was just a feeling.'

'And it still doesn't make any sense?' Declan asked.

Lana shook her head. 'No sense whatsoever and it's driving me crazy.'

The sound of a scream made all three of them jump up at once.

'Emma!' Lana screeched as she ran towards the bathroom, crashing through the door to find Emma lying naked on the floor of the shower, the water continuing to pour on top of her.

Lana quickly shut off the tap and grabbed the nearest towel, wrapping it carefully around her sister.

'Emma?' she whispered. 'Can you hear me?'

Aria and Marlene both stood by the door. 'What can we do?'

'We just need to get her out. Declan? It's ok, I've wrapped her in a towel.

He leaned over the shower and carefully lifted her up, carrying her into the girls bedroom where he placed her on the bed.

'She's still out,' he said. 'She must be having a vision.'

Lana nodded as Marlene appeared with a few more towels, placing some under her head while she gently mopped much of the water from her hair.

'Should we try and wake her?' she asked.

Lana shook her head, 'She needs to see it through to give us a better chance of finding them.'

Emma had the faintest sensation of being moved, but she didn't care. She was beneath the water again, but this time she wasn't alone. She'd been sitting silently there at the bottom of the lake when all of a sudden something was thrown into the water in front of her. It startled her so much that she screamed. Coming to her senses, she saw the object was large and heavy. Whatever it was appeared to be wrapped in something... a rug? Her eyes opened wide as she rushed to its side, unravelling the thick, heavy carpet until something rolled out of it.

It was the hair she noticed first. Long strands of blonde hair, moving gracefully through the water. She screamed, swimming away until she knew she had to go back. Slowly swimming towards it, she completely unravelled the carpet until she found the corpse of a beautiful woman. Her eyes were closed. More death. Sadness filled her every fibre once again as she tried to pull the body out of the water, but she was so heavy. Emma struggled until the corpse's eyes flew open, forcing Emma to scream out for the second time.

She wasn't dead? The woman's eyes turned a different colour and suddenly she was grappling to grab hold of something, anything. Her nails caught the side of Emma's face and she cried out in pain.

'Moraaiiinnnne,' the woman sang as she flailed about.

'Wait!'

Emma tried to yell but the muffled sounds of the water did little to help. 'I'm trying to help you. Let me help you. Stop fighting me and let me help you.'

But the woman's eyes suddenly changed back. The eyes of a corpse once again. It stopped moving and the body began to fall deeper and deeper beyond. Emma was helpless to do anything but watch until eventually, the body was swallowed by the darkened depths of the lake.

Emma's eyes opened suddenly and she coughed, struggling to sit up.

'Emma? It's okay, you're safe. You're safe,' Marlene reassured her as the tears began in earnest this time.

'Hey,' Lana said, sitting beside her and holding her hand.

Emma looked down and noticed she was wrapped in towels and her hair was still wet.

'What happened?'

'You had a vision in the shower and screamed. We thought we'd better get you out and somewhere warmer.'

Emma nodded before shaking her head, tears flowing faster now.

'Did you see something, Sis?'

'It was just a body in the lake. It didn't tell me anything about Eleanor,' she sniffed.

'It's okay,' Lana said, squeezing her hand. 'It might be a clue.

Don't disregard anything yet. You get dried up and into something warm and then we can talk about it, alright?'

Emma nodded, blowing her nose on the tissue that Marlene handed her.

'You're going to be alright, Emma,' she whispered as they all left her alone in the room to compose herself and get changed.

'I'm going to be alright,' she whispered to herself. 'I'm going to be alright.'

Ten minutes later, Emma entered the living room and smiled the best she could.

'Hey,' Declan said, standing up. 'Come on. Sit down and tell us what you saw.'

She nodded and repeated everything from the vision before continuing, '... and I think I need to swim again but not just anywhere. There's a specific lake I need to go to. There I'll understand what all this means.'

'Do you know which lake?' Aria asked.

'Moraine Lake,' she said matter-of-factly.

'How do you know?'

'She told me.'

Declan nodded. 'Okay then, we're headed to Moraine Lake. Do you want to rest first?'

But before he could finish the question, Emma was already putting on her coat and boots.

'Oh, okay. Let's go.'

OTHER BOOKS IN THIS SERIES:

Daisy Madigan's Paradise
The Ghost of Josiah Grimshaw
The Temporal Stone
Looking for Lucy Jo
We Stand Against Evil

ABOUT THE AUTHOR

Suzy Turner wrote her first chick lit novel in her early twenties, but it wasn't until much later that she decided to focus on writing full time. It was during a visit to Canada in 2009 when the ravens within the dark eerie forests of British Columbia called to her. The story of Lilly Taylor was born soon after and the first novel in The Raven Witch Saga was created. Suzy has since published several more urban fantasy books (under her pen name SG Turner) and contemporary women's novels.

Having lived in Portugal since childhood, Suzy, who is originally from Yorkshire in England, loves to travel. She finds inspiration wherever she goes. Old decrepit buildings, graveyards, cathedrals and castles are just a few of the things that can be found within the worlds of her urban fantasy books, and her contemporary women's fiction novels are filled with fun friendships, ordinary people in extraordinary circumstances and quirky characters you'd want as friends.

Suzy lives in the Algarve with her husband, three cats and a dog, where she does yoga every morning and bookish stuff for pretty much the rest of the day!

For more books and updates, visit www.suzyturner.com or www.chilloutpress.com

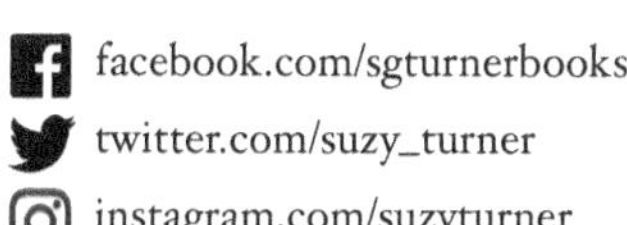

ACKNOWLEDGMENTS

First I'd like to thank one of my favourite authors and online pals, Melissa Pearl, for taking the time out to beta read for me. Melissa, you are truly an amazing YA and NA author – I've devoured practically every one of your books and I am in absolute awe of you. So to get your opinion on my own work, well, what can I say? I am so incredibly grateful. Thank you.
My other beta readers, as always, are amazing. I feel so lucky to have you in my writing life. Jill, Brittany, Debra, Mary and Jean. I heart you girls! Thank you for your hard work.
To my awesome editor, Andrea. You work so hard to help improve my writing in every way and I'm looking forward to working with you on lots more books in the future.
As always, I know I wouldn't be in this fabulous position right now if it wasn't for my wonderful readers. You keep me going with your words of encouragement and you make me want to be a better writer – something I hope I achieve in every book I complete. Thank you for purchasing my books, reviewing them and getting in touch. It really does mean the world to me.
My fellow authors and bloggers who have become real (virtual!) pals. I'd be lost without your words of wisdom and encouragement. I love that you are all so supportive of me. Thank you.
And finally, to the wonderful friends and family members who I've

lost over the years. I'm not going to list you because, sadly, there are so many of you. But I know you're all looking down and watching over me as I go through my writer's journey. All of you inspired me to become the woman I am and I miss you terribly. Thank you for loving me just for me. This book is for you.